Shop-Bought Flowers

About the Author

Short story writer and primary school teacher, Yvonne Dykes is part of the diaspora of Irish immigrants who settled in Notting Hill during the fifties and sixties. Growing up in a large Catholic family enabled her to collect vivid, compelling stories. There are many elements of *Shop-Bought Flowers* based loosely on true events. A published author, you can find her work on the Fairlight Books website (fairlightbooks.co.uk). Yvonne lives and works in London.

Shop-Bought Flowers

Yvonne Dykes

Copyright © 2024 Yvonne Dykes

The moral right of the author has been asserted.

Apart from any fair dealing for the purposes of research or private study, or criticism or review, as permitted under the Copyright, Designs and Patents Act 1988, this publication may only be reproduced, stored or transmitted, in any form or by any means, with the prior permission in writing of the publishers, or in the case of reprographic reproduction in accordance with the terms of licences issued by the Copyright Licensing Agency. Enquiries concerning reproduction outside those terms should be sent to the publishers.

This is a work of fiction. Names, characters, businesses, places, events and incidents are either the products of the author's imagination or used in a fictitious manner. Any resemblance to actual persons, living or dead, or actual events is purely coincidental.

Troubador Publishing Ltd
Unit E2 Airfield Business Park,
Harrison Road, Market Harborough,
Leicestershire. LE16 7UL
Tel: 0116 2792299
Email: books@troubador.co.uk
Web: www.troubador.co.uk

ISBN 978 1805143 055

British Library Cataloguing in Publication Data.
A catalogue record for this book is available from the British Library.

Printed and bound in Great Britain by 4edge Limited
Typeset in 11pt Minion Pro by Troubador Publishing Ltd, Leicester, UK

For Chris

Part One

One

Evelyn Frances Ryan
b. 29th October 1987

2019

There's no sanctity here amongst the dead of Kensal Rise cemetery. Evie's ma is buried in the shadow of a kitchen island-sized monument belonging to a couple of brothers. They were villains shot by rival drug dealers. According to Bea, Ma was once a friend of the family.

Evie clambers up the slope to place flowers in an iron vase. It is welded to the marble that surrounds her mother's grave. When her sister Bea explained to the stonemasons that Ma would appreciate a vase for some fresh-cut flowers, the heavy Gothic urn was recommended as it was theft-proof. She rips the plastic wrapping from the white roses her sister bought from the supermarket and places them in the rain-filled vase.

Bea, suitably funereal in black, stands below her and recites a Hail Mary. Evie is seven months pregnant and has dressed more liberally in a thick cardigan and leggings. Her coat strains to cover her bump. Nothing formal or tailored fits now she's the size of a hot-air balloon and the cold slice of sharp wind at the graveside justifies her layers.

Bea says a curt Amen and glances at her watch while Evie, noticing a clump of rotting leaves on the gravel, stoops awkwardly to remove it. When she rises a figure comes into view. There's a man standing amongst the gravestones. He's alone and although it's impossible for her to be sure at this distance, he's staring at her. She watches him and is alarmed by the way he seems to stare back. Surely if he meant no harm, he would turn away or move on.

'You say that every year.' Her sister's voice cuts through the cold air.

'I didn't say anything.' Evie stares at Bea, small and dark against the sepulchres and monuments reaching to the horizon.

'The stone's more worn than last year. You always say that. Every time we come.'

'Well, it is.'

'Every year. What's that?'

Evie looks up as if the answer is hidden in the blanket of white winter cloud. If she doesn't count the actual funeral, it's twenty-one years. Ma would have been sixty-nine, a perfect age to have a grandchild. Her sister scowls and shrugs.

'I didn't say anything just now.' Evie checks to see whether the man is still present but the space he occupied is empty. Perhaps he wasn't staring at her after all.

Bea inhales, her nostrils flaring like a miniature thoroughbred before she turns away. She walks tentatively, arms out, tiptoeing over icy cracks. Her nipped-in waist and full skirt give the impression of a ballet dancer in heavy wool.

When Evie slips her arm through Bea's she feels the rigidity of her elder sister's frame against her own soft form. She spots the stranger again as they pass the lodge. Walking away this time, his heavy boots fur trimmed and good quality. His puffer jacket can't hide the fact he has the bent outline of an old man.

Bea stops suddenly.

'What? Is it that man? I'm sure he was watching us.'

'He's probably harmless but a couple of women were assaulted in this cemetery recently. It was in the newspaper.'

'Is no woman safe these days?' Evie tuts.

'You're more likely to be assaulted by someone you know, actually.' Outside the gates, the stranger hails a bus and gets on.

'Maybe he thought I was alone.' Evie shivers.

Her sister's bones relax against her and Bea smiles. An apology for her sour mood or relief that the man has gone?

'Shall we have lunch?' Bea asks. They find a cafe where they take a table inside by the window. 'To get the benefit from any remaining daylight,' she says. The sunshine through the glass seems to wrap them in a warm companionable silence interrupted only by the gurgle of the coffee machine.

'When you were young, you were so beautiful. Whichever room you were in was lit with sunlight.' Bea smiles into the middle distance through the window.

Evie follows her sister's gaze and sees a playground full of children climbing, spinning and swinging. The adults are watching the toddlers as they launch themselves off on their adventures, overstuffed ragdolls in their winter ski suits. It stirs a memory. 'Do you remember when we went to Kensington Gardens and I got lost?'

Bea looks at Evie for the first time since they sat down and touches her throat; it's a light, nervous grip on an emerald necklace that belonged to Ma.

'You were both running around shouting. I could see your legs, but you couldn't see me,' Evie says.

'You said you were playing hide-and-seek.' Bea raises her eyebrows. 'Ma was beside herself.'

This memory, like so many others, is not Evie's alone; it's a montage. She provides the first scene — white legs and cotton hemlines flitting through a tangle of branches — but there is nothing after that so Bea fills in the gaps.

Her sister is squinting as if the sunlight streaming in at the window is causing her pain. Evie notices the unusually thick beige powder set in the creases around her eyes.

'Ma was terrifying. I often wonder how you've turned out so…sane,' Bea says.

'I never knew where I was with her. She'd be laughing one minute and the next she's giving me a slap on the backside.' Evie turns her face to catch the sunshine.

'You mustn't worry about talking to yourself. I do it all the time. So did Ma.'

'I didn't say anything. You must have heard someone else.'

'Perhaps Ma was trying to contact us from beyond.' A glint of mischief plays around her sister's eyes and lips. The waiter brings lunch and she makes a point of asking him where he is from, having detected his accent. He's from Argentina and Bea tells him of her trip to Buenos Aires for a catwalk event. If Evie didn't know her better, she would think Bea was flirting with him.

'I'd like to look into our ancestry.' Evie announces this as though she's thought about it at some length.

Bea chews. Evie watches as her tongue drives the food off her front teeth. 'There are some papers,' she says at last. She's swallowing hard so the muscles of her neck stand out like slender organ pipes. 'In a box. In my room. But don't go poking about without my say-so.'

'Oh. A moment ago, I was your little ray of sunshine.'

'Well yes, you were no trouble. But Ma had a past. You never knew her like I did.'

'Didn't know my dad either,' Evie says.

'I've told you before. He left her and stole the rent money. End of.' Bea pushes her plate away and continues to look at the playground. 'I think tracing our ancestry is a fabulous idea.' Bea raises her face to the light once more and closes her eyes. 'There are some cousins in West London.'

The food is surprisingly decent for a place tucked away down a side street. Evie's baguette is overfilled and fresh. There is artwork on the walls and the coffee leaves no trace of bitterness. She eats everything except the brittle crusts as her gums are tender from pregnancy.

The waiter asks Bea if there is anything wrong with

her lunch as she's hardly touched it. She makes it clear that the sandwich is delicious but she lacks the appetite to do it justice. Evie pays at the counter, ordering a cinnamon bun for the train journey home.

Before they part, Bea buttons Evie's cardigan, pulls her coat around the bump and zips it up. 'A girl,' she says. 'I wonder whether she'll have our auburn hair or Ma's red?'

'Or black hair like Max?'

'Red, I bet. You must have a boy next, to look after her.'

'Give me a chance. Anyway, Gertrude will look after herself.'

'Do you have to call her that? It makes her sound like a cow.'

'It's a Max thing. Better than She. It.'

'Keep her snug then.' Her sister tiptoes to kiss Evie's cheek.

The train pulls out of Paddington. There is nothing outside the window except the blackness of a late November afternoon punctuated by flares of light. Evie sighs and stares into the darkness rather than at her double in the window and wonders whether she's serious about looking up her ancestry. She had grown up thinking her conception was the last selfish act of a desperate woman. An afterthought. A ruse to keep a man from running away. Whereas Bea, darling, precious Beatrice Mary, was the adored first child.

How often had Evie walked into a room only for the conversation between Ma and Bea to end abruptly. Their heads close together excluding her from their snug little chat. What were the conspiracies whispered so fervently and furtively? Bea at fifty-one seems older than her years. Burdened, perhaps? It feels like it.

As the birth gets closer, the chasm between them seems to have nothing to do with their difference in age; it's made deeper and wider by Bea's unshared past life. The ancestry research might throw light on Ma's past too. But it's not about finding an uncle who won medals for bravery in the war or a great aunt who was a suffragette. Evie wants to know what to expect when the baby arrives.

She remembers the cinnamon bun and retrieves it from her bag. It has stained the brown paper wrapper with butter and is softly squished. She pushes the whole doughy mass into her mouth, swallowing it in two delicious gulps. Max meets her at the station in the car. He drives as if there are eggs balanced on the dashboard. He asks after Bea and she tells him that Bea seemed a bit off with her and that there was a weirdo at the cemetery.

Their house still smells of new build. They had to sacrifice original features and easy transport links for something affordable. It's on a private estate with clipped hedges and pristine looping roads that take them round and out again. The location is what estate agents call sought after as the River Thames is nearby. There are quaint, well-preserved villages that line its verdant banks. Bobbing boats are tied to pontoons along their stretch of water although a dense evergreen hedge masks this view. This doesn't bother Evie because the sudden reveal of sunlight glinting on the water as they skirt the conifer screen is a constant delight.

After dinner, she clears the coffee table of exercise books and planning sheets and stuffs them in a tote bag. Her maternity leave from her teaching job starts at Christmas. As soon as she's lowered herself onto the sofa, her head drops and she finds it difficult to keep her eyes open.

'Did she mention your dad?'

Max's question jolts her awake.

'No, it's still Mr Unknown.'

'Pity,' he says. 'She must know about him.' He grabs his laptop. 'I think it's mean, if you ask me.'

'She wasn't around at the time Ma was seeing him. And anyway, I haven't really pushed her on it. I'll find out when I do this ancestry thing. It'll be my project. You can get your DNA checked and everything.'

Max is as curious about Evie's dad as she is. Must be something to do with starting a family. Although, he was genuinely delighted when his aunts clubbed together to commission a Ryan family tree. It was a wedding present, all maroon curlicue writing on green linen. It hangs in the hallway and when the front door opens, the wind lifts it ever so gently, as if Max's forebears are welcoming her home.

The television is on mute while Max catches up on work. Evie yawns making a mental list of what to prepare for tomorrow's lessons. Then she kisses Max goodnight and leaves him with his screen. In the bedroom, Gertrude rolls a limb over her bladder and Evie peels off her clothes, throwing them on the new nursing chair. Her body tingles with the relief of being freed from her layers and she stares at the little heap of washing.

She's just thinking she must get on top of the household chores when the necklace Bea was wearing slips out of her cardigan pocket and slides like a green silk ribbon onto the floor. Evie snatches it up from the carpet. Did her sister put it in her pocket? Or did it fall off her neck? She panics. Bea will worry if it's the latter. Evie rings but the phone goes to voicemail. 'Hi, it's me. I found your necklace. I've got it in case you're worried.' Looking at the solid silver clasp, she reckons it didn't come off without her sister's agency. She doesn't know this for sure but Bea has given her a good excuse to visit the house.

At Paddington Station, Evie heads towards Bishop's Bridge Road, intending to get a bus. But the building works for the new Elizabeth Line catch her out and they have been diverted. She walks to Westbourne Grove, pausing to pick up an outrageously expensive fruit tart as a contribution to lunch. An overpriced pot of hyacinth bulbs takes her fancy and she buys it as a gift for Bea then cuts down the back streets towards her old home. By the time she arrives, her legs and lower back are aching and she leans on the gatepost. The white stucco front is stained by old leaks, there are plants growing out of the gutters, the window frames are flaking and the front path is cracked. Next to its swanky neighbours the house looks shabby.

Bea answers the door. Her hair tumbles in clumps of unwashed strands. Her blue eyes sparkle as always but the skin around them is puffy and dark. Today it seems the doorbell has woken her and she's not expecting Evie, despite the arrangement made during the week.

She's wearing a mismatch of loose layers: a beautiful silk kimono with a cherry tree design sags in places it shouldn't; a beige woollen gilet, slack around her shoulders, is secured with a hair stylist's clip at her breast. Bea works for an haute couture designer down a little cobbled mews in Mayfair. She assists in the creation of sumptuously tailored garments, cutting the patterns and making up samples. She used to travel with the design team and has pinned clothes onto the world's most beautiful men and women. She tells anyone who asks that it isn't glamorous, it's a job.

Evie places the hyacinths on the hall table and follows her sister through to the lounge. It looks as though she is moving house. 'What's happening? Where are you going?'

'I'll explain all.' Bea disappears down the three steps to the kitchen.

The room is full of cardboard boxes and bags. There are old suitcases: brown leather ones secured with cracked belts, round vanity cases, the type you see in vintage markets, and there are chocolate boxes. These are huge, their landscape-painting lids bulging from all the stuff they hold.

Bea appears. 'This is it,' she says. 'Us. Ma, John. Your grandparents…'

'You said there was a box in your room, not an archive.'

'Well, I had some free time and I thought…'

Bea flops onto the sofa opposite Evie. The tinted-glass coffee table stands between them. Like everything in the room, it has been here for decades. The Heal's sofas and the Schreiber sideboard would be considered design icons now. The ancient leather armchair by the window, John's chair Bea calls it, is scarred and split in places but still elegant. Only the television belongs to the twenty-first century.

'What you said about tracing your ancestors is a waste of time. We're from low stock. There's nothing but drudgery, criminality and poverty. Max won't thank you.'

'It's nothing to do with Max.'

'It's a waste of your time. You should be concentrating on…Gertrude.'

Evie scans the model village of boxes Bea has assembled. The dusty fingerprints on the rooftops must be hers. 'So, you've gathered together all this history for what?'

'I was going to throw it away.'

'No you weren't.'

'You have every right to go digging. I can't stop you, but you need to know there are some unpleasantries.'

'What sort of Unpleasantries?'

'Not ones I want to discuss.' At the singing of the kettle, Bea stands and walks out of the room. The kimono seems to fly after her like a trained kite.

Evie leans forward and lifts the lid off the nearest box, but on Bea's return, she sits upright again as if she's been caught raiding the biscuit tin. Bea places a tray on the table. The cups rattle as it hits the glass and the tray itself is swimming with spilled tea.

'Well, it's all here.' Bea waves a hand and Evie is transfixed. Her sister's fingers are trembling. It's a rapid uncontrolled quiver that sets the cherry tree branch along her sleeve swaying in a breeze. 'You can help yourself. I won't get in the way.'

'Bea? Are you ill?'

Bea pulls her sleeve down to hide the worrisome hand. 'A little.'

Two

Bea 2019

Evie's legs are wide apart, flanking her bump. Her grey sweater partially hides a white shirt, an old one of Max's. Bea can tell by the stiffness of the collar and cuffs. She is an ensemble of dull grey and off-white. It's sad that Evie has let herself go during pregnancy and the visit to the cemetery was simply disrespectful.

'Are you sick?' Evie asks again.

'No, actually I'm not. As I said, just a little.' Bea thinks of Dr Khan's advice. Best to avoid stressful situations until the test results come back. Keep calm and find a distraction. So she has spent every evening since the bloods were taken pulling out the contents of cupboards and drawers.

The box at Evie's feet contains the mould-spotted funeral cards for great-grandparents, grandparents, aunts and uncles. There are certificates, some of them with an X in place of the signature where the relative was illiterate. Bea half-hopes this is all Evie wants. The ancient past. 'I've put it here for you to sort through.'

'Thank you. I will. What is it?' she asks.

'It's our past. Everything from gas bills to—'

'What do the doctors say?'

'They think it's a repetitive strain injury, nothing to worry about. You know what they're like up at the surgery.'

Evie fetches her rucksack and holds out the necklace.

Bea laughs. 'No, silly, I put it in your pocket as a surprise. I want you to have it.'

'It's yours and if I'm honest, my neck's too big for it. I'll never wear it.'

'You could lose weight after the birth. Is there a local gym you could join?'

'No. I won't need to join a gym. I'll be breastfeeding.' Evie's indignant frown seems to dim the light between them.

'You annoyed with me, Evie?'

'Yes. No. I don't know. You were so weird the other day. And you're ill and you didn't tell me.'

Bea sighs and conjures a contrite smile. 'I'm sorry.'

'And I don't talk to myself.'

'It must have been the wind. Sorry.'

The magic word sweeps the frown from Evie's face but there is still unease. She doesn't tell Evie she can hardly hold a needle let alone thread one. The shaking doesn't happen every day but when it creeps up on her, she has trouble with handles. Pans, brooms, cups, all tricky. Thankfully, her sewing machine is still under her control, the familiar vibration a frenzied metronome to the rhythm of her jangling nerves.

She treads carefully amongst the boxes and throws the emeralds in a drawer. It seems every decision she makes these days is overthought or not thought through. Those bloody emeralds. Why didn't she just say, Here you are, Evie, they're yours now. She would have taken them with good grace. A gift to celebrate the birth of the baby or an early Christmas present. Instead, Bea has made her anxious. What did Evie say in the voicemail? She didn't want her to worry. It should be the other way round. Bea turns and smiles broadly, inviting collusion. 'Shall we search our ancestry?'

Evie opens the chocolate box at her feet, a muddy Joshua Reynolds on the lid. It contains amongst other things, the birth, marriage and death certificates of Grandma and Grandpa Fuller. There is a photograph of the two of them outside number twenty, Prescott Drive.

Their bungalow on the outskirts of West London seemed like a toy house when Bea was little. It was filled with heavy brown furniture and busy wallpaper. Bea had asked Grandma how she got up to bed. At the time, they had all laughed and the anecdote was circulated so that it became a family joke. As the years went by, the innocent remark mutated into an insult. A judgement on Grandpa Tom and Grandma Kath's council-house status. Ma became the rich relation and what a joke that was.

Evie takes pictures of the certificates. 'So, Grandma was a laundry worker at the local hospital and Grandpa was a ganger.' She looks up ganger on her phone. 'It means he built roads,' she says.

'I don't remember him working when I was young. Ma kept out of his way for years.'

'Why?' Evie asks.

'She always said he didn't approve of the way she was carrying on.'

'Was she doing something Unpleasant?'

'There's time for all that later,' Bea says, summoning Evie into the kitchen for lunch.

Evie is shocked at the state of the old fitted units. She offers to help pay for someone to come round to fix the drawer fronts that have fallen off and replace the sealant around the sink. Bea ignores the assault of kindness by cutting bread and tossing salad. They eat. At least Bea tries to as lately her food lies heavily on her. It's as if a squat cross-legged troll lives under the bridge of her diaphragm. She feels a little envious of the way Evie tucks into her food with such relish.

They talk of small things that cause no harm. Evie and Max are thinking of getting a dog, a pair of ducks from the river flew into her garden the other day and Max has been given a big fraud case to work on. He's only been at the law firm a couple of months. He's thrilled.

'What a brain he has,' Bea says. 'How do you keep up with him?'

'I'm quite capable of understanding his work. And there's lots of things he doesn't know. He's never read Joyce, for instance.'

'Well, you make a fine couple. The pair of you are well suited.'

After they have eaten, Bea swipes up the plates and instructs Evie to choose another container from the family depository while she clears the table and washes the dishes.

Bea returns to the lounge to find Evie has picked a brown suitcase that belonged to Ma. There is a pile of stuff already retrieved, stacked up and wobbling next to Evie's feet: squashed shoes, a broad-brimmed hat, the crown of which has caved in, and Ma's make-up bags, thickly caked in foundation and powdery residue. There are clothes, magazines, photographs and some vinyl records still to be excavated. Bea remembers stashing the case and its contents up in the third-floor bedroom after Ma died.

Evie pulls out a little miniskirt. It's a tiny thing – beige wool with a check pattern.

'That waistline measures eighteen inches,' Bea says.

'I've certainly fallen far from the tree.' She holds the skirt so that it sits on her bump.

'You always liked your food.'

'Now what did she say to that when anyone commented?'

Together in unison, they wail, 'She's a growing girl.' The echo in the room and the two voices merging together make it sound as though Ma is calling from the kitchen. Evie puts the skirt to one side and picks up a photograph in a walnut frame. Bea fetches her glasses and leans over to see what Evie is staring at.

'Ma loved that photo of her and Dad.'

Evie places the photo on top of the skirt. 'Your dad.'

Bea is about to say that John wasn't much of a father and that for all his good looks he was a brute when Evie holds her head to one side.

'She's like his trophy. The way he's holding her arms and he's pointing her towards the camera. He could be holding the handles of a gold cup.'

Bea had lived with the picture on the mantelpiece for years. Well, at least for as long as John was around. Holding the old walnut frame in surprisingly steady hands, Bea notices John's broad shoulders and how Ma is overwhelmed by them. To Bea, she looks like a cardboard cut-out he has just placed on a shop floor. The ones that deter shoplifters. She can't see her mother as any sort of trophy, more a possession. Her father seems to be saying, 'Don't steal my stuff.' Bea places the contentious image on the table.

Evie lowers herself down to sit on the floor and rest her back against the sofa. She crosses her legs at the ankles and her body is transformed into the voluptuous softness of a reclining Henry Moore sculpture, a pose Bea could never achieve.

Evie lifts out a hymnal, faded blue barely touched, bearing the owner's name. Ma's name, Rosemary Kathleen Fuller. Next a set of flimsy papers, folded for so long they are tearing along the creases. She unfurls one of them. 'Holy Trinity Church Dance. Age limit strictly fourteen to nineteen. Admits one.' She struggles with the date on the slip but settles on March, nineteen sixty-six. She arranges the skirt, the ticket and the photo together. They tell the story of Ma when she was a girl. 'She would have been fifteen.' Evie runs her hand over the objects as if gently rousing them from sleep. Her face is set in thoughtful concentration.

Bea follows her gaze, and the skirt, photograph and ticket form a triptych raising Ma from the dead. The dry scent of vanilla and acetone from her make-up bag lingers, pulling her into her mother's past. She imagines Rose. Fifteen, tiny waist, long legs. Dancing.

Three

Rosemary Kathleen Fuller
b. 12th November 1950

1966

Rose Fuller stands in front of her bedroom mirror teaching herself to dance like Mick Jagger. Her feet shimmy to the right, then to the left. She lifts one foot an inch above the threadbare rug before sliding it a fraction more and repeating the move with the other foot.

Rose hasn't yet mastered the timing on the arm swing and wrist clap, but she reckons for a girl, the feet are enough. The Holy Trinity Church Dance isn't quite a Soho nightclub but there's music, ginger beer and boys.

Mum calls from the kitchen and Rose takes a deep breath before turning off the radio and pulling her long red hair into a ponytail.

'What the bloody hell is this?' Mum's mouth drops open.

Dad is uncharacteristically speechless when he clocks her miniskirt.

It's beige with a brown check running through it and she's teamed it up with a white roll neck sweater, perfect for the early spring chill. The new shoes are fab. They're shiny patent beige courts. She had started a Saturday job in Peepers a few weeks back. It's the best thing that has ever happened in her entire life. 'It's my uniform,' she lies. 'I always have to wear the clothes from the shop in case people ask me where I got them from.'

Mum holds a hot dinner plate, awash with meat and gravy, using a grubby tea towel to keep her fingers from burning. The kitchen smells of beef dripping. 'Is it a lingerie shop you're working in then? Go and put some clothes on.'

Dad looks away and rubs the back of his fat neck. 'Do as your mother says or you're not going anywhere.'

Rose's mother is a put-upon, dowdy old woman who has never felt the need to control her frizzy brown hair. She has the most repulsive swollen ankles, which she blames on a painful and dangerous birth – Rose's.

'You can drop that sarky face while you're at it.' Mum practically throws the plate onto the table.

It's not Rose's place to talk back. She knows there'll be a hiding if she does. It's not fair she's the only child and the sole target of all their meanness and rage against the world. She didn't ask to be born. Rose runs the length of the corridor back to her room and puts on a long circular skirt with pink rosebuds on white calico. It looks like she's wearing a curtain. The fabric hides the fact she's still wearing the mini underneath.

Her best friend, Carol Lafferty, calls for her. She looks great in a belted summer dress as she's got the bust and hips for it. Rose is a broom to her dustpan. That's what they say at school, although her boobs have been itchy lately and she hopes they're growing. Rose slams the door shut behind them. She bends over, lifts the curtain and shows the door her miniskirted arse before running gleefully up the basement steps.

'How's the job going?' Carol asks.

'Great. I get a clothes allowance.' Rose dips into the shadow of a cobbled mews and removes the curtain, rolling it up and stuffing it into her new red bag.

'Give us a twirl then,' Carol says, and Rose obliges.

'God. You look like Twiggy. You're such a bitch. Get me a job at the shop, will you?'

'I might, you know. One of the full-timers says she's leaving and I'm going to ask my boss for her job.'

'You're leaving school?' Carol looks horrified. She is all round eyes and round mouth. It suits her general roundness.

'Well yeah. I mean what is the point?' There is no point. The teachers don't say so but they sigh a lot when they hand back her homework. Her mum and dad couldn't give a fig. They want her out earning. 'See, Carol, if I can get twenty-five quid a week working in a shop that sells the most fabulous clothes, which I can get for practically nothing…well, I would be doolally not to. Right?'

They laugh and link arms. Carol shivers and their pace quickens as the lights of the church hall draw near. Father Patrick, a clever old letch and overseer of the do, thinks the souls of the young ones are easily corrupted by pop music and dancing.

He explained his reasons for organising the dances one Sunday morning after Mass. 'The church dance will enable me to provide the popular music and the modern dancing our young people crave in a safe environment.' There were nods from the men but the creak of the pews was deafening as the mothers shifted in their seats.

'We don't want them to stray Up West and get involved in the ungodly shenanigans of that infamous place. Do we now?'

The direct bus route from Westbourne Grove to Piccadilly Circus put the fear of God into the Godfearing clergy. The youth of the parish, as far as they were concerned, were bound for Hell if they were to board the bus unaccompanied by priest or nun. A mile away, the underbelly of the serpent that is Paddington crawls with fallen women, and Notting Dale, in the opposite direction, is a cesspit of destitution. But Piccadilly is a singular sort of sewer altogether, so they say.

The dance floor is well lit, but the long fluorescent tubes throw the walls of the place into shadow. Rose swears everyone is gawping at her legs. She was half expecting to be turned away. But the Fathers are all busy.

There is a wooden table where one is dispensing glasses of ginger beer. Swirls of dust picked out by the light, the shed skin of Catholic congregations, shower him as he drops coins into an old biscuit tin. Rose and Carol buy a penny glass each and gravitate towards other girls from their school.

Father Patrick has his back to them and is talking to a man with rolled-up sleeves and braces standing behind the record player. The Father is censoring the music. One small pile for God and a taller pile for the Devil. The music soon draws Rose to the middle of the hall where figures, emerging from the shadows, are gathering. It is both thrilling and scary. No one else is wearing a skirt like hers and she's desperate to try out the Mick Jagger.

The girls place their handbags and drinks on the floor and stand around them. The opening bars of *The Last Time* belt out of the record player and everyone starts moving.

At first, she just sways, unsure of whether this is the place to unleash her talent. Then she makes the first tentative shuffle to the left. Then another to the right. Her arms rise for the wrist clap, but she resists. She's not Mike Yarwood. Rose lifts her foot and shimmies back to where she started and she's got it. The drumbeat works into her bones, the guitar electrifies her sinews and she's on *Top of the Pops* with the lads.

But her shoes are new and the floor has been polished. There are no worn bedroom rugs to stop her sliding away under her smooth soles. To her dismay, she is unbalanced by the slippery parquet with its frictionless veneer. Her legs part in an ungainly scramble to keep upright. She falls onto her backside. One foot kicks a glass and ginger beer trickles a sticky path across the floor. Her bottle-green school knickers are exposed and everyone is roaring with laughter. Except Carol, who has her hands clamped over her face. She's such a good mate.

Rose's shame is complete when Father Patrick pulls her up by her roll neck and escorts her out of the door. She is shaking with embarrassment and his words come sharp and cruel.

'I will be speaking to your father and you can expect harsh words, Miss. I will be advising him to keep you in your room and burn your wanton little skirt on the fire.'

'But, Father, it's the fashion. Don't tell me dad.'

She knows he will speak to Tom, as he's done before, and she'll get the belt. She starts giggling uncontrollably. A response to her fear and the idea her skirt is wanton. It was the skirt that led her into temptation.

'I will pray for you, Rosemary Fuller.' Father Patrick nods his head like a vigorous automaton. The old priest raises himself to full height and points a nicotine-stained finger as he declares, 'In the meantime, Miss. You are barred.'

Rose can't stop laughing now. There are tears in her eyes as The Holy Father strides into the hall, sweeping past Carol who is clutching the red handbag. Carol joins in the sniggering and Rose crosses her legs sure she's going to piss herself.

'First person to be barred.' Carol hands her the bag.

'Not the last, I reckon,' Rose says, taking the bag and pulling out the old curtain.

'You're a legend, Rose. I'll see you Monday at school, yeah?' Her friend slips back into the hall.

When Carol opens the door, Rose hears the man with the record player announcing the next song. His voice is stilted, hesitant. He's not a real disc jockey like the ones on Radio Luxembourg but some bloke who happens to own a Dansette and a bunch of forty-fives. She doesn't resent the fact that her friend goes back in. Rose would do the same.

Later, the Laffertys will send out an army of brothers to escort her home. Which is unlucky for Carol. Whereas Rose is already planning her escape from her parents, her friend has no hope of getting up to any West End type shenanigans with her mob.

Rose doesn't bother trying to get back into the dance nights at first. They are for kids anyway. Carol says she must ask Father Patrick for a second chance and that she shouldn't be embarrassed by the accident. According to her, all the girls are wearing minis and she makes it sound like they're all falling over. The way Carol tells it, Rose has invented a new dance. But the marks on her thighs are pretty bad. Dad really went for it, holding her down with his big fat hand on her spine, her cheek squashed into the crumbs on the kitchen table and his hobnailed boot on her foot. Luckily, Peepers sell these great ski pants that loop under the feet. They look cool and her boss says not everyone can wear them.

For Rose, there is always an upside to everything. The girl who works at the shop on weekdays leaves and Rose waves a goodbye to the school gates. She gives the concrete block of modern incomprehension a two-fingered salute. Carol and some other girls are at the window of one of the science labs. They are waving madly. She waves back and blows kisses like she's Esther Williams at Cannes until the girls turn away in one sharp synchronised movement and disappear.

Rose gives her mum ten pounds a week for her keep and stows a few pounds in her Post Office savings account when she remembers. Her parents never asked for her money. They don't enquire into how much she earns and it's as if there exists an unspoken rule: don't mention housekeeping; coins for the gas meter; don't complain about the quality of the meat or the fact there's no cake for Sunday tea. A bit of bad luck must be endured without comment.

Conversely, a bit of good luck should be snatched up and acted upon immediately as it is guaranteed not to last. More importantly, the good luck must be kept hush-hush, shared only amongst the immediate family, as to involve others leads to catastrophe.

Like last summer when Kathleen proudly announced that by being careful with the housekeeping and a small win on the bingo, she had finally saved enough money for a holiday. ''Ere, Tom, get down the phone box and book a family room.' Kath had handed over a black-rimmed advert for a guest house on the Kent coast. She gave him an empty envelope with the address neatly written in capital letters. The instructions were clear: book the room, go directly to the Post Office, buy a stamp and send the landlady a deposit to secure the booking. Kath handed the precious pound notes to Tom who stuffed them in his wallet.

Once he'd gone, Kath and Rose set to cleaning the flat. Then after a cup of tea and a salad cream sandwich lunch, they took it in turns to search the wardrobes, planning their holiday outfits.

It was late in the day when Tom arrived home. He was limping.

'What happened?' Kath's face was a mixture of anger, suspicion and worry.

'I got mugged, girl.'

Despite her bulk, she knelt with the agility of one half her age and tended to his ankle. Tom howled as Kath peeled off his boot and sock. Then she stopped. 'Have you been drinking? You have, ain't ya? Did you book the B and B?'

There was a strangled reply interspersed with groans and yelps as Kath wrapped a bandage around the swelling. 'I went to the Alex for a pint. Just one I swear. Then I went to the phone box and some Herbert opened the door and snatched me wallet.'

Kath must have gripped the swollen ankle with more force than she intended because Tom let out a deafening scream that bounced off the kitchen walls. 'Stupid cowson. What ya doing?'

'I haven't touched yer.'

Kath stood, hands on hips. 'So, the deposit money's gone?'

'It's not my fault!' Tom raised his voice and Kath did likewise.

'You've had a skinful. You chancer!'

Rose ran out of the kitchen. Limping or not, Tom was handy with his fists and she didn't intend to stay around to witness it. She fled to her room; the sound of an almighty row muffled by closed doors.

Tom's two weeks off work and no wages meant the money Kathleen had saved was used to pay the rent and feed the meter. For some time afterwards, she rarely spoke more than was necessary and when she did it was through gritted teeth. Especially when she learned from Sylvie, the neighbour, that Tom had been in the Alex for well over an hour boasting about taking his family on holiday. A glimmer of happiness had been snuffed out by Tom's inebriated inattention and feckless boasting.

To celebrate the bit of extra money Rose is now bringing in, Tom treats them all to fish and chips. They sit around the kitchen table eating greedily. Mum has a brew on the go and Rose butters slices of white bread. They make chip butties and the sounds that fill the little kitchen come from deep down inside: the growl of anticipation as the paper is unwrapped, the gurgling of empty stomachs and the soft belches of contentment.

Rose is always hungry. It's as if she has a little puppy inside her yelping for food but right now, the puppy is well happy. She licks the salt and vinegar from her fingers and closes her eyes when cold butter melts on hot chips. 'Wish we could have this every night.'

'It's fish on Fridays, Rose.' Dad speaks through a mouthful of food.

'It's a treat. Isn't it? It wouldn't be the same if we had it every night.' Mum pours hot tea into mugs. They take turns sharing the spoon to stir in their sugar.

'We could have fish and chips every Friday then,' Rose says.

'We'll have it when I say so.' Dad sits back, places a hand on his big round belly and picks his teeth.

'I could buy it for us with my wages.'

'No thank you,' he says.

'Why not? I don't mind.'

'I mind.' He removes the stubby wet finger from his mouth and bounces it by the side of his plate. 'I am the one who puts food on this table. It is my job.'

'I'm only saying—'

Tom picks up his knife and bangs the end of its handle down.

'You've said enough,' Mum says. 'Your dad pays for dinner.'

Rose offers to wash up, sending her parents into the front room to watch telly. They won't move unless they need to piss or fetch a bottle of stout. She takes the old belt from its hook on the back of the kitchen door. Its worn brown leather, stretched by years of misuse, is scarred with pale striations that resemble the skin at the top of her thighs. Rose twists the leather around her knuckles as her dad has done for years. She throws it off and it unwinds itself.

Wrapping it in the newspaper that held the fish and chip supper, she walks out to the dustbin and throws the rubbish inside. The metal lid clangs with a satisfying echo that follows her back into the flat.

Four

Rose 1966

The Fullers have a kitchen, living room and two bedrooms in their basement flat. The rooms run off a narrow corridor where a single bulb glows dimly. The back wall of the kitchen bulges with damp and the ornate ceiling plaster is riddled with cracks.

A glass-panelled door at the end of the corridor leads to a small yard graced by the outside toilet. Rose's old pram still stands by the back wall, useful for when Kathleen needs to carry coal or potatoes, and a tin bath hangs on a sturdy hook. Out the front at street level, a broad flight of external stone steps, smooth and worn, leads up to the main house. The last tenant upstairs was a filthy-mouthed brothel-keeper.

When Rose was eleven, the brothel-keeper, Scary Mary as she was called by the neighbours, was arrested. Rose and Kathleen had just returned from the Saturday shopping trip, Kath wheeling the old pram. They had seen the Black Maria parked outside their house.

'Not before time,' Kath had said.

They had stood on the pavement and were soon joined by others. Mary's mouth was painted a vivid shade of red and a scrape of blue eyeshadow filled the creases around her eyes. Her sagging body was wrapped in a flowery dressing gown tied at the waist and her breasts swung low under the robe. Two policemen, skinny in their navy serge, tussled with her on the stairs.

Kath had clasped her hands over Rose's ears. Her mother had probably intended to protect her from the woman's language, but the grip on her head meant Rose was unable to look away and she could hear every foul word.

The old madam was screeching insults and spitting as the coppers took their truncheons to her thighs and buttocks. 'Get the fuck off me. Bastard pigs,' she screeched. 'I'll tear the balls off yer.' With every blow from the truncheon, she had lashed out at the officers with long red talons, directing kicks at their privates when given a chance. 'You wait until I tell Inspector Bryan. He won't be happy. Ow! You coupla cunts.'

'What did she say?' the old man who lived two doors down asked the crowd around him.

'She's gonna tell Inspector Bryan,' Sylvie piped up.

'He's her best customer.' A voice behind Rose caused a ripple of laughter to skim through the audience.

Although Rose was old enough to know Mary was a very bad woman, there was something heroic about her attempts to free herself in this uneven battle. She was Boudicca fighting two Roman soldiers, lacking only the armour and a chariot.

As the struggle continued, the parting of her robe exposed the ripe, bushy mound of her fanny. Rose had never seen such a thing and was in one breath revolted and enthralled. Her mother had let go of her head by now, too busy talking to the neighbours to notice the woman's state of undress. They exchanged stories about the shameless girls who worked for the brothel-keeper and the men who kept them up all night with their comings and goings. Eventually, the two policemen managed to cover the old woman up and get her handcuffed. When the van roared out of sight, the only evidence there had been an incident was a pair of grubby pink satin slippers on the stairs, misshapen moulds into which Scary Mary had poured her bunioned feet.

Sylvie had taken them from the step as if she were picking up after her dog and thrown them in the dustbin. 'Gawd knows what they've seen,' she said.

'Let that be a warning to you, girl.' Kath had kicked the brakes of the pram and shoved Rose in the back towards the basement gate.

The bombed houses at the end of Rose's street have been bulldozed. Hammering and endless drilling fills the air during the day. At night there is an eerie stillness behind the hoardings that hide the new flats. Some are occupied. According to Sylvie, they have inside toilets and baths, balconies, and windows the length of the walls. There is central heating in every room, and it's included in the rent. 'You can leave your front door open and everyone looks out for one another like they did before the war,' Sylvie says. When he heard this, Dad told Mum to go down the council office and sign up for one.

They have few callers. Dad's relatives live in a new town out Essex way and Mum's sister, Vi, lives in Ruislip. They exchange Christmas cards but Vi never visits. It's not the same as it used to be, she says. The rent collector, the man who comes to empty the gas meter and the milkman make their brief calls. Mike from Enright's Department Store is Rose's favourite visitor. He brings a suitcase full of necessities and premium items to buy on tick.

He looks like Lionel Blair with his collar-length hair and shimmering shirts. They're sometimes blue, and sometimes a daring dusky pink. He has a dark tan that seems to last all year round and he carries a large brown leather suitcase full of cellophane-covered clothes. Anyone watching him descend the stairs would think he were a glamorous uncle returning home from overseas and not the tally man. It's spring and with the season comes a change of stock.

'Good morning, Kathleen. Lovely to see you. And look at your Rosemary. What a doll! I've got a fabulous line of frocks, new in. She'd look smashing in them. How's that leg of yours? Mr Fuller well?'

'Tea, two sugars, Mike?' Kathleen signals to Rose who turns away and fills the kettle.

Mike places the suitcase on the kitchen table and Rose and Kathleen ooh and aah over the high-value items he is trying to flog them. He holds up a lemon summer dress which gives Rose an electric shock when she touches it. 'Looks like it's just stepped off the pages of *Vogue*,' he declares.

'No thanks, Mike. It's not her birthday and besides she's got this job at a boutique. Haven't you, Rose?'

Mike's alarm flickers across his face at this news. But he rallies. 'That's all very well for young Rosemary, but you'll be wanting something more sophisticated.' He pulls out a gold sequinned cocktail jacket. 'This is a reproduction of one Grace Kelly wore. Try it on, love. I've only the one left in your size. You'll kick yourself if you miss out.'

Kathleen pulls the jacket on and tiptoes to catch her reflection in the mirror above the kitchen sink. The sequins glimmer, giving her cheeks a healthy glow.

'Perhaps I'll buy it you,' Rose says.

'Don't be daft. Where am I going to wear it? The bingo?' Her mother slips the jacket off and returns it to Mike.

'I tell you what. I'll do you a discount seeing as you're one of my best customers.' Mike holds the jacket up to the light bulb and it glitters provocatively in the dimly lit kitchen. It's as if he's trying to hypnotise them.

Kathleen buys a new girdle for herself and socks and vests for Tom. They are bought as replacements for the dull grey ones that are no longer fit for purpose. She has a little book to tally up her payments. Mike has a similar book but his has a leaf of inky blue carbon paper. She needs to pay a few shillings to clear last month's debt, then a small amount to begin her new instalments. They write identical figures in their books. Mike uses a fancy pen with gold bands around it and as he writes he tucks one ankle around the other. Rose reckons that the sole of his left shoe is threatening a hole. The tally man re-packs the suitcase with a precision that reminds Rose of a soldier packing his kit bag in war films. He tells Kath to ring head office in case she changes her mind about the jacket. Her mother smiles in response to Mike's permanently beaming face as she says her goodbyes. But Rose detects the usual cloud of regret hanging between them.

Not long after Mike's visit, Kathleen tells Rose that a family from Trinidad called the Stanleys have moved in upstairs. Her mother uses an insulting epithet to describe her new neighbours and Rose tuts. She tells Kath to be kinder and for this she receives a lengthy racialist rant.

Evangeline Stanley is gorgeous: slim, hair swept up like a Motown singer, the skin of her round cheeks dark and smooth, even though she's probably in her forties like Kathleen. Rose is too polite to ask where the husband is, but the two young lads are well brought up, she can tell. Sylvester, the older one, is ten and Linton is seven. Rose sees them helping their mother clear out rubbish, sweep the steps and run errands.

Her new neighbour takes in clothes for repairs and alterations but mostly she makes up patterns her customers bring with them. Rose has seen the women, Black, smart in their fitted dresses and little jackets, the sort of outfits the women in her family wear to weddings. They wait on Evangeline's top step, polar opposites of the dirty old men who stood there when the rooms were rented to Scary Mary.

When she first met Evangeline, Rose had been on her way to work. Her new neighbour was struggling with her shopping bag on the stairs. Rose had introduced herself and offered to help with the shopping but Mrs Stanley refused. Rose understood why.

There was blood. Pink blotches stained the canvas bag. Bulging out of the top was a mound of mottled grey rind. A dead animal.

'What is it?'

'Goat,' she had said, heaving the bag onto the steps.

'Goat?'

'Kid goat, for a curry. It's cheap and has better flavour than lamb or beef. When it's cooked, you can have some.' The woman's handbag was slipping from her shoulder and Rose rescued it. The shopping swung awkwardly between her legs and pale pink blood smeared her smart beige raincoat.

'You'll need to wipe that down sharpish,' Rose said.

'I will. Don't fret about me, sweetheart. You mustn't be late for work.'

'It's alright. I'm opening up today. I work in a boutique.'

'You're too young to be the boss, nah?' Mrs Stanley had reached the front door and took the handbag from Rose. 'You the boss?'

'Me? No. I'd like to be one day. Welcome to Westbourne Park, Mrs Stanley. If you need anything, I'm just downstairs.' She'd waved a cheery goodbye and run to catch her bus.

Dad is furious. For three days, the smell of the curry drenches the walls of the whole house with a spicy perfume that slowly fades to a single fragrant note. Rose inhales the scented air and her mouth waters.

But Kathleen sprays a throat-clenching air freshener that makes Rose gag, the hiss of the aerosol as waspish as her mother's nasty little comments. When Dad comes home, the two of them sit and moan about the decline of the neighbourhood.

'Why don't you ask Evangeline to open the windows upstairs if you're so offended by the smell?' Rose says, fed up with the constant criticism.

'Evangela, is it?' Dad chokes on his stout. 'Don't you be fraternising with her upstairs. She's got two kids and no fella. She's a wrong 'un.'

'It's Evange*line*. And you can't be so quick to judge. He might be in some war somewhere.'

'War? What are you talking about?'

'He might be a soldier in the Commonwealth.' She sits in the armchair nearest the door. A cold draft that deadens the flesh in all weathers creeps in and she gathers her long legs up to keep them warm.

'Soldier. Commonwealth. I swear some of the things you come out with.' Dad sneers. 'They don't allow Blacks in the British Army.'

'There were Black American GIs in the war. Why can't there be Black soldiers in England?'

'Don't talk about what you know nothing about. They're ain't no Black soldiers in Her Majesty's armed forces. I know. I was there.'

The gate swings on its rusty hinges and shortly afterwards there is a faint knock. Rose waits until Mum nods before getting up to answer the door.

Sylvester stands in the shadowy porch, hunched and awkward. Rose asks him to come in, but he shakes his head. 'Mum says to give you this.' He holds out a dinner plate covered with another dinner plate.

'It smells amazing.'

'Who is it, Rosemary?' Mum shouts from the front room her voice closer than expected.

Sylvester takes a step back. 'Can we have the plates back when you're finished?' he whispers.

''Course. Tell your mum I'll bring them up later.'

He turns away and takes the stairs two at a time. Mum comes into the kitchen where Rose is eating her second dinner. 'What's that?'

'Sylvester's brought me some curry. Isn't that kind?'

Dad pokes his head around the door. They've been eavesdropping. 'You're not going to eat that?'

'I bloody well am.'

The sauce is thick, brown rather than grey, studded with celery and carrots. There are dumplings, firm on the outside, fluffy inside. As Rose lifts the meat to her mouth it falls away from the bones. There are tastes she has never experienced, deep layers of fragrant spices, herbs and a bubble-gum sweetness.

Alone in the kitchen, Rose eats. Head down, slurping gravy, sucking the marrow from the bones and licking the dish clean. She scrapes the leftovers into the kitchen pail, washes the plates and takes them upstairs. Sylvester comes to the door and she tells him to thank his mum. She cocks an ear at the drone of a machine coming from somewhere inside.

'Sewing machine,' Sylvester explains.

'I'd love to learn to sew. I was rubbish at it in school.'

'Mum's, like, always sewing. She sews in her sleep.'

'Did your mum make that shirt?' Sylvester is wearing a

fitted shirt with a broad collar and cuffs that shines goldy-coloured in the evening light. He looks down at his chest and nods. 'Well, I best get downstairs. Tell your mum that dinner was the best thing I have ever tasted in my life. And I mean it.'

Rose unwraps a toffee she has found in her pocket. It's good to have an excuse to be out in the night air. Warmed by her second dinner she stands on the top step and looks down at the street. She is looking forward to June, when the milkweed and privet blossom bloom in the front gardens. She wonders if anyone has thought of making an air freshener out of privet blossom. It's a clean, fresh fragrance, like mown grass, that masks the urine smell rising off the pavements. Unlike her delusional parents, she knows the neighbourhood has been a shithole for as long as she can remember. Dirty, run-down and full of old drunks pissing up the walls in broad daylight. No wonder the council is tearing it down.

Across the road, Sylvie's curtains twitch. She must have seen a few things from her window when the brothel was in business. Local punters still need somewhere to get a hand job and they have plenty of opportunities around here. The prostitutes hang about outside the Duke of York pub as bold as you like and there's a woman in one of the houses on Powys Square who sits at her window with no bra on.

Mum and Dad ignore these facts, preferring to think of the area as an idyll, a little enclave of people like them, all rubbing along together having survived the Blitz. Kath conveniently forgets that she was once a foreigner herself.

After a few rum and blacks, she's quick to tell Rose about the time her family fetched up in Ladbroke Grove fresh from Cork. Signs in the windows where rooms were for rent stated, 'No Irish, No Blacks and No Dogs.' Kath tells her how she walked home from school with her sister, Vi, and they ran into a group of local boys who called them Gypsies, spat at them and mocked their Irish accents. Maybe the people moving to the area now feel just like her mum did back in the day.

Instead of seeing Westbourne Park for what it is, a crime-riddled slum area where people would rob their own grannies for the price of a pint, her parents complain to each other about how the outsiders are taking the jobs, the houses and the women. Rose straightens out the silvery toffee paper and makes her way down to the basement. She throws the wrapper in the dustbin and notices the bones from her second supper. Someone has already emptied out the kitchen pail.

Five

Rose 1966

Sharon Clements, pronounced Clemo, is gorgeous. She speaks like Rose imagines Princess Margaret speaks, dropping little French phrases into her conversation like Rose drops profanities. She wears the top range in her shop. This summer it's about wearing white: white drop-waist dresses; white half-length boots and a white turban over her peroxide hair. 'Only practical, darling, if you travel everywhere by car,' Sharon declares.

She has taught Rose lots of useful things: how to apply make-up properly, what hairstyle suits her – short, close cut around the neck and fringe swept to one side – and how to eat without looking like a starving docker. That was what Sharon called her when they went for breakfast one morning.

Peepers Boutique is Sharon's own business. The clothes are designed by her friends and there are two other shop assistants. Lizzy, dark-eyed and small like Elizabeth Taylor and Jean, buxom and blonde. 'The Range' as Sharon says. According to her fashion philosophy, adding Rose to the staff, with her red hair and skinny frame, means she has a collection of assistants who represent her customers. These customers drift in, quietly choose an item and drift out again. There are many dull moments when rails are re-hung, window displays are updated and money is counted and banked.

Occasionally, Sharon's friends hang out at the shop. An art school crowd, they linger over the coffee Rose makes them, talk about artists she's never heard of and try on clothes which they never buy. One of them is a photographer called Marcus. Sharon believes that Rose's red hair will look fabulous in print and persuades him to take her picture.

Upstairs from Peepers is a tiny flat accessed by a spiral staircase which Sharon calls her Kensington slum. One room is painted brilliant white. The shop logo, a pair of wide-open eyes looking up into a forest of black lashes, adorns one wall. A lamp on a tripod throws a hot beam into the room.

As Rose changes into the outfit Sharon wants her to wear, green tartan cape over a matching mini dress and peaked cap, Marcus is replacing film cartridges. He is tubby and has a skinhead cut that doesn't suit his head. A man needs a smooth domed bonce to get away with a number two. Marcus's head is broad and compressed as if it had been sat on when he was a baby. He is wearing a boiler suit like the one her dad wears for work. He hasn't even noticed Rose has stripped down to her underwear and she's determined not to get all shy and immature around him.

This is the future. A modelling career, as Sharon says, is every girl's dream, foreign travel and stacks of money in the bank, an independent life. The money part sounds alright to Rose, but she gets sick on long journeys so isn't bothered by the travel bit. The lights heat the room and her armpits are already damp from the itchy wool.

Marcus gives her a brief smile and barks instructions. 'Like stone, love.'

She's taken aback by the accent. He talks like Sharon and it sits incongruously with his skinhead cut and workmen's overalls.

He's sweating and puffing. 'No emotion,' he says into the camera and steps up on a ladder to take a shot from above. 'Don't move, Puss.' He isn't happy with the lighting and jumps down to adjust the lamp.

The cap keeps slipping down towards her nose but he doesn't seem to care about how ridiculous she looks.

'Wait there, Puss.' He too is sweating and wipes his palms on what Rose thinks is a tea towel before realising it's the blouse she's just removed. He is about to raise it to his head.

'Oi! The cheek of it.' She snatches the blouse off him to inspect the damage and the little cap rolls across the floor.

'Sorry, sweety, thought it was a rag.'

'For God's sake.' She shakes out the blouse and puts it over the back of a chair. 'Anyone would think it's hard work.' Rose places the cap back on her head, willing it to stay put.

'I beg your pardon?'

'Taking pictures.'

His glistening face, slick as her own armpits, is inches from hers. 'It *is* bloody hard work. It's art. But you wouldn't have a clue about that, would you?'

'Very sorry, I'm sure,' she says, her mouth as dry as sandpaper.

Marcus leaves the room and she hears a tap running nearby. She wonders whether to shout out for a glass of water but decides against it. Instead, she adjusts the cap so that it sits at a jaunty angle and takes up her pose with a renewed determination to please.

He returns and without warning, collapses at her feet onto his back.

She steps away and squeals. 'What the f…?'

Marcus roars. 'What are you doing? Get back into position.'

'No way. You're a pervert.' Rose closes her knees and clutches the skirt.

'This is impossible. Forget it. I'm not putting up with this.' He turns over to haul himself up on all fours and her kitten heel accidently skewers his hand. The air is filled with a string of expletives as he kneels at her feet.

Her lips twitch at the corners and she chews her cheek to keep from laughing. As if the screaming photographer had had enough trauma, the cap falls off her head and the stiff plastic peak bounces off the bridge of his nose.

'Bloody oiks.' He spins around the room collecting his gear, muttering curses and sucking his hand before storming out amidst the clank and scrape of his ladder and tripod. Downstairs, there are voices raised in argument.

Rose waits for Marcus to return, watching the door, unsure whether to stay or go.

Sharon's snow-white turban appears. 'Rosie, *ma chérie*? Marcus has had to leave for another appointment. I need you downstairs *tout de suite*.' She stares through thick black eyeliner and takes a drag on her ciggy.

'Sharon?' Rose turns so that her boss can unzip the tartan dress.

'*Oui*?'

'What's an oik?'

'It's a slang word for a hip sort of girl.'

The shop floor is quiet, Sharon is in the little back office, Lizzy is at lunch and Jean stands at a long pine table re-folding knitwear. Rose tells her that Marcus wanted to take photos up her skirt and Jean laughs.

'Marcus isn't into girls. And he is a very talented artist.' Jean raises her eyes, directing Rose to look at the black and white images displayed on the walls. Lizzy and Jean pose in the white room upstairs. Unsmiling, Jean is no longer an affable shop girl. She is hardened around the edges on Marcus's instruction. Lizzy's pitying brown eyes stare down at Rose like the Virgin Mary. The girl who Rose replaced stands on a hilltop in a cape which billows in a ferocious gale. Her hair covers most of her face and she stands with her fists on her hips.

Rose sees these pictures every day but never really looks at them. Today they seem altered. The one on the hill is about to step off her windswept cliff to give her what for. She slinks into the back office and makes coffee, hoping she has the chance to apologise to Marcus one day.

Later, as they lock up, Sharon invites her to the pub with the rest of the staff. They sit on high bar stools and are joined by others. The old couple who own the antiques shop next door are already at the bar and the man who sells fruit and veg on the corner soon joins them. The jukebox plays *Spanish Harlem*, and someone buys a round. Rose is given what Sharon is drinking, a ruby tumbler of Campari and soda on ice.

Sharon lights a cigarette then offers the carton to Rose. Carol sometimes allows Rose to breathe in the fumes from ciggies she's nicked from her brothers. But she draws the line there. Sharing a fag is unhygienic, you can get cold sores, she had explained. Rose confesses to the company she has never partaken.

They become animated by the confession and encourage her while Sharon demonstrates her smoking technique. She exaggerates each step, peppering the lesson with French instructions. Rose does as she's told and coughs into her wrist as the smoke stings her nostrils. The people around her laugh but she has another drag, catching her reflection in the mirror behind the bar. With her Campari and soda in one hand and a cigarette in the other mimicking Sharon's pose, she doesn't recognise the imposter.

This girl isn't the Rose who gets a belt for her cheek or the pupil with down-at-heel school shoes that pinch her feet. This is the Rose who has arrived in the big grown-up world and wears her hair and make-up like the models in *Vogue* magazine.

'He's a lucky man,' somebody says. It's a male voice. Rose blushes, turns away from the mirror and glances along the bar. But none of the men sipping their pints look her way.

One after the other the little group relate their experiences of their first smoke. The antique dealer's grandmother had offered him a cheroot when he was twelve. His grandad had died of lung cancer and the old bird had wanted company. Lizzy says she used to steal her teacher's supply from his desk.

But the fruit and veg seller trumps everyone. 'I had my first smoke when I was eight. It was during the Blitz. There was an air raid and we had to scarper to the underground. I was with me mates larking around, so it was alright. When the siren sounded the all-clear we ran up the stairs and there was rubble everywhere.'

'It must have been awful.' Sharon is sympathetic and the antique dealers nod in agreement.

'The fronts of the buildings had collapsed, and you could see inside the rooms. There were clocks and pictures still hanging on walls.'

While the fruit and veg seller takes a long drink, Rose notices Lizzy and Jean exchanging a look. They roll their eyes. It's probably because they are sick to death of war stories whereas Rose has been taught to listen with respect.

The fruit and veg seller continues, 'We walked down the road, all of us not speaking. Speechless we was. Then we saw this black coat lying on the road up ahead. We went closer and it was a woman just staring up at the sky, blood on her face. Stone dead. She had this packet of fags all squashed up in her fist. Like she'd wanted to take them with her when she'd copped it.' He stops to take a drag on his Woodbine, closing one eye as the smoke rises. 'To this day, I don't remember who done it, but one of us half-inched the packet. A full packet. Poor cow was probably on her way home from the tobacconist when the siren went.'

Everyone is still. Rose reckons they are all thinking the same thing as her. That the fruit and veg seller pinched the fags. He chain-smokes and is always miserable. Like he keeps a nasty little secret.

'Whose round is it?' Jean says brightly. The pleasant hum of small talk resumes and someone feeds the jukebox to lift the mood.

Rose tries to focus on the conversation as it flows from fashion trends to music then gossip. She is handed more Campari and sodas until she feels sick and words come out of her mouth all of a muddle. When Jean asks her what she's doing on her day off, she can't remember the name of the department store on Church Street where she intends to go shopping for tights.

A man she doesn't recognise thrusts a tumbler in her hand, not the pretty pink drink, but something dark that fills her nose with fumes. He offers her another cigarette which she smokes as if she's been smoking all her life. He laughs when she tells him she's an oik. Rose tries to listen to the stranger over the background chatter and the records on the jukebox, but she can't follow what he's saying. The pub has filled up and she's jostled by people trying to get to the bar. The stranger is standing so close she can make out the porous hair follicles on his upper lip. His mouth moves but there is no sound.

He puts a hand on her knee and her stomach heaves, her skin grows cold and she's going to vomit. Rose looks around for Sharon but her boss and all the others have disappeared. She fumbles for her coat and handbag and slips off the stool. As she heads for the door the stranger blocks her way, but she pushes his chest with a flat palm and tells him to fuck off. Once outside, the pavement rears towards her and she throws up.

The shillings for her keep clatter noisily all over the kitchen lino and someone has opened the door of the front room. A television audience laughs. She pukes into the outside lavvy, immune to the cold. In bed, the ceiling swings up then crashes down before whirling around several times as if God were stirring the room with a cocktail stick. Jordan's. She remembers. Jordan's is the name of the department store on Church Street. Rose falls asleep dreaming that she is the black-coated woman on the bombed-out street. She rises off the gritty pavement, screaming at the fruit and veg seller. Blood pouring from her head, she chases after him as he legs it. She wants her fags back.

Six

Evie 2019

Gertrude is kicking. It's a vicious attack and papers slip off Evie's knees. Bea comes over and rests her hand on the bump. The hand, which had been shaking uncontrollably an hour ago, is quite steady and her long fingers search for the little prods and pokes coming from within. She giggles when Gertrude kicks so hard it makes Evie swear.

'Can I stay the night?' Evie asks.

'Max will worry about you,' Bea says. She looks nervous.

'I just can't face the journey.'

'I'll call you a cab.'

'But this is great. We never talk like this.'

'You've got Max to bore you now.'

Bea is busy shoving photos back into the suitcase. Evie needs to move. Her legs and backside are numb from sitting on the floor. She struggles to her feet and sits on the sofa.

'That's hilarious.' Bea smiles.

'What?'

'The way you got off the floor. Like a desperate sea lion.'

'Can I stay? I can order a takeaway and we can watch a film.'

Bea is deciding. Her thoughts flit across her face. Yes. No. Awkward. Love to have you. Maybe. Eventually she agrees.

Max tuts down the telephone when Evie tells him. She imagines him blowing out his cheeks as he's deciding whether to quibble about it. She suggests he come and pick her up on Sunday and take her and Bea to lunch.

Evie insists on a walk down the market. She persuades her sister to throw a long coat over her kimono. Bea scrapes her hair up into a neat little chignon, hauls on some boots and wraps a grey scarf around her neck.

'No, not that one,' Evie says. 'It's too dull. Here.' A bright pink scarf is hanging from the coat hooks in the hall as if it's been repurposed as home decor. When she throws it around Bea's neck, the colour returns to her sister's cheeks.

Bea and Evie follow an old familiar route to the Bella. No one calls the Portobello Road by its real name. It was always the Bella or Portobella, the end letter sounding more suited to the local accent, to Ma's accent. They cut through the backstreets and use the walkways of the housing estate in the shadow of the Westway.

The queue at the Lisboa bakery isn't really a queue, but a huddle of good-natured bon vivants anticipating sweet, delicious pastries and catching up on their news. They join the hubbub and buy a box of small delicate cream-filled cakes before mooching around the stalls of Golborne Road. It's more like Portobello used to be. The crowds thin out after the Westway overpass and it's easier to stroll.

Evie notices the changes from when she was a girl. Amongst the fine china and bric-a-brac there are prayer mats and tagines and stalls selling fried fish and couscous. The greasy fry-ups Ma used to treat her to are still on the menu in the cafes but there are vegan alternatives. It seems every other dish has some take on avocado. The bread is sourdough instead of white sliced and the tea is Earl Grey or English Breakfast. Not the thick brown sludge that tasted like rusty metal.

The shutters are coming down on the shopfronts and the darkness of afternoon is alleviated by the streetlamps. Stallholders fling open the back doors of little vans as they pack up. It seems as though Bea's hands have turned into a barometer for gauging her sister's health. Evie can't help but glance at them and now Bea is holding the box of pastries, they are in clear view.

Bea stops abruptly. 'Do you want one now?'

'What?'

'A cake? Do you want a cake? You keep looking at the box.'

'No thanks. I'll wait.'

Some people are queuing outside the pub on the corner of Falmouth Road. Except it's not a pub anymore. It's an oyster bar and fine dining experience according to *Time Out*. Bea slows down when she reaches the pub. 'A little local history, perhaps? A bit of context for your family tree? This place was once notorious for prostitutes and drug dealing. The Laffertys used to deal here, from what Ma said.'

'Who are the Laffertys? Do we know them?'

'We see two of them every time we visit Ma.'

'At the cemetery?' Evie thought for a moment. 'The next-door neighbours with the big kitchen island monument.'

'It was called the Duke of York back then. I remember when I was young, Ma hung out here. She was very low at the time. I suppose she was lonely. John rarely visited.'

'This isn't one of your Unpleasantries is it?' Evie scans the menu. 'Jesus, look at these prices.' From Bea's reaction she realises her voice is too loud.

'She wasn't designed to live alone and she liked a drink. Back in the day there was a shellfish stall outside. Ma used to bring home a pint of prawns or cockles and welks. I can still taste the vinegar.' Bea puckers her lips. 'Peanuts on the bar. Pills and weed in the toilets and prawns on the stall. That was the Duke of York back then.'

'And the sex workers?'

'Sad, fragile girls who were pimped out by the Lafferty brothers. You could research the Laffertys. It might add a little bit of local colour to our boring family history.' Bea moves away from the pub with its group of would-be fine diners stamping their feet and blowing their hands against the cold.

Evie follows. She knows the area had a bad reputation back when Ma was young but had never been interested enough to find out what that had entailed. Selfishly living in her present, she wasn't aware of what Ma, or Bea for that matter, had experienced before she came along. Her sister was right. If she's going to carry out this research, finding her dad along the way, she would need to put her family and their lived experiences into context.

Seven

Rose 1967

Rose has been forgiven for succumbing to the wanton miniskirt which has been assigned to the back of the wardrobe. The crypt of the church is now a youth club and Rose tells herself she's only going to chaperone Carol. She wraps up warm for the chilly evening air. Demure in her ski pants and roll neck.

Her best friend is besotted with a lad called Tony from the local boys' school. All her time is spent clinging to him in the shadows. He wanders over, says a barely audible hello to Rose then whisks Carol off to a far wall. She joins her ex-school chums by the new pool table and drinks Panda Pop. They talk about their forthcoming exams. How they have a fabulous teacher who is passionate about girls doing well at school. This teacher says there is nothing to stop a girl from being a dentist or a journalist if they want it badly enough.

Rose laughs. 'You're kidding. Do you know how

much it costs to go to college?' She has no idea how much college costs but saying it sounds as though she has more experience of life. She tells them she was photographed for a magazine. When they ask where they can buy it, Rose tells them it's French. Only available in Paris. Eventually, Carol's brothers arrive. Rose signals to her friend who moves swiftly, distancing herself from Tony. He melts away without leaving a trace. Her three older brothers, chewing gum, cocky and dapper, cross the dance floor.

Paul, the eldest, winks at Rose as she says goodbye to Carol. He ducks his head and whispers, 'Alright there, lovely?' His lips brush her ear and hot needles pulsate between her legs.

Why does it take all three of them to fetch Carol? Her street isn't particularly dangerous. Maybe Kath is right. She's hinted enough times that Carol's family are dodgy. That they're mixed up in all sorts of shenanigans, like fencing stolen goods and a bit of drug dealing. If so, the boys would have made enemies of other gangs, making Carol a target when she's out on her own.

The Fullers and their acquaintances are quite partial to getting goods on the sly. Tom says it's a war-thing. When someone stands at the bar with a joint of beef or a bit of jewellery and asks for a couple of quid, everyone is interested. Paul certainly looks the part of local villain with his lily-white hands and shiny shoes. He's broad-chested and handy with his fists. She worries for Carol's beau.

Rose walks home. As she passes the new council block, the streetlamps come on. A tarpaulin ripples in the wind and somewhere out of sight there is the clink of metal hitting metal. Without thinking, she turns down an interior footpath and in minutes she's standing under the brick tower. The wall is studded with windows and balconies and some of the flats have been let so that dusk is pierced with lights from within. A little patch of tarmac by the path has been given over to a yellow seesaw. She sticks out her foot and pushes down so that the seesaw rocks. As it stutters and squeaks in its cumbersome manner Rose imagines being married to Paul.

She's heard there are flats especially for young couples who want to start a family. Paul and Rose could ask for a two bedroom and, as more sprogs arrive, they could get a bigger place. She could watch from the balcony as the children play on the seesaw. Paul and Rose. Rose and Paul. Their names would look perfect on wedding invitations, on a notice board in Holy Trinity or a marriage certificate. The deep shadows formed by the walkways and balconies make her fearful – like the dark alleyways Kathleen warns her about. She turns and hurries back to her street.

She only wants to get married so that she can leave the basement behind, get out from under the size nines of her bully of a dad. Besides, Carol's whole family are dodgy and she would be mad to marry into it. She's distracted by her thoughts and doesn't notice the stranger before she bumps into him. Her toe kicks a static shoe and then her shoulder connects with the solid wall of body before her brain engages. 'Sorry,' she says, stepping back.

He's much older than her, same height, but broad-shouldered. He has a builder's stance, stocky under a smart coat. He is strikingly handsome with barbershop pomade in his hair and a strong jaw. He just stands there. She doesn't feel afraid, he's not digging his hands in his trouser pockets or leering.

'My fault entirely. I startled you, I'm sorry.' He offers her his hand. 'John O'Dowd.'

Rose can't recall anyone shaking her hand in greeting. Up to now, shaking hands was for Sunday Mass. What was she thinking of? Going to that church dance with all those school kids. Miss Rosemary Fuller works and earns her own money for God's sake. She can go Up West if she chooses, go to nightclubs and dance. Piccadilly beckons. Perhaps the bus has just arrived in the form of this handsome gentleman. She takes his hand, which encloses hers completely. 'Rosemary Fuller,' she says breathlessly, tilting her head to one side with all the coy elegance and charm she can muster.

John Patrick O'Dowd, House Renovator according to his business card, is one of life's true gentlemen. Rose sniffs the little rectangle of card before she rings him. It smells of spice mixed with tobacco and spray starch. So far, he has taken her to the pictures, the occasional long drive out to Richmond Park or Kew Gardens, and for her sixteenth birthday, he took her to a West End club where he bought real champagne and they danced until one o'clock in the morning.

Tom and Kath first meet John after he takes her to see a film at the Kilburn State cinema. The first feature was about a Black female pilot who served in the RAF. As the car pulls up outside the basement steps, Rose hears the dustbin lid clatter. Tom is tipping vegetable peelings into the dustbin as she opens the gate. 'It's not bin night, is it, Dad?' Rose asks, peering down at Tom's bald patch. Dad knows he's been caught out and she's glad he looks sheepish. Rose leads John down to the front door and all four settle in the front room.

There are a few questions from Dad. What do you do for a living? Whereabouts are you from? Looking at the three of them, Rose decides that John is more relaxed about this situation than they are. She is glad he's kept his coat on as he's sitting in the draft. There are awkward pauses that would normally be filled by the partaking of a drink but John has politely declined.

'This is a cosy room,' John says. He looks up, scanning the high ceiling with its cornicing and picture rail loaded with soot.

'We need a bit of painting doing. The skirting boards and such. Do you know anyone?' Kathleen asks, wrapping her thick cardigan around her chest.

''Course he does. He's a property developer.' Dad doesn't follow this up by calling Kathleen a silly cow or worse and Rose is relieved.

'I've a team of builders working round here. They could drop by and take a look.' John pulls out his wallet and gives Tom a card. He asks Kathleen where she's from in Ireland and she tells him the family are from Cork. 'I've cousins there. The O'Rourkes out by Blackrock.'

Kath shrugs. 'I left Ireland when I was seven. Don't remember much about it. Except the rain.'

John nods and there follows a discussion on the

comparative qualities of Irish rain and the rain in their adopted country. When he leaves, Mum, Dad and Rose stand in the hallway.

'He's too old for her,' Mum says.

'She needs someone mature, with a bit of common sense,' Dad says, glancing at the card in his hand. 'Keep her in check.'

'He's got his own business. That's alright.'

Dad rubs his head. 'Looks like you've got yourself a very nice fella. You'd better be good to him or he'll be off.'

Rose's parents take themselves to bed and she returns to the front room. The feeling of smallness she felt by the tower block returns. Others, older with more experience in life, are directing her. Kath, Tom and John seem to be pulling puppet strings and she's on the end of them. You better be good to him, her dad had said. In the hall they had talked as if she wasn't present. Perched on the arm of the sofa, the fire embers glowing amongst the white coals, she feels twelve years old again. She puts her nose into the neck of her pullover and her leg swings back and forth.

No. It was she who had decided to say yes when he offered to walk her home the night they met. And it was her decision to take his delicious little card and walk down to the phone box to ring him the next day. But there's a niggling doubt. A little voice whispering in her head. Especially when they are in his car and the kissing is accompanied by a little fumbling inside her. He goes no further, adjusts his groin area, then considerately fixes the legs of her knickers.

Why doesn't he want to take her? Why stop? There's

cover enough down the mews or behind the hospital. There's a back seat that would do. Or why doesn't he take her back to his place in Edgware? The answers are too unwieldy for Rose to think about this late at night.

She pulls herself up from a slouch and catches John's aftershave on her sweater. She thinks about changing her scent from the insipid eau de toilette she usually wears and investing in something more potent, a Christmas present to them both. She wants him to smell her when he is driving away. The back door closes and the bolt is drawn with a thud.

Kath calls out from the darkness along the corridor. 'Rose. Turn out the light and make sure the door's locked.' All further thoughts about John are snuffed out with the task and the happy prospect of a trip to Whitley's perfume counter.

She doesn't see him every day of course. He's running his business and Rose is at Peepers. No one seems to stay for long at the shop. Lizzy and Jean both leave and Rose is Sharon's assistant manager now. She has more responsibilities: checking the cash at the end of the day; running the work rota for the new part-timers and choosing the outfits for the window display. The best perk of the job is that she gets to wear the top range. The mini is out, pretty much, and the maxi dress is in, according to Sharon. Rose is showing more boob than Mum and Dad approve of, but John loves it.

For working Saturdays, she gets a day off in the week and John has asked her to meet him at the Self-Serve Café on Westbourne Grove. He says he's doing a bit of business with the owners and tells her to wait. Then he enters a door at the back of the cafe in between the vending machines that line the walls.

The metal-ringed white table she sits at is spotted with burn marks. From somewhere above her, the muffled sound of jazz music can be heard. Rose thinks she is alone, then a movement out of the corner of her eye makes her jump. There is a woman sitting inside a booth. Her short peroxide hair is wiry and her roots need doing. She is there to dispense change, according to the sign on her window. Rose smiles in her direction, but the woman's eyes are lowered as she reads a magazine. The only movement she makes is a lick of her index finger when she turns a page.

Rose lights up a cigarette and buys a coffee from one of the vending machines. It's boiling hot and watery, hardly tastes of anything, so she leaves it to one side. Smart-suited men walk in, ignoring the woman in the booth and the watery coffee, and go through the door John disappeared behind. As they pass her table, they turn and throw admiring glances in her direction until she too lowers her head and ignores them.

She waits for what seems like an hour. The machines buzz intermittently as if they are struggling to function. Lights seem to flicker as she stares at them. She reads the labels: Tea, Coffee, Hot Chocolate, Ham, Cheese and Pickle. She notices that some of the labels are unlit and she can't make out the writing on these. Every so often she glances over at the woman in the booth but her head is stuck in the same position. Studying her roots, Rose guesses the woman is auburn. John eventually emerges from the door buttoning his overcoat and grinning. He seems pleased with himself.

'Did it go well?' she asks, stubbing out her second cigarette.

'Yes, darling. You're my lucky charm, that's what you are.' He kisses her lightly on the lips.

'Ahh, that's nice. Glad to help out.'

'Come on, beautiful. Got something to show you.' He grabs her hand and they walk up Westbourne Grove towards the Bella. He stops outside a grand three-storey house and the keys rattle as he unlocks its black iron gate. There is a *For Sale* sign in one of the downstairs windows.

The inside smells of fresh paint and new carpet. There are high ceilings, huge windows and air. So much air Rose inhales as if she's in the Swiss Alps. He leads her down a small flight of stairs to the kitchen and she can't help but compare it with the dark, greasy cubbyhole in her mum and dad's basement. This is bright, with a Formica-topped orange table, and chairs that have a matching cushioned seat. She runs one hand along the sleek brown worktop and pauses at the back door which opens onto a yard. The grass glistens with winter frost.

'All mod cons,' John says, waving his hand at the stove. 'They say the way to a man's heart is through his stomach. Whoever buys this house won't be able to fight the ladies off.' He laughs at his joke and Rose smiles with him. 'This was a shithole when I bought it.' John rubs his hands together. 'A family from Trinidad lived in that room.' He points in the direction of the lounge. 'Dad, Mum, her sister and loads of kids. They had to share a toilet on the first floor with a bunch of nonces and prossies who crawled out of nests like rats, sniffing around the dad for money and sniffing around the kids for God knows what. Poor bastards.'

'What happened to them?'

'All evicted.'

'John. No…'

'The family were fine, Rose. Believe me, they ended up in a nice flat down in South London. I don't know about the rest of them. Don't care. Look at this place.' He sweeps his arms wide. 'Do you know what I am, Rose?'

She cocks her head on one side and waits.

'An alchemist.'

'Come again?'

'An alchemist takes base metal and works it into gold. I'm an alchemist.'

She repeats the word to get her tongue around it as John comes over and nuzzles her neck.

'Rose, there are bedrooms upstairs. Two floors of them. The master bedroom's like something out of a Hollywood movie.' He pulls her closer to him. Her skin tingles and an electric current seems to whizz right down to her fanny. She is so up for this she gasps. He squeezes her arse and she feels the strength in this hands. He's a man used to manual labour.

'Care to see the master bedroom, madam?'

They have sex for the first time. He fetches a towel from the bathroom and lays it across the bedspread while Rose removes her panties. He grunts and groans as an unseen blunt object struggles to enter her. She is distracted by the room: there is no bulb hanging from the light cord, only a net curtain at the window, and the pale pink bedspread they are lying on is the only bed linen covering the mattress.

John has to withdraw to open her up with his fingers. Her body arches intuitively and she is tempted to reach down to keep his hand at work. But he is too quick for her and his shallow breaths and small helpless cries continue until with one last shudder, he comes.

When he withdraws, she feels the sting of rubbing, like new shoes on a heel. She giggles, and he asks her why she's laughing. 'Lucky there were no viewings,' she says.

'That'd be something to behold. You're so beautiful, Rose.' He wraps the condom he had used in a hanky, slips it into his pocket and balls the towel up in his fist.

'I need to see your mum and dad soon,' he says while he's lacing up his shoes.

'Why?'

'Bit of business.' John clocks her blush and grins. 'What did you think I meant?'

'Nothing. Just…'

'Come on, girl, we gotta go.' He holds out his hand. 'I can't marry you, Rosie. I never said I could marry you, right?'

She nods. 'I'm not silly.'

'You still want to be my girl?'

''Course I do, you fool.' She smiles but her heart sinks into her stomach.

In the days that follow, John takes her to other properties that are dressed up for sale: a flat in Elgin Avenue, a house in Ladbroke Grove and a mews house down a cobbled alley which her parents had always told her to avoid. The alley has been cleaned up, the houses, tiny but smart, have been transformed by John's alchemy.

He is at the bar when Rose, Tom and Kathleen arrive at the Princess Alexandra. They grab a table as the pub starts to fill up with regulars. Tom nods in the direction of a couple of old men and Kathleen talks to a woman she works with before settling in next to Rose.

John fetches drinks and announces he has bought their house. The previous owner had signed over the deeds with the sitting tenants included in the deal.

'So, you're our new landlord?' Dad looks uncomfortable.

'For the time being.' John sips at his pint.

'What do you mean?' Rose asks.

Dad's eyes narrow. 'I'm not sure what you're playing at, John, but I don't like what I'm hearing. It's not easy to find a place with a reasonable rent these days.'

'Ah, now you see,' says John, 'I have a plan. A plan that will benefit everyone. Your good selves, yours truly and even your neighbour, Mrs Stanley.'

'What plan is this then?' Mum asks.

'Rose tells me you've been on the council list for one of the new flats. Well, if I hand you an eviction notice, the council will have no alternative but to rehouse you.'

'Eviction notice?' Mum whispers and looks over her shoulder.

Dad sits back in his chair and rubs his hand over his head. 'Now wait a minute. What's the guarantee we'll get one of the flats? We might end up on the streets.'

'It's not complicated, Mr Fuller. I've done it before. With the right paperwork, you'll have your pick of the two-bedroom flats. You might even get one of the houses on the ground floor. Imagine. A bit of garden to work in. What do you say to that?'

The company is silenced. Rose's parents look at each other as if they are telepathic.

'What if we don't get given a place? What if the block's full?' Mum asks.

'Then I give you my word your flat will be completely refurbished to the highest possible standards and you will retain your current rental agreement.' John lays his hand on his heart.

'I've seen what John's houses look like,' Rose says. 'They're palaces compared to ours.' She can't keep the excitement from her voice.

'It's a win-win whatever way you look at it,' John says.

He buys more drinks and her parents start imagining their furniture in one of the new flats. Rose, cheered by the prospect of leaving the basement, offers to go to the bar.

While she's there, someone leans into her. He places a hand on her shoulder blade and rubs it. Rose flicks her body and the hand is removed. The man persists. 'Hello, beautiful,' he says. He's swaying and slurring and there is spittle in his beard.

'Piss off.' Rose is firm.

'Tha's not very nice, is it?' He's tall, there are white dribble stains on the lapels of his jacket. She looks over her shoulder but there's a line of drinkers between her and the table. 'You want business, darlin'?'

For a second, she thinks that he knows what she does with John on her days off. That somehow it shows on her face. A knowing expression or a posture assumed to signal that she's no longer a virgin. Rose shouts above the noise of the drinkers. 'How dare you! Get away from me. You pervert.'

The whole pub stops. John pushes his way through the static crowd. He talks quietly and explains that Rose is his girl, that the fella's had one too many. He advises him to go home. She's amazed at how calm he is and wonders why he hasn't landed one on him. The man mumbles and backs away as John takes the drinks over to the table. Rose is shaking so John fetches her a double brandy.

Kathleen and Tom use the incident to prove once again that the area has gone downhill. That the Black people have brought drugs into the area and the fella at the bar is probably out of his nut on something. Rose is sure he's pissed but decides not to argue as she is soothed by the brandy and John's reassuring palm pressed on the small of her back.

Just as she recovers her composure, the drunk from the bar lunges at them through the line of people. He has a knife. It flashes above his head and the crowd shrieks as he swings the blade down towards John.

Tom leaps up and, in one decisive movement, upends the heavy table and rams it into the man's chest. Glasses smash, the knife arcs, the crowd parts like the red sea as foaming beer splatters them. The attacker is on his back, pinned to the floor. The shouts and hollers of an avenging gang of locals fill the pub. Their fists and boots pound his prone body. The woman who talked to Kath earlier takes off her shoe to batter the man's head with its heel. Stools rock, glasses smash and the landlord barks, 'Take it outside, you lot.'

The group of men aiming kicks and punches move like one fearsome set of limbs, hauling the lanky stranger out onto the street. The door swings shut and muffles the sound of the kicking. The barman picks up the table and wipes it down before offering them drinks on the house.

'That's how we deal with pervs round here,' Dad says, looking at John with contempt. 'Drinks on you, I reckon.'

Rose watches as any respect, any trust, her mum and dad held for John slips away like the beer dripping off the table onto the pub's carpet. The magic spell has been broken and the talk of the new flat is nothing more substantial than the melting ice cubes in Kath's rum and black.

Eight

Rose 1967

The summer passes without an eviction notice being issued. Tom has made it clear he doesn't trust John. Kath is at the bingo afternoon session with Sylvie. Tom sits brooding at the kitchen table while Rose is mopping the floors. He's watching her and she can see he's got something to say. 'What's the matter?'

'Your fella's dodgy,' Dad says.

'But Dad. You need to move out of here. Mum's legs are playing up. She can't do the stairs.'

'He's dodgy. I've heard things.'

'What sort of things?'

'He's in with some nasty geezers, a Soho outfit. Clive Lafferty says they're running…clubs.'

'So? Clive's selling drugs. It's common knowledge they sell pills down the Duke of York. Anyway, what's wrong with clubs? I've been to clubs with John. Really posh ones.'

'Well these ain't posh and I don't want you hanging around them. The Laffertys say he's working for a gang mixed up with the Krays.'

'Like the Laffertys, you mean?'

'No. Not like the Laffertys otherwise we'd be alright. Just watch yourself, girl. I don't trust that Paddy.'

Rose leans on the mop. 'The Laffertys are Paddies.'

'Bleedin' Nora.' He uses the tone of voice reserved for nitwits and fools like her and Kath. 'The Laffertys are *our* people. And don't you forget it.'

'The Laffertys aren't trying to get you a council flat, are they?' Rose squeezes the mop out and takes a broom to sweep the basement. She hears a great sob coming from the steps of the main house, drops the broom and runs up to see Evangeline leaning against the balustrade holding a letter. 'What is it? What's happened?'

'Your man came through for me and I got one of the new flats. Praise God and Mr O'Dowd. Praise the Baby Jesus.' Evangeline puts her hand to her eyes and the tears flow.

'Why are you crying? That's amazing!' Rose smiles and her heart swells at the thought that John has made this happen.

'I know, I know. But we been in this place for a year and every day has been shaming.' Evangeline sniffs and wipes her eyes with the heel of her hand. 'I never see such a shabby run-down hole.'

'But you've got the new flat now. It'll be fabulous. I'm so happy for you.'

'And you'll come and visit, and I'll teach you how to sew.' Evangeline smiles. 'You say thank you to your John for me.'

'I will. And I'll help you move.' Rose likes the sound of Your John and thinks she might start saying My John. Now that Evangeline has got her new flat, surely Dad will tell *Her John* to send them the notice. Or is Dad going to be a pig-headed, selfish git all his life?

It's Evangeline's moving day and one of those mornings where the sky is deceptively blue. The sun shines but a brisk early autumn breeze makes it necessary to wear a headscarf. Rose has chosen an orange one peppered with red flowers and she's wearing a dark shirt and jeans in case she gets grubby. Not that she thinks for a minute Evangeline's rooms are anything but clean. She just knows her own home too well. She trips lightly up the stairs to her neighbour and knocks on the door.

There is no furniture decent enough to warrant a removal van and most of it isn't Evangeline's to take away. Every wobbly chair leg and rusted bedstead will go in a builder's van, according to John. Evangeline has picked up four lovely high-backed dining chairs from Golborne Road recently. They are second-hand but in good condition and the little troupe of removers, Rose, Evangeline, Sylvester and Linton, carry these and various overstuffed bags in a packhorse procession to the new council block.

Mike the tally man has arranged to meet Evangeline at the flat so that she can order new furniture. He is looking really smart these days in his shiny Italian loafers. While Rose and the boys lug boxes and suitcases back and forth along the street and up along the balcony, Evangeline arranges two dining chairs in the bare living room and apologises to Mike when she discovers the kettle has not yet arrived.

'Mrs Stanley, lovely to meet you. Congratulations on your new tenancy. Rosemary has told me you're a tailor. I much admire the rag trade. My father was also a tailor, God rest his soul.' They sit in a beam of sunlight in front of the large windows and Mike opens his catalogue. He uses his suitcase as a desk, laying out his order book, gold pen and retractable tape measure on its surface.

Evangeline flicks the pages, ignoring the cornucopia of hostess trolleys and fancy lava lamps. Efficient and businesslike, she makes her selection and stands aside as Mike measures and checks the dimensions to ensure they fit. He tries to persuade her to buy a dining table after admiring her chairs, but Evangeline knows they come up for sale second-hand on Golborne Road. She'll wait. The living room door is closed when Rose and the boys return with more belongings. The door opens and Mike's last words echo through the flat. 'Now, I can do you a good deal on the table, Mrs Stanley. If you change your mind, give us a bell.'

'Thank you but I am fine with what I've ordered.' Evangeline is having none of the hard sell and the faint frostiness Rose picks up in her tone sends out a clear signal.

Undeterred, Mike's smile is as sunny as the light flooding the room. He secures the cash deposit with a rubber band before lifting his hat. 'Lovely doing business with you, Mrs Stanley.' And to Rose, 'Give your mother my best wishes, young lady.'

Other families are moving into the block that day. Leaning over the balcony, Rose spots Mike drumming up custom. As he talks to a woman holding a washing basket full of indeterminate belongings, he points his finger up at flats where, presumably he has taken orders. He waves in Rose's direction and his gold-coloured watch sends its frantic signal all over the walls.

Evangeline leads them all back to the old house for one last check. On the way, she buys four bottles of Coke from the corner shop. They sit on the stone steps and sip at their drinks. The boys are excited, asking their mother if they can have a telly. Evangeline laughs and says they'll have to get paper rounds to pay for the rental. Rose feels the breeze as her body cools down from her labours. She wishes she had brought a cardigan.

A dark blue Cortina slows down in front of them. The man in the front passenger seat winds down the window and Rose thinks he is going to ask for directions. But then she clocks the skinhead haircuts and tattoos. All three passengers and the driver are holding beer bottles.

Her whole body stiffens. They are sneering at her and passing round insults loud enough for all to hear.

'N— lover.'

'Chocolate whore.'

'She needs a slap.'

'Dirty cow.'

Rose gets to her feet and looks down at the thugs. Heart racing, the heat of blood creeps up her neck. She's had enough. Sick of her mum and dad's racist comments. Sick of the vile treatment her Black neighbours get at the corner shop where the White owners make them wait until the Whites are served first, and now these cretins are insulting her and her friends.

She's about to get off the step and give the men in the car what for but feels a tug on her shirt.

'Get in.' Evangeline's whisper is urgent. They turn and walk up the steps. The men in the car make monkey noises. 'We just ignore. You hear.'

Sylvester and Linton both kiss their lips in a show of defiance and the sound must've carried down to the men. The car door swings open. 'Oi, Oi!' one of them shouts. Then the sound of breaking glass followed by a bottle smashing against the Stanleys' door. Mocking laughter erupts from the street below and the car door slams shut. The driver revs the engine.

Rose snaps. 'Bastards. You bastards.'

Each man inside the Cortina raises a middle finger. Without thinking, she hurls her Coke bottle right back. It hits the boot.

'Oh, sweet Jesus. What have you done?' Evangeline whispers. The car jolts as the driver brakes hard and the passenger doors open. The men stand in the road, all denim and Doc Martens. 'Rosemary! Get here, now!' Evangeline and the boys are already inside the house.

'Come on then, bastards. What you got?' Rose walks down the steps to confront them. One of the men steps forward. He is everything she expected: mean eyes, ugly mouth set in a snarl and anger emanating from every pore.

'You cow. You dented me motor!' the driver squeals, swiping broken glass off the boot with his sleeve.

The thug nearest to her steps up onto the pavement. Spittle foams on his lips as he spews a torrent of filthy abuse while the others jeer.

Rose's heart is thumping; her brain is blank. But lovely, kind Evangeline has been insulted. 'Don't you come round here—'

'I am gonna slap you right up.' The angry git grabs her throat.

'Leave her alone.' Evangeline is close behind.

But the grip on Rose's throat tightens and panic rises as she tries to catch her breath. Then she stares at the opposite side of the street and her body slackens. The thugs all turn as one, following her gaze, the hand dropping away from her neck. Evangeline steps in between Rose and the skinhead. She is clutching a broken chair leg.

Neighbours are gathering. They walk with a sense of purpose towards the car. Some have returned from shopping and are carrying bags; a White woman with a baby in a papoose stops opposite them. Two young Black men, Sylvie's student tenants, skip down her steps and Sylvie herself hangs out of an upstairs window, a fag in one hand, her little dog held close to her chest. A burly White man Rose recognises as a bailiff jogs closer to stand with the students. The sense of confrontation is palpable.

'Can we help you gentlemen?' one of the students asks.

The thugs react quickly, the angry git who had grabbed Rose's throat backs away and swings himself into the passenger seat. The audience is treated to the sound of a thud as his head connects with the doorframe. Mocking laughter springs up, drowning out his curses as the car pulls away.

'Cowards! The bloody lot of you. That's it. Run back to the pond you crawled out of,' Rose shouts after them.

From her upstairs window Sylvie shouts, 'Good girl, Rosie. You showed 'em. Good afternoon, Mrs Stanley.'

Rose follows Evangeline up the stairs to the old rooms, where an upturned chair is missing one of its legs. Shaking and dry-mouthed from the encounter, Rose wished she'd held onto her drink. Sylvester is leaning against a wall, eyes down. Rose can feel his supressed anger.

Linton is hanging out of the window. 'Bastards!' he yells.

Evangeline issues a sharp smack to his behind. 'Never use that language around me again, young man. And Rose, I'll thank you to keep your cussing to yourself.' She takes Rose's face in her hands. 'You've a good heart, Rosemary.'

Later, Rose meets John in the Duke of York. They have stopped using the Alex in case her parents are there. This pub is rougher. There are prostitutes hanging around but John is always at the bar before she arrives so she doesn't get hassled. She gives him the keys to the now vacant rooms and he kisses her cheek as he pockets them. One of the Lafferty boys, Rob or Colin, she can't tell which, sits at the far end of the bar deep in shadow. 'Over there, John. It's a Lafferty,' she whispers, remembering Tom's warning.

He laughs, throwing an arm around her shoulders. 'That wee lad in the corner there? He's one of the Laffertys?'

He buys a drink for the boy, then waves when he sees the barman present the glass of whisky.

Rob Lafferty approaches. 'O'Dowd?' Rob's chest is out. He stands with legs apart; a lightweight boxer preparing to be hit. 'My father sends his regards.'

'Good man. And same back to him. It's John, by the way.' He holds out his hand which Rob ignores. Rose imagines two bull mastiffs facing each other for a fight. Rob turns his back on the hand and places the drink back on the bar untouched. The pub is still. No one is drinking. The barman is nowhere to be seen.

Rob returns and his face is close to John's. 'This is our pitch, O'Dowd. Tell your Mafia mates to go back to Soho.'

'I'm afraid it's not that simple, Rob. Maybe you and your brothers would like to meet my friends. You could be very useful to them with your local knowledge.'

Rob laughs. 'You're right there. Local knowledge goes a long way. Your pals are out of their league. Know what I mean?'

'My business associates are in a league of their own, son. Come on, Rosie, we need to find some more refined company.'

He takes her to a Greek restaurant in Bayswater, but she finds it hard to eat. The day has been momentous: first the joy of moving Evangeline into her new flat; the racist aggro boys with their hatred; then Carol's brother Rob and her John confronting each other. She's tired, holding back tears that she knows John won't appreciate. He's paying for a lovely meal; he's bought wine. He sulks when she doesn't look as though she's enjoying his company. He's sulking now.

'What?' John asks.

She tells him about the aggro boys then asks, 'What're you doing, John? Gettin' involved with this gang? Dad says—'

'I don't want to hear what your dad says. He's a fool. Now you listen.' He leans towards her. 'My business associates are just that. I don't get involved in how they earn their money. I just help them out by keeping their money clean. I'm legit, Rosie. I do up houses for a profit. The Maltese give me loans, so to speak. You have to understand that. Nothing going on around here, Officer. Got it?'

'No, John, I've no idea what you mean.' She rests her tired head on her fingers.

'Did you get the number plate of that car?'

'No, I didn't think to.'

'Pity.' John throws his cutlery down and wipes his mouth with his napkin. 'Come on. Got something to show you.'

He takes her to a house on Falmouth Road he has just finished refurbishing. It has the same layout and features she remembers from the house he took her to when they first had sex. 'What do you think?' he says, rubbing his chin. He seems nervous.

'I think it's lovely, the best yet.'

He has chosen a really gorgeous wallpaper for the living room. It's a cabbage rose pattern in a ghostly grey and silver. The sofas and armchairs are covered in the same patterned fabric and a long brown radiogram takes up one wall. A streetlamp sends a stream of light through the big bay window. 'Do you like it? Would you live in it?' He moves over to stand behind her and slips his arms around her waist.

'Like a shot. If we had the money. Although imagine me mum cleaning this pile, with *her* legs.'

'No. I mean you. Just you.' He nuzzles her neck.

'Are you asking me to marry you?' Rose frowns.

He pulls away sharply and steers her towards the sofas. 'You know I love you, Rose. You make me very happy, Rosie. I would like you to live here—'

'With you, John. Will it be our house?'

'Let me finish, girl. It's a place where we can be together in private.' His curly fringe drops free from its layer of pomade and he looks younger. 'It's a lovely house. You could make a nice little garden out the back there.'

'You really can't marry me. Can you?' Her lip trembles. 'Are you going to explain why? Or do I have to work it out for myself?' She runs to the front door but he grabs her arm and stops her.

'Didn't you hear what I said? I love you. I told you already. We can't get married.' His grip loosens, and he steps in close. 'What's marriage, Rose? It's a business deal. That's all.' He is stroking her face and each tear that drops he catches on his thumbs. 'My part of the deal is to go to work and earn money. My wife makes sure I have a clean shirt and she provides me with a couple of brats.'

'You've got kids? You never said.'

'It's a dull old business, my wife and kids.'

'You'd leave them if you really meant that.'

'What we have is love. We're free.'

'But what will people think?'

'Who cares? What we think is what matters.' He kisses her ear. 'You'll have this beautiful palace to yourself. I'll stay as often as I can. We'll have parties. We'll stay in bed all day. It will be just us. Our romantic love hideaway like Elizabeth Taylor and Richard Burton.'

She turns her face away from his. 'But what about Mum and Dad?'

'I don't fancy Tom and Kathleen, Rose. Give me some credit, girl.'

She giggles and he takes her, right there, next to the little marble-topped telephone table. The mirror above it thumps the wall with each thrust.

'Come on, girl. We'll have fun. I'll look after you,' he says afterwards.

'You have to promise. Promise me that you'll look after me.'

'I promise to look after you. Buy you chocolates...' He tickles her sides, she squirms. 'I'll buy you sexy knickers...' He tickles her harder and she giggles, swatting him away. She tries to catch her breath between the fits of laughter. He grabs her hand, pulling her up the stairs. They are both giggling, as though they've had too much to drink. He sweeps her up with the ease of a man holding a doll and the laughter subsides as he carries her into the bedroom.

Nine

Rose 1967

New Year's Eve brings a knees-up at the Alexandra. Rose, Kathleen and Tom are there as is Sylvie and a couple of her tenants, the White ones anyway, and the bar is heaving.

Kathleen and Tom have wandered over to where Clive Lafferty and his wife are sitting. If there were a best seat in the house, it would be theirs. As for Carol's brothers, they sit at the bar in a neat semicircle, smoking cigars and sipping at the best whisky. Paul looks common in his brown loafers. His brothers in their off-the-peg grey suits and unruly hair remind her of the squab pigeons that wander dazed and confused on the pavements. She suspects they've taken something other than whisky.

Carol sits with her and they talk of old school friends and the teachers who they admired. Rose tells Carol she is assistant manager at Peepers and is earning a fortune.

'I left school at Christmas,' Carol announces. 'I had to pass a maths exam for me job. It was a piece o' piss really.'

Carol fumbles around in her handbag for her ciggies, but Rose is there first and they both light up.

'Are you still seeing Tony?'

'Yeah, well sort of.' Carol explains that Tony is a bit shy in front of her brothers so they have to see each other on the quiet. 'It's one of the reasons I left school. I can meet him in town after work.' Carol looks up at the bar where Paul is raising a glass in their direction. She nods and Paul brings over two fresh drinks.

'Alright, lovely? Good crowd tonight.' He smiles at Rose. 'Your boyfriend coming?'

She blushes. 'Don't have a boyfriend, Paul.'

'The old geezer, the one who does up the houses.'

'Oh him. Yeah, it's not serious.'

'Tell him Paul Lafferty sends his regards.' Carol's brother bends forward and pinches her cheek, his face uncomfortably close. 'You won't get pissed and forget now, lovely?' He smiles but it's a gargoyle's snarl. 'You didn't thank me for the drink, girl. Where was you dragged up?' Paul is loud. Nearby drinkers pause and look over at the little table. He laughs for too long and Rose is secretly pleased to discover that he sounds like a braying donkey.

'Thanks, Paul. Happy New Year and all that.' She knocks the drink back, the sweet-sour liquid burning her throat as he walks away. Rose buys a round, then another as Carol says she doesn't have any money on her. Carol hasn't asked her about John but the alcohol makes Rose brave. As the old year fizzles out towards its final moments, Rose tells her everything. 'He's a lovely bloke. You'd like him. Takes me to some nice restaurants. He's got a car and everything.' There are at least two Carols staring back at her. 'We could go out for dinner. You, me, Tony and John.' She blinks and tries to focus. 'He's asked me to move in with him. But…I'm not sure.'

'I wish you'd told me. Paul knows more about it than I do. How's that?'

'Your Rob saw us in the Duke of York.'

'What does Tom and Kath make of him?'

'Ooh.' Rose shakes her head. 'You know what they're like. Miserable old sods.'

They both laugh and suddenly there is uproar. The chimes of Big Ben ring out. There is a crush in the bar as old and young get to their feet. Clothing is adjusted as nineteen sixty-eight crashes noisily into the world. There are kisses given and kisses received, soft wet kisses on the lips, dry old kisses on cheeks. Everyone tumbles outside to sing *Auld Lang Syne*. The lusty La La Las of a conga ring out in the freezing air.

Rose clasps Carol's generous hips as the line wobbles from one end of the street to the other. Some unseen reveller holds Rose's waist and pulls her back. It's as if her legs are trying to dance through treacle. Next, there is a raucous rendition of *Knees Up Mother Brown* – pantyhose exposed to the night air for all to see – then the *Hokey Cokey* so rambunctious Rose worries about her mum keeling over.

'You put your right arm in, your right arm out…' The revellers shout the words as they form a circle. Rose has a view of the pub and watches all three Lafferty brothers gather together in its shadowy porch. She sobers up at the sight of Paul. He's staring at her, the streetlamp highlighting his grim features.

'In, out, in, out. You shake it all about…' She will not be sending John any regards from the Laffertys.

'You do the okey cokey and you turn around…' Rob Lafferty has fetched Carol over. She's leaning against him as she staggers towards Paul.

'Oh, oh the okey cokey. Oh, oh the okey cokey…'

They tower over her friend, their faces bent and Paul's big white hand on her shoulder. Rose thinks they are telling her off for getting drunk, for making a fool of herself. Perhaps she flashed her knickers when they did the knees-up.

'Knees bend, arms stretch, ra, ra, ra.' Tom and Kathleen appear, wrapping themselves in their coats and scarves ready for home. 'Happy New Year, darlin',' Kath says, her voice raw from singing at the top of it. She gives Rose a hug.

'Don't stay out too late or you won't get in,' Tom says.

'Happy New Year to you too.'

They move away and Carol appears. It's as if there is a line of people waiting to speak to her.

Carol shoves Rose in the chest.

'What was that for?'

'Paul said you've been fucking this…this old fella all over town.'

'Carol. It's not like that—'

'Anyway.' Carol wipes the snot and tears from her face with her forearm, raises her chin and points. 'Paul says you're a right slag and he doesn't want me to see you again.'

'What's your brother got to do with the price of fish? Grow up, Carol.'

'Fuck off, Rose Fuller. Fuck off, slag.' Carol's eyes stream with tears. She turns and staggers up the road to where the warm interior of her brother's car is waiting for her.

John has bought Rose a leprechaun key ring that has a bell inside. It clangs as she takes it from her handbag. She opens the door of the house on Falmouth Road with a shiny set of keys that are so new they scratch her fingers. She switches on the boiler as the winter is shaping up to be a cold one. Every time the heating clicks over, she thinks of the miserable damp little flat she has left her parents in and hopes they'll have enough council points soon to get a flat in the new block.

Tonight, John is going to throw a party for his business associates from the Self-Serve Café. She had to ring Selfridges Foodhall in her lunch hour to order canapés and a side of ham and some drinks, every sort, to stock the bar he's installed. He rearranges the living room, pushing the sofas back against the walls while she fixes bottles of spirits into the optics. The bar is a solid walnut affair with mirrored shelves that shimmer in the lamplight. It transforms the room into a members' only club.

'One day, I'll own a real pub. In Spain. Right on the seafront,' he announces. 'John's English Pub.' He puts a record on the radiogram. 'You'll be the barmaid, and when we're not entertaining the punters, we'll be dancing in the sand.' He swings Rose around to the Chords' *Sh-Boom*.

'Will we be together every day?'

'Too right. You're going nowhere, Rosie Fuller.' He sings along, 'Life will be a dream, sweetheart.'

He tries to undo her zip but she pats him off. 'Later,' she whispers. 'We've got company coming and you haven't told me anything about them.'

'You don't need to know much, darling. You just need to look gorgeous.'

'But if I know what they do, I can talk to them. The Queen never meets anyone without a full report on who they are, what they do—'

'We're entertaining a VIP from Malta. He's investing in the business, Your Majesty.' He grins then wipes a nervous hand across his chin.

For the party she wears one of the top-range dresses from the upcoming spring season. Full and floaty, it has a plunging neckline that ends in a broad waistband. She teams it with flat pumps as otherwise she towers over John in her heels. It's easier to solve the dilemma of what to wear than to dwell on being sent to Coventry by her parents and Carol.

Tom and Kathleen haven't spoken to her since the day she moved in. Carol won't answer her phone calls and when she had visited Carol's house, her dad answered the door and told her to clear off. Like she had been caught nicking the milk off the doorstep. And now John is inviting his business associates, his Mafia friends as she thinks of them, to their house.

John comes into the kitchen where Rose is putting prawn vol-au-vents on a dinner plate. 'Don't use that crap.'

He leaves the kitchen and returns with a large box. 'Use these.'

Rose opens the lid and inside, carefully wrapped in layers of tissue, there is a dinner service. The dishes are white with a border of red roses and gold spots. She holds an oval serving platter up to the light and sees a pearlescent glow through it. 'Quality John,' she whispers.

'Too right. Be careful. Don't you go chipping them.'

'No. I mean that's what I'm going to call you from now on. Quality John.'

He takes the plate from her and squeezes her waist. 'That's me, alright.'

Somehow, she's stuck behind the bar. She had been cutting lemons and filling the ice bucket when the guests started to arrive. The men had offered greetings in a heavy Mediterranean accent. They were accompanied by a group of English girls, blondes wearing last year's coats and patent boots. They had come over and admired her dress then ordered drinks as if they were in a real bar.

Unable to get away, she has become the barmaid at John's English Pub. The evening goes well with everyone getting merry thanks to her generous measures. John replaces the Matt Munro album playing on the radiogram with Elvis and some of the Maltesers, as she now calls them, grab their girlfriends and dance. They swing them around too fast and the girls tip and sway. There is a high-pitched squeal as a heavy brass lamp threatens to keel over when someone knocks into it. The men grip the girls tighter in order to save them from falling off their heels. They steal kisses and when *Love Me Tender* comes on, they cop a feel.

Eventually, the heels come off and the three English girls are dancing to Motown. The men gravitate towards John. Rose reckons that sometimes, it's more interesting watching the fun than having it. She drinks a steady stream of cocktails she has invented while John's group talk business. They lean in, hands raised in gestures that convey the seriousness of the points they are making.

Rose has met a couple of John's colleagues before. They hold bottles of beer and refuse her offers of something stronger, maintaining a quiet seriousness, whereas the Maltesers are all smiles and laughter. Tommy Beresford, John's solicitor, is also here.

'What can I get you, sir?' Tommy comes and sits on one of the high stools. He's big, likes his grub and the booze has made his nose as red as a beetroot.

'Gin and It, please, sweetheart.' He lights his cigar while she mixes his drink, finishing it with a glacé cherry on a cocktail stick.

'There you go, sir, that'll be two shillings and fourpence.' She holds out her hand, grinning at their little role-play.

'My word. Prices have gone up at this establishment. I might have to take my custom elsewhere.' His voice is rich, layered in fat.

'I blame the government,' Rose says. 'Have this one on the house, Mr Beresford.'

He smiles, picks the cherry out of the drink and pops it into Rose's mouth.

She comments on Tommy's suit and says she has a friend who is a tailor who would give him a discount on his made to measures. They laugh as she demands a drag on his cigar, and she chokes on it with much drama. 'My God, Tommy, that is disgusting. How can something smell so good and taste so wrong?' She takes a gulp of her drink. 'John likes a cigar. I'd like to get him some.'

'I'll send a box over, next time I'm in Havana.'

'They have to be the best for Quality John.'

Rose says this at the exact moment the music on the radiogram comes to an end and the guests are quiet. A ripple of laughter litters the room. One of the taller Maltese men bends his ear to a short, stocky individual and they talk rapidly. The needle on the record fills the air with a constant scratch as it digs deeper into the vinyl. No one is moving. She guesses the stocky guy is interpreting for the tall guy.

The taller man laughs and points his glass at John. His arm sways with the amount of booze he's put away. John stares expectantly at this man. Rose holds her breath, her eyes fixed on John. 'Quality John,' the tall man says. He speaks again to the little guy next to him. 'I am Quality Marco. I like business with Quality Englishman.'

There is an explosion of laughter, more of relief than mirth, the room breathes again, and Rose takes a long drink.

'That was fun,' Tommy whispers. 'Let's have another one of your delicious gins, Rosie, and let's tweak the volume a shade lower.'

There is more dancing, but Rose won't dance, and she's given up the barmaid job, preferring to sit on the stool next to Tommy. Her head rests on one fist and she has a stiff vodka in the other. 'He's not even English,' she whispers, referring to John. 'Irish all the livelong day. Like Val Doonican.' Her elbow falls off the edge of the bar and she slops vodka down her front.

One of the girls staggers over. 'Can I have a gin and It, please?'

'Help yourself.' Rose takes a cigarette from a small green onyx box on the bar and Tommy lights it for her.

'Er. Excuse me.' The girl leans on the bar. 'Aren't you supposed to be serving?'

'I'm on my break.'

The girl splashes a drink into her glass before returning to her friends.

When the Maltese take their leave, it's all very good-natured. Lots of long handshakes and clasping of shoulders. She is relieved to see John smiling as the men come over and kiss her on both cheeks. She doesn't understand what they are saying. They're probably too drunk to bother with English, but the little stocky man says she's a Quality English something. Someone grabs his collar and slaps the back of his head.

The radiogram lights are off. Tommy sits on the sofa; his wide belly working as a shelf for his glass. John sits on a dining chair and there are a couple of others who have pulled up chairs to sit close. These men have rolled up their shirtsleeves and loosened their ties as if they are off duty. Rose fetches them each a whisky before refreshing Tommy's glass. She catches the name of Lafferty but the talk amongst the men is silenced each time she enters the room.

She sits in the kitchen smoking and drinking the last of the gin. She's not wanted next door. There is the sound of men laughing. Tommy's voice booms then there is the noise of scraping chairs and heavily exaggerated yawning as the men prepare to leave. Rose stands in the hall to say goodnight, prolonging the talk, telling John's colleagues to bring their wives and girlfriends to the next party.

Tommy is particularly sweet. 'We must have lunch, Rose. You won't mind if I take your lovely lady out for a bite to eat?' He looks at John who laughs too loudly.

'I reckon she'd be safe with you, old fruit,' he says.

The door closes and they are alone. He turns to look at Rose and it's like he's deciding what to do. John places a hand on the wall and mutters something incoherent into the space between them.

Rose doesn't move. 'Come again?'

'Stupid little cunt! Don't *ever* talk about me in company.' He showers her face in spittle and punches the wall beside her head.

Ten

Rose 1968

John's side of the bed is empty. Her hips ache and her arse hurts as though it's been through a mincer. She hadn't had the balls to say no when she awoke in the middle of the night to find him on top of her. She just let him do what he wanted and what he wanted was new and painful and she had cried softly to herself after it.

It was her penance for the embarrassment she had caused him. She shudders at the memory of Tom's words the first night he had met John. She had to keep John happy and this was more important now that he was Tom and Kath's landlord. She had messed up royally last night.

The street is empty. A deep winter silence hangs over Falmouth Road. The luminous green numbers on the bedside clock tells her it's ten. There is something about having a bad night that stirs in Rose a need to make things better, to have a good day despite the shitty things that happen. She gets it from Kath, she reckons.

Kath and Tom used to have almighty rows in their bedroom. There'd be banging and crashing. Kath in tears and Tom swearing. Then Kath would be at the breakfast table the next morning and she'd cook eggs and bacon for everyone. Or she would announce a trip to the pictures or some such treat. Rose understands why she did that. It was to banish the bad stuff that happens and to consign it to the past as quickly as possible.

Today, Rose is on a mission. She just needs to sort her undercarriage out before she leaves the house. An Epsom salt bath helps. She isn't intending to do a good turn for John. She hates him at the moment. But there will be a good outcome for him if her plan works. She figures she will benefit too. Better than that, if everything goes well, Kath will be made up.

Rose makes her way down to the council offices. People sit in straight rows facing a wall of cubicles, a solemn, compliant atmosphere pervades and the room is quiet considering the numbers present. She winces as she takes her seat. A toddler comes over and leans on her knee. He looks directly into her eyes and raises his hand. There is half a damp rusk stuck to his palm. She smiles and whispers, 'No thank you, little man.' The boy smiles back at her and slaps the biscuit into his mouth. A woman calls to him and he pulls away, waddling off, having drooled spittle and crumbs in Rose's lap. She takes her cigarette packet out of her pocket and lights up. Her smoke drifts upwards and joins the smoke of others.

The good idea that had surprised her on waking was simple. Rose wants to tell someone about her mum. She wants to explain how Kath is having trouble walking. About how her job at the St Charles hospital laundry has given her swollen ankles. The years of standing all day long, feeding the machines with bedlinen, have taken their toll. She needs to tell the council how the basement flat is full of mould and damp and that her parents have to fill a tin bath to wash. Her mission is to get them a higher priority on the council's housing list.

A man in a greasy raincoat comes to sit next to her, his hands in his pockets, fiddling with himself. She stands and walks away, finding a seat nearer the front in between two women. She's too hungover to make a fuss. The aspirin she took is wearing off and she's down to her last cigarette by the time her name is called. The disjointed voice over the Tannoy tells her to go to window eleven.

Rose is face to face with a softly spoken young man with slicked-back hair, thick glasses and an accent like Tommy Beresford. She describes the basement flat: the dangerous steps down to the front door; the outside toilet and tin bath. She gives a heart-wrenching performance while describing her mum's swollen ankles. The man behind the glass, who has been taking notes, nods sympathetically, talks in deferential whispers and tells her he will contact her parents directly.

Afterwards, she goes round to see them, stopping off at a flower stall in Ladbroke Grove to pick up some pretty daffodils wrapped in brown paper and secured with string.

Kath puts them in the little white enamel jug that has stood on the windowsill in the kitchen since Rose was a child. 'You what?'

'I've been to see the council, Mum.'

'You could have told us first, Rosie. Give us a bit of warning,' Tom says.

'You'll have to get a phone put in. When you get the new place.'

Mum is cooking. The smell of damp greens and boiled potatoes fills the little kitchen with a homely fug. Peppery sausages spit under the grill. Rose hasn't been back to the flat for a while and there is something unexpectedly comforting about its familiar rooms. Sitting at the kitchen table, their elbows almost touching, she has a sense of belonging which she couldn't recall having felt before.

'They say they're coming to visit?' Mum asks. They talk about making a good impression for the council. About mopping the floors, cleaning the skirting and tidying the backyard.

Then Tom stops abruptly. 'Has he put you up to this?' Her parents look at her suspiciously.

She never speaks to them about John. They disapprove of what they call her modern arrangement. 'No. I haven't told him about it.'

'You need to clear out your room. Or I'll have to bin your stuff,' Mum says.

Rose asks if she could have her old dressing table.

'Why not. One less bit of tat to carry,' Dad says.

Rose walks home from her parents' place congratulating herself. She has set wheels turning. John will be delighted with her. He will tear out the innards of her old house and tart up the outside. He'll make a fortune. Mum and Dad will get a lovely new flat and they'll be made up. She's almost bursting with excitement and practically skips home in her eagerness to phone John. It's amazing what you can do when you find yourself in a fix.

But he's not around when she rings the office. Someone tells her he's away on business for a few days. She immediately phones Evangeline to invite her and the boys to dinner next Sunday after church.

Unlike her parents, Evangeline has no problem with the modern arrangement. Rose has a chicken in the oven, she has peeled potatoes and there's a big head of cabbage chopped up in the saucepan. When they arrive, Rose takes Evangeline on a tour through the house. They end up in the lounge where the boys are playing cards. Evangeline runs an expert hand up the chintz curtains. 'Good quality, Rose.'

'John's got good taste for a man,' Rose says.

'Do you think it's his taste or someone else's?'

'What do you mean? His secretary? Or his decorator?'

'You know what I mean.'

'Erm, I think he gets stuff from a catalogue.'

'I must teach you to sew, you know.'

'I'd like that. Thank you. Perhaps I'll make some new curtains.' They peer at the bare patch of yard outside the back window.

'You got that little yard out there, Rose. It's a shame not to tend it,' Evangeline says.

'I will one day, but with work, I'm too busy.'

'Linton and Sylvester could help. It would be good for them.'

'I'd need to spend money on it.'

'John's got money. We've seen him riding around in his new car. Very fancy leather seats. What is it? A Rolls Royce?' Evangeline laughs.

'No. It's a Jaguar. He isn't that rich.' Rose laughs at the idea. 'Besides he doesn't spend money unless it leads to a profit. There's no point in spending any more money on this place.'

'But it's your home. It's not the business.'

Rose is reminded of John's words. Marriage is a business. A contract between a wife and husband. She would never be John's wife and where was the bit of paper to say this was her home? 'I suppose so. Maybe I'll ask him to get someone in to clear the garden for me.'

After lunch, Rose and Sylvester carry the dressing table from the basement flat, crossing the roads, dodging prams and trying to keep the thing balanced between them. Linton runs back and forth, gripping the heavy mirror that threatens to capsize the thing, shouting instructions. 'Step up on the kerb', 'Mind the dog poo' and suchlike.

Rose puts the dressing table in the back bedroom and fetches the rosebud-patterned skirt from her old suitcase. Evangeline explains how to cut it up to make a trim. After the family leave, Rose applies a lick of white paint to make the table look fresh. It's not a bit out of keeping in the sunny back bedroom.

As a reward for her endeavours, she opens a bottle of vodka. It's become her favourite drink and she pours a generous glass, adds ice cubes and Coke and takes a good slug of it. 'Just the one,' she says to herself as she walks upstairs to run a bath. But Rose, pink and cosy in her bathrobe, has another and another. As she pulls herself up to bed, she stops and sits heavily on the stairs. Terrible thoughts crowd in. John doesn't love her anymore. His wife has demanded he stays at home. He's abandoned her because her mum and dad are friends with the Laffertys. He could send those awful Maltesers to chuck her out of the house.

If he did throw her out, would her parents welcome her back? The thought of having to go and live with them makes her cry, even if they do get a nice new flat. The whole *I told you so* thing would be monstrous. The tears drip down her cheeks and splash on her knees.

The phone rings and she grabs the handset before she gets to blow her snotty nose.

'John?'

'What's the matter, girl?'

'Nothing. I missed you, that's all.'

'I'm on my way over. I've missed you, baby, I've got you some chocolates, your favourites.'

She's so relieved to hear his voice she can't speak. She daren't speak.

'And a baby-doll nighty from Harrods. Can't wait to see you in it.'

'Thanks. Sorry about the other night.'

'S'okay. You didn't mean anything by it. What's the matter?'

'Nothing. I was asleep.' She brews strong black coffee, takes aspirin to clear her head and brushes her teeth.

There's no time to run another bath so she has a nun's wash at the sink. She puts two fresh glasses on a little silver tray, almost dropping it in her haste to make everything perfect. She scans the rooms for untidiness and is satisfied that there is nothing John can criticise.

Eleven

Rose 1968

Tom and Kathleen Fuller take possession of a neat little home with a small garden out front and a larger one at the back. There is an airy living room, one bedroom, fully fitted kitchen and an indoor bathroom and toilet. It took the council all of four weeks to make them an offer. But it's not in the new block.

On account of all the suitable ground floor flats being spoken for and the urgency the council placed on rehousing Tom and Kath, the nice man from the council offers them a bungalow in the leafy suburb of West Ruislip. They almost bite his hand off when he tells them as Kath's sister, Vi, moved out that way a couple of years back. John offers a van and driver to move their stuff. There's only room for three at the front so Rose takes the underground and a bus.

When she arrives, a smiling Vi greets her. 'Rosie. Lovely to see you. They're upstairs sorting the bed out. Nice chap you found.' Vi nods towards a young man Rose has never seen before who is unloading tea crates. Once inside the kitchen, Rose's eyes are drawn to the large window and the garden outside.

'It's a bit overgrown,' Vi says as if reading her mind. 'But Tom'll get it sorted. We can always lend him our lawnmower.'

'It's nicer than mine.'

'Well there's a surprise. Listening to Kath, you live in a palace.' Vi lifts the hem of her blouse and shakes it to cool her skin. 'You going to marry this fella then, Rosie?'

'Erm, I might. In the future.'

'Would be nice to have a wedding in the family, hey? Kath always said she wanted grandchildren.'

'S'pose. I'm a bit young yet.' Vi is holding cutlery and Rose offers to put it away. The chink of metal as she throws it in the drawer accompanies the whistle of the kettle. 'Imagine Dad mowing the lawn? I bet he never thought he'd be doing that.'

'Well he wouldn't be doing it in Westbourne Park. All those blocks of flats.'

'They're not so bad. Some have balconies. But it's nothing like here, Vi. You're so lucky.' The sound of the van's engine and Kath's repeated thank yous signal her parents' approach. 'Is there a fish and chip shop somewhere? I could run down and fetch us lunch.'

'No need, love, I made a sandwich for your mum and dad.'

Tom and Kath spill into the room, both carrying kitchen paraphernalia. The washing up bowl is stacked with tea towels and dishcloths and the old laundry pan Kath uses for boiling whites is brimming with opened packets of groceries. The boxes are squashed down to prevent spillages.

'My bloody feet are killing me.' Kath has a sweat matching Vi's shining on her brow. The family resemblance is strong.

'Where's the tea, Rosie? I'm gagging.' Tom pulls one of the old kitchen chairs to the table and sits. He doesn't bother to fetch one for Kath or Vi so Rose drags the set across the floor.

'I'm glad I'm out of that basement.' Kath sighs and with a gesture very like her sister's she fans her face with her new rent book.

'The area's not what it used to be. When I told Clive Lafferty we was moving out he said he's thinking of moving out too,' Tom says.

'Is that old git still going? I thought he'd be dead by now,' Vi says.

'You might want to think about moving out here, Rose.' There's a look of hope in Kath's eyes.

'Can't. Can I? I'm working.'

'You still at that shop?' Vi asks.

'I'm the manager now.'

'That's right,' Tom says. 'Best stay put.' He slurps at his tea and it spills down his vest. Kath scolds him and fetches a cloth, embarrassed by her clumsy other half.

Rose visits every Sunday at first, bringing flowers to brighten the place up and arranging a phone to be installed on a hall table just like the one at Falmouth Road. But the visits become less frequent. Rose tells Kath that the Saturday girl has been let go at Peepers and Rose is working six days instead of five. In a way, the distance between them and her long tiring week is a blessing because Rose has discovered she's pregnant.

She hasn't seen much of Sharon lately and when her boss phones, she only wants to hear about the takings. Which is annoying because Rose needs Sharon's advice as there's no one else to confide in. Then out of the blue, Sharon invites her to lunch. Rose is relieved. Who else can she talk to about getting an abortion? Evangeline is properly religious and not just the paying-lip-service type of Catholic that Rose has become. Kath, who already disapproves of her modern arrangement, will most likely never speak to her again. That's if Tom has anything to do with it. He's more concerned with keeping in with the Laffertys and what he says goes in the Fuller household. Kath having to explain to Vi that the baby is illegitimate would be shaming. Rose doesn't want that for her mum. As for John. Well, he's another problem entirely.

On the day of the lunch, Sharon and Rose head towards Olympia to a little Italian place. They sit downstairs in the dark brown interior. Murals of Italy, colour-washed in blue, adorn the walls. They order spaghetti alla Bolognese and a carafe of red wine and Sharon fires off questions about the customers, the bestsellers and the takings. Suddenly, her boss reaches across the table. She takes Rose's hand and squeezes it.

'What's the matter?' Rose asks.

'The lease is up on the shop and the landlord has hiked up the rent. I can't afford to keep it going.'

'Oh.' Rose laughs on an exhalation then stops.

'What's funny?' Sharon withdraws the hand.

'I thought you were going to tell me you're ill. Or someone's died.' Rose offers her commiserations and her boss relaxes. 'When are we closing?'

'This Saturday will be our last trading day. Take what you want from the rails. I've had to go in a different direction.' She tells Rose all about her new venture leasing a stall in a market on Kensington High Street. Her plan is to sell vintage clothes–beautiful furs and silks, cocktail dresses and grannies' day dresses.

Rose is listening just enough to seem polite as her pasta congeals.

'I jump in the car, tootle around church jumble sales and pick up beautiful things for next to nothing.' She offers Rose a cigarette and they light up. 'I even hopped over to Calais on the ferry last week and snapped up some divine lace undies.' The imminent shop closure and the inevitable redundancies are forgotten in a heartbeat. 'I'm sure you'll find something else, Rose. You're a top manager. Selfridges or Harrods will hire you like a shot.'

'All the best with your new stall. I think it's right for the moment. Clever you,' Rose says. She raises a glass to toast Sharon's new venture and this pause creates an opportunity. 'I wanted to tell you my news anyway. I'm having a baby.' The words come out as if she's delighted, without a hint of the desperation she feels inside.

Sharon congratulates her, pours more wine and offers another cigarette. 'You won't need to work,' she says. 'You'll be a terrific mamma. You're such fun.'

'Actually, I was going to ask you if you knew anyone who could help me.'

Sharon didn't need an explanation. She smiled. 'Why would you want to do that?'

'So I can keep on working. I'm too young. John's got a family already. I thought you'd know someone who could…'

Sharon nodded her head and lowered her voice. 'I do know of a clinic but it's prohibitively expensive and you'd need to pay a couple of doctors to get you in.'

'John can pay.'

'He might not want to. Sorry, Rose. I won't help you. It's the wrong time totally. Haven't you read the papers?'

'What about?'

'There's a law going through Parliament. They're making abortion legal. You should keep up with the news.'

'When? When will that happen?' Rose can't control the excitement in her voice.

'End of the year, maybe next year. *Je ne sais pas.*' Sharon shrugs.

'It's too late for me. I need to deal with it now. I mean in the next few days.' The door had suddenly closed on the solution. Rose slouches back in her chair and swigs the wine in her glass.

'Have the baby. John will be responsible for it. You won't need to work.'

'But I want to work.'

'God! Why? Isn't that what every pretty young thing wants these days? Someone to pay their bills for them. To take them out to dinner and pay for all the shoes and clothes and holidays?' The bitterness in Sharon's words fills the space between them. Brought on perhaps, by resentment. Her youth having slipped by as she immersed herself in the business of earning her own living. Throughout her time at Peepers, it had been what Rose herself had aspired to. Then John had come along and changed all that. She didn't need to work, but work was liberating. Before they part, Sharon opens her handbag and places an envelope between them. Inside is a cheque and a reference. They promise to keep in touch.

As the bus makes its way down Kensington High Street, Rose stares out at the buildings. Her commitment to John is binding if she has this baby. Being the mother of his child is a high-security prison compared to marriage. Is that how she feels about John? Is that how much she has come to resent him?

John is sitting on the edge of the sofa. He's rubbing the knuckles of his right hand. His jaw is set rigid and there's a day's growth around his lips. He looks worried, like a villain from a detective series who's about to be charged. Rose fixes him a whisky and ice. 'For fuck's sake, Rose. You could have said something sooner,' he says.

'There's no way I'm getting rid of it. I'm brought up Catholic.' She's rehearsed this line since meeting Sharon. That was a week ago. It didn't sound convincing in front of the mirror. It feels even less so now.

'I know you are,' he says. 'You're a good girl.'

'So, I can keep it then?'

''Course. You keep it. I'll see you both right.'

He swallows the whisky and puts the glass in her hand.

He nods towards the bar and she fetches him another one. She drops the lid of the bottle and it rattles on the surface. 'I'll need baby things. You know I've lost my job at the shop. I don't have any money.'

'We'll go shopping. Get you whatever's needed. The best stuff.'

She's made steak and onions with mash and gravy and they go through and eat in the kitchen. He asks after Tom and Kath and she tells him they are fine and no they don't know about the baby. He falls silent and she doesn't interrupt his thoughts.

'Why not?' he asks after a while.

'Hmm?'

'Why haven't you told Kath and Tom about being up the duff?'

'I wanted to tell you first.'

'The problem is, Rose, I've been away some nights.'

She has been anticipating his response, playing out various scenarios in her head until they became ridiculous. Now the moment has arrived, fear crawls over her skin. 'What's that got to do with anything?'

'I have a reputation. I'm an alchemist, remember?' There is no anger. 'I won't be taken for a fool, Rose.' He eats quickly; the muscles of his forearms taut, his fist clenched around his fork. 'A woman who keeps secrets from her husband makes him a fool. That's an old Italian saying.'

'You know what I do. I don't have any secrets.' She was going to say more. Tell him she has spent most mornings throwing up, cleaning the house and reading magazines. She wants to ask him if he knows what his wife does at his other home when he's here. But she keeps quiet and so does he. They could be sitting in two kitchens in houses on separate streets. She can't see his eyes as they are hidden by his thick black eyebrows.

Finally, he speaks. 'If I find out you've been messing around with another fella while I was away. If it comes out and looks nothing like me, I will drive you to Little Venice and throw you and it into the canal.' He finishes his food, scraping the last slick onto his knife and licking it off. He stares at her, his eyes devoid of feeling, blank and unreadable.

As her middle gets rounder, John's mood becomes grimmer. Business seems to be booming, money flows but at what cost? John rarely comes to the house without a group of Maltese business associates in tow. They talk in hushed conversations, grim-faced and serious, whilst she pours drinks and hands round plates of sandwiches. The company has been widened to include a couple of police officers.

She's woken in the early hours one night by someone ringing the doorbell. It's a strong continuous blast. Slipping out of bed, she creeps onto the landing and in the darkness catches the conversation that's going on by the front door.

Ian Campbell, one of the police officers, is demanding money. 'Let's be frank, John, you are implicated. I can help you.'

'Get out, Campbell. You're drunk.'

'It'll be in the papers tomorrow and your friends are responsible and you know it.'

'It's nothing to do with me, old son. So best be on your way.'

'A thousand pounds. It's nothing to you, hey?'

'Look, Ian. You'll wake my wife. You don't want to do that.'

John sounds reasonable, appeasing the young policeman as he holds onto the wall for support.

'John. John, mate. A thousand pounds and I can deal with it. Keep the heat off.'

'We'll talk in the morning. Come to the office and we'll see what we can do.'

'It'll be all over the papers tomorrow.'

'Tomorrow, son. Come to the office. Tell us what's occurring down the cop shop and you never know, we'll come up with something. A holiday for you and the wife and kids. How's that?' John places a hand on the man's back and guides him out the door.

'But John. They're dead. The two lads are dead.'

'All the better for you, Ian. Dead lads can't talk.' John closes the door and covers his face with both hands.

The two lads who had died weren't named in the local newspaper but everyone in the area knew who they were. Rob and Colin Lafferty. According to the paper, they were found dead in a car outside the KPH pub in Ladbroke Grove. They had died from gunshot wounds to the head and the murder had all the markings of a gangland killing.

She bought the papers to read the reports: a couple of columns, then an article on the lethal gangs that have carved up London. Finally, a short paragraph that said the police had no new leads. By the time of the funeral, the paper had dropped the story altogether. She'd got wind of the date and time the boys were being laid to rest and left Falmouth Road, covering her bump with her rain mac.

Amongst the sea of black-clad mourners streaming down the steps of Holy Trinity she sees Tom and Kath.

'Go away, Rose,' Dad hisses.

'Get home. Please love.' Her mum holds her elbow, trying to push her away from the gathering crowd outside the church.

'What for?'

Tom glances over his shoulder. 'You're not wanted here,' he says.

'It's your John. He's a wrong 'un. He's not here an' all, is he?' Kath looks to left and right.

'No he isn't. I'm here to pay my respects, that's all. I've not been invited to the church but I can say goodbye here, can't I?'

Tom pulls at the knot in his tie, 'Suit yourself.' He turns away, dragging Kath by the arm as she pleads for her daughter to go home.

Two carriages pulled by black-plumed horses carry the coffins. Mrs Lafferty looking pale and unsteady is supported by Mr Lafferty senior. And there is Carol. Her eyes wide open, staring as if she were quite driven mad by it all. It seems to Rose her ex-friend is somewhere else entirely. There is a man she doesn't recognise holding her around the waist. If he let go, Rose was sure Carol would drop to the floor.

One day, Carol will see sense and they will talk it through. Especially now she has lost her brothers. There's nothing like bereavement to bring people closer together. They'll take up where they had left off and become friends again.

Then with frightening clarity, she realises she is implicated by being John's girlfriend. Bile rises in a painful surge as she cottons on. How could she be so stupid? She swears to herself. Her parents are right. She isn't wanted here and she was mad to come. Rose spins around to get away but Paul Lafferty is standing in front of her. She feels sick and wants to throw up.

He stares over her head towards the hearses. 'Has he sent you to rub shit in our faces?'

'I'm here as a friend.'

Paul is crying. His chest heaves under his black coat. 'Carol isn't your friend. Will never be your friend while you're with that brown-nose, O'Dowd.'

'I don't know what you mean. You're upset. Stop talking like that.'

'You've betrayed us, Rose. Your mum and dad are ashamed of you.'

'No, Paul, that's not right.' Rose turns back to look for Tom and Kath in the crowd. She needs them to tell Paul that isn't the case. But she can't spot them.

Mr Lafferty senior rolls down the window of the black limousine. 'Get that bitch away from here and get in the car.' His voice drips pure hatred and it cuts into her.

Paul's voice is calm. 'You tell O'Dowd he's a dead man.' He steps off the kerb then turns abruptly. In front of the assembled crowd of old friends and neighbours, in front of a crowd that includes her parents, he spits on her shoes.

Twelve

Rose 1968

She should be overjoyed. Rose and John should be sitting together looking at catalogues, strolling around department stores buying furniture, choosing names, attending the midwife classes together at the ante-natal clinic. Instead, she knits, cleans the house, shops down the Bella and in the evenings, watches the television set.

She tells Kath that she's pregnant over the phone.

'Oh sweet baby Jesus. Is he going to marry you then?'

'Not just yet.'

'What's he said then? When is he going to marry you?'

'I don't know. I thought you'd be pleased. Vi said you wanted grandchildren.'

'Not like this, Rose. For God's sake, what've you got yourself into?'

'I'm going to be a good mum and John is going to be a good dad.'

'What am I going to tell Tom? He'll go spare.' Kath

whispers as though Tom is close by. There were no congratulations or offers to help. She's on her own as far as this baby is concerned.

John should be sitting with her in the evening when the baby kicks so that he can feel the real, living person that she's holding for him. Their baby. When he does visit it's to drop off housekeeping money. The street watches with a mixture of disdain and jealousy as vans from Selfridges pull up outside. Delivery men bring boxes and bags to her door and she signs for everything: the cot and highchair; baby clothes; Beatrix Potter-themed wallpaper and linens. John organises for a chap to come around to decorate the nursery and put the new furniture together.

'Your uncle said you wanted yellow paint.' His accent is Irish.

'My uncle?'

'Mr O'Dowd. Sorry,' he says. He disappears into the nursery, refusing the tea she offers. Grabbing a coat and a bag of knitting, she walks the short distance to Evangeline's flat. It's getting nearer to the due date and she craves the company of her old friend.

They sit in Evangeline's sunny lounge, Rose knitting the baby a cardigan while Evangeline hand smocks a dress in delicate pink thread. She is convinced that the baby is a girl. 'Mothers are better off with girls. Boys are wayward.' Evangeline is quite serious.

'Linton and Sylvester are hardly wayward,' Rose says. There is evidence of study around the flat. Textbooks, dictionaries and jotting pads are neatly stacked on the sideboard. Her eye is drawn to a photograph of Evangeline and her husband on their wedding day. Her husband is sombre in his dark suit and when she looks closely, Rose can see Sylvester's strong jaw and serious eyes. They break from the sewing to stand amongst the pots of tomato plants and marigolds on Evangeline's balcony. Birdsong fills the air.

Would it be possible to persuade John to come and live with her when the baby is born? Did she even want that? Or could she get out of Falmouth Road and get rehoused by the council? Leave John and his criminal friends behind her? Rose had never seen the lack of a husband as a hindrance for her friend. Evangeline is a great mother.

'Where's your husband, Evangeline?'

'I'm a widow, Rose. Clayton passed.'

'I'm so sorry.' It had never occurred to Rose that this was the case. She had always pictured Mr Stanley living with a second wife with other children, if she had given him any thought at all. Evangeline isn't a wrong 'un, like her father had insisted. She is a widow.

'What happened to him?'

'Got into trouble with the police.'

'Oh I'm so sorry. Don't tell me if—'

'He was a bus driver. Me and the boys stayed at home in Trinidad while he came over to find work.' She pauses and looks down at the little yellow seesaw, the size of a child's toy from where they are standing. 'Too cold out here. Let's go inside.'

Evangeline takes up the little dress and her needle but they rest on her lap. 'He came over in sixty-three and saved and saved and saved until he had enough money for our fares. We were so excited. I can't tell you how much the boys missed their father.

'He'd given me an address. My God in Heaven, me took so long to find the place it was nearly midnight. We were walking the streets with our suitcases. My hands and feet were raw. Linton was sleepwalking.' Evangeline smiled.

'So, he'd found a place for you all?'

'He had. But he wasn't there when we arrived. The other men in the house said we could stay the night, but we'd have to go to the police the next day. Clayton had been involved in an incident.'

'What sort of an incident?'

'They wouldn't say. I just lay awake all night. Not knowing, you see. Being so, so exhausted and not knowing what had happened, or what to expect. I prayed to Jesus and all the saints an' it was the worse night of my entire life.'

There is a terrible stillness; even the birds stop singing.

'You don't have to tell me anymore, Evangeline. If you don't want to.'

'A *altercation*, the police called it. On his way home from working the last bus. Police said him were *loitering*. Clayton died because he was out late. How can a man driving the las' bus not be out late? An' him in uniform?' Evangeline stiffens as she confronts her memories. Then she relaxes as if she had taken foul-tasting medicine that had finally slipped down her throat. She takes up her needle and thread.

'Oh my God, Evangeline. You hear about these things but... I'm so sorry.'

'God's plan for me is none of my business. I just get on wi' it.'

'What about the boys? They must've...'

'They miss him.'

'Did you get a solicitor? What about...?'

'Hah. Stop now, foolish girl. I had no money for a solicitor. I had other things to be getting on wi'. Like finding work to pay for a sewing machine.'

Rose falls silent. Evangeline's tragic story reminds her of an August bank holiday two years ago. Rose, Carol and a couple of friends had walked up to Acklam Road to witness the Carnival. They heard it before they saw it: whistles and drums; endless chatter; laughing and singing combining to fill the warm air with joy. Like the sound of a fairground moving through the narrow hot streets.

A crowd of people of all ages, White and Black, surrounded two open-backed trucks. Rose had a clear view of the first truck. Men in brightly coloured shirts, their skin gleaming with their efforts, were blowing saxophones or playing oil drums. On the face of it, everything was good-natured and harmonious. Rose had wanted to join the crowd snaking its way towards the Bella. She was almost off the pavement with her need to dance but her friends all shook their heads.

'It's not for us. Anyway, we're not dressed for it,' Carol had said.

'Just stay a minute. Walk with them.'

'We're going for a tea and KitKat. You can suit yourself and stay if you want.'

Rose had turned for one last look. The crowd had thinned and somehow the music was more subdued. All she could focus on were the policemen that lined the route. They stood in front of the shops and cafes on the opposite side to her. Maybe a hundred of them. She remembers them now as a static border of bodies in blue serge. Stern disapproving mouths set in white faces and helmets too low to see their eyes. Disengaged and threatening, they had stolen Carnival from the people on the street. They had sucked up the goodness and left a bitter taste in her mouth.

Had they been there? The bent copper, Campbell? And in that line of blue, had there been the officer responsible for Mr Stanley's death?

In the early hours of the first of September, Rose wakes in a thick black world of outrageous pain. She screams as if she's being killed and is disgusted by the wetness around her thighs and lower back. The pain cuts across her hips and she turns to slide off the bed, knowing she must get to the telephone. Her lower half is overcome by an urgent hammering and with every surge, she howls like the vixens that roam the back gardens.

On all fours, she crawls to the top of the stairs fearing a fall and imagining both her and the baby dying from loss of blood or head injury. The pain ripping her body in two subsides and she grips the banisters to edge her way down on her bottom. A streetlight shines through the glass panels of the door and she's aware of her thighs visible through her soaking nightdress. It makes her blush.

She whines like a smacked dog as she grabs the telephone handset. Another wave of agony overcomes her and this time, she finds herself screaming out for her mother. A flashing light appears outside the door and she has managed to wrap a coat around her shoulders. Evangeline had told her to pack a bag and leave it in the hall. When they take her to hospital she has the bag, her coat and as much of her dignity as she can muster.

It's a girl. A slight, serious-looking dolly with thin arms and legs like her own and a face that is the image of John's even though it's impossible to pick one feature the same. John is studying the baby. He smells of brandy and cigar smoke and she wants to tell him to sober himself up. When he kisses Rose's cheek, his stubble scrapes her skin. The baby wakes, her arms reach up and John reacts as if she is holding her arms out for him. 'She's beautiful. She's got the look of my grandmother about her. Well done, Rose. Well done.'

Rose turns away, exhaustion and relief and something else stirring inside her, fighting for ascendancy. A need for her own mother or Evangeline, someone who will take care of her, guide her through motherhood. She feels unready and knows nothing about the life she has carried for nine months. She closes her eyes tight and while John cradles the baby in his arms, she tries to block out the image of him pulling her out of a car on the bridge at Little Venice and throwing her in, baby and all.

'Beatrice,' he says. 'We'll call her Beatrice Mary after Granny O'Dowd.'

Rose feels a wet kiss planted hard on her lips and tastes the brandy he has been drinking. It's delicious, like Christmas cake. He whispers another slurred well done and is gone.

She must have dozed off. The sun splits the ward in two and she is warmed by its rays but the opposite beds are in shade. At first, she doesn't recognise the woman who is walking along the white linoleum, turning and bending around to peer behind curtains. When her sleep-sticky eyes focus, she realises it's Evangeline and she wants to cry.

'Well done, Rose. You did it.' Evangeline sits in the chair by the bed.

'Never again,' Rose says.

Evangeline smiles. 'I said the same with the first one.'

Beatrice cries and together they respond but it's Evangeline who is swifter, more assured. She holds the baby, cooing gently as Rose tells her about the birth, the lovely midwives and the stitches. 'She couldn't wait to get out. I almost had her in the ambulance.'

'She's beautiful. Perfect. God bless her and praise Him for her safe arrival.' Evangeline's soft tone is drowned out by insistent crying. 'She wants to feed.'

'Oh God, I can't. I don't know how.' The panic rises and Evangeline shushes her. She places the baby at Rose's breast and they watch as the tiny bundle attempts to latch on. Her little face is screwed up in frustration.

Evangeline guides the mouth by gently pushing her cheek towards the nipple with her forefinger. It looks like a giant's finger against the tiny head. Then the baby relaxes and begins to suckle. As the warm sunlight streams down on them, Rose is reminded of figures in Holy Trinity's stained-glass windows.

Beatrice is a strange creature. Her forehead is usually furrowed and Rose thinks it was the tortuous birth. She's seven days old and they've been home for three of them. The nurses had put Bea on formula milk as she refused to give up screaming through the night. She wasn't thriving on the breast, they had said.

John feeds the noisy bundle, sits her on his knee to burp her then holds her to his chest. This is the first night he has slept at the house since Beatrice was born. 'She's just like Granny O'Dowd when she yells like that.' John holds the crying baby in his arms. Barefoot, his braces dangling at his sides, he paces the bedroom floor. 'My granny was a legend.' His voice is soft. 'She was tiny like this little one. Sharp eyes too. I remember they were like the black beads in her rosary.'

Rose, lying in bed, feels as though he is telling her a bedtime story.

'Dad said the family used to dodge the rent man and the police by moving from one flea-ridden Dublin hovel to the next. Abject poverty it was. She used to give my aunts and uncles a hard time but not my dad. He was unusual. Seven children dropped out of her one after the other like parcels in the sorting office, they said. My dad was her eighth and there was a scandalous rumour that the parish priest was the father, not Grandad O'Dowd. My dad was special.'

Rose's eyelids close. The baby has ceased howling and is moaning in stops and starts as if deciding whether to listen to the story or not. The floorboards creak as John continues. 'My father had intelligent eyes. Everyone said it. And a broad forehead. I've the same. None of the others are like him, so he could've been the priest's.' His voice drifts across the room.

'"Mrs O'Dowd, you would be well to think how you can encourage this wee boy and give him an education. There is nothing as good an investment as educating a child," the priest said.'

'What? Word for word?' Rose lifts her head from the pillow.

'Near as damn it. "And what would an educated child do in my house, except mock us?" said Granny.' John bent his head closer to the baby.

'He'll not, Mrs O'Dowd; he will make you comfortable in your old age. This is the one. Spend time and money on this little fellow and reap the rewards at your leisure.'

'My aunts and uncles hit him and sold his books out of spite. Granny beat them all in retaliation, according to my dad.'

He comes close to the bed and Rose holds out her arms to take the baby. But John turns to pace again as Beatrice howls. 'Declan, that's my dad, got a job as a civil servant in the Office of Public Health. The priest was delighted but regretted that he hadn't chosen a career in the service of the Lord. Granny told him it was a fight between de Valera and God and de Valera won. Dad bought her a nice little cottage in Blackrock before he left for London. We used to visit but she was old by then. Still yelling at everyone and swearing like a navvy.'

Rose smiled up at him. 'You're lucky to have all those aunts and uncles.'

'Ah, they're the biggest bunch of freeloaders you ever encountered.'

She had enjoyed listening to the story. He has revealed a part of himself. John The Alchemist has let her in and one day, when Beatrice is older, she will share the story with her. It is a good moment and it gives Rose hope.

Thirteen

Rose 1971

Three years older. Rose is three years older. In the dim light of the bedroom, she draws her hands down her sides, taking pleasure in the way soft flesh yields to her touch. She no longer mourns the loss of her slight teenage frame. She runs her fingers through her hair. It's glossy and she wears it long, the way John likes it.

Rose dresses in her most provocative outfit. Her hipster flares reveal a tantalising glimpse of belly and a tight jumper accentuates her fulsome boobs. Her hair is ruffled, just as it says it should be in her magazine. She has planned a seemingly spontaneous blow job which isn't exactly stated in the article but is implied.

Rose checks on Bea, asleep in her cot, and tiptoes out of the nursery. She waits in the kitchen drinking vodka and Coke. She's heard that vodka doesn't smell on the breath. John is due over tonight and there's a party planned for his business associates. They are celebrating and she wonders if it's to do with the Laffertys' clubs being raided. It was all over the papers. *Scotland Yard Clean Up.* was the headline. Clive has been arrested for living off immoral earnings. No mention of Paul or Carol and no mention of the Maltesers. She sighs. 'Wait until Scotland Yard cop on to this lot.'

When she hears the key in the door, she adjusts her boobs and smiles as she makes her way up from the kitchen to the hall. 'Hey, John. Missed you.' Her kiss is wet and sexy, pushing into his mouth, pressing her body into his.

'Bea asleep?' John asks as she undoes his belt and drops down onto her knees. He emits a little tug of breath as he comes and scrabbles in his coat pocket. She rises and taking the proffered hanky, wipes her mouth.

They stand at the newly named *Cocktail Bar*. A pink neon sign on the wall behind her makes the bar top glow. She fixes them both a drink then lights his cigar. John inspects the lounge, checking the room is ready for the poker game that will go on into the early hours. He checks the labels on the whisky bottles and asks after Bea.

'She counted to ten today. And I asked her to give me a red brick. She only went and did it and I thought let's try again to see if she knows her colours. So we sat for ages on the carpet and guess what?'

'She knows her colours.' He smiles and nods his head at this news. 'She's a clever girl. You need to encourage that, Rosie.'

'Red, blue, green, yellow. You should've seen her. Giggling every time she got it right.' Rose lights a cigarette as John sucks on his Havana.

'She takes after my dad. He was a clever man. I told you about him.'

'And your granny.' She waits for him to ask about her day but he doesn't so she tells him her news straight out. 'I took Bea to Kensington Market today. Saw Sharon.' And as casually as she could, 'She asked me if I could work Saturday.'

'What'll you do with Bea?' John's face is a picture: as if he's been asked to name all the kings and queens of England. In order.

'I thought you could have her. Take her to the zoo or something.'

He snorts. 'The zoo? For God's sake, Rosie. Give me a break.'

'It's just one day and you'll have loads of fun. She's so clever.'

'Forget it, girl. I've a business to run. You don't need to work.'

'I want to work. It'll get me out of the house—'

'What d'you want to get out of the house for? This house not good enough for you?'

'No. John, I love this house. I just thought you could have some time with Bea and I could get out and earn some money. You're away so much.'

'You've got work here, Rosemary. You are earning your keep here, girl. Have you forgotten you have a child?'

'I know, John, but I need some time for me.'

'What are you talking about? You need to stop reading those magazines. They're filling your head with shit.' He bounces a finger off his temple and ash falls from his cigar onto the carpet. '*Time for me.* What utter rubbish.'

Shop-Bought Flowers

Rose mouths an insult as she leaves him and fetches a cloth to rescue the carpet from the hot ash. She has come to realise that she is the mistress to a man so like her father she may as well have stayed put in the basement.

The guests gather for the poker game. Rose is fetching drinks. Smiling as she greets each player. She has cultivated the fantasy that she is delighted with John's world and she adores all his fascinating colleagues. Rose reacts when wolf whistles greet her entrance. 'Come on, lads, stop that,' she chides. As John's girl she is unequivocally not for sale, unlike the girls they bring to the house.

Tonight, Marco watches her as she moves around the room. She is unsettled and she's glad that John is engrossed in conversation with a group of men. From behind her, John shouts, 'Fetch the man a drink, Rosie. He's dying of thirst over there.' He is pointing to Marco.

She offers him his drink but before he takes the glass, he brushes his fingertips down her breast. 'If you were my special lady, I would lock you up.' He whispers into her ear and sniffs her hair. 'You smell like honey.'

She can't speak. The smile, the mask she wears so easily, is rigid but her breathing threatens to expose her fear. She turns to face the thinly crowded room. John has his back to them.

Marco rests his hand on the base of her spine. 'Meet me tomorrow. Savoy Hotel at two. We will eat oysters and after...' His hand follows the path of her spine and he finds a spot that sends hot coals tumbling through her body.

John is talking ardently to a nervous young man who looks like a rookie copper. John only needs to glance in her direction and he would see Marcos eyeing her arse as he rubs it. With all the brass neck she can muster she blurts out, 'You naughty boy. What am I going to do with you?' She wags her finger and winks at him and he laughs as though it was all a big joke.

There is a bottle of John's good malt on the kitchen table. She unscrews it and pours herself a generous glass. At first, it burns and she wants to throw up in the sink. She fights the urge and has another. She tops up the bottle with a cheap brand so John won't accuse her of drinking his special tipple. She drinks the cheaper brand, mixing it with ginger ale to make a whisky mac. Tommy had made it for her one night.

She wishes he were here. He would ask John if he could take her out to lunch like he always does and instead of letting John answer for her she would say, 'Yes you can, old chap. You bloody well can. What time? Where?' Footsteps bring her out of her seat and scurrying into the hall. A man she doesn't recognise is taking one of the girls upstairs. He lifts her skirt and pinches her arse and she giggles in that nervous but I'm pretending to like it way that all the girls do. She wonders if that's how she sounds.

John comes out of the lounge. The smell of cigar smoke signals his arrival.

'Where're they going?' she whispers.

'Where d'you think?' He's tired, rubbing his eyes after hours of poker.

'What're you doing letting them use the bedroom? We've got Bea upstairs. What if—'

'They wouldn't hurt Bea. They have kids of their own. And anyway I'd tear their balls off.'

Rose follows him upstairs. 'It's horrible, John. I don't want these girls around Bea.'

He stops and looks at her as he unbuckles his belt. 'I'm just going in for a piss. Want to watch?'

'I don't want prostitutes using the bedroom.'

'What're you going to do about it? Go back and live with Mum and Dad?'

'We could do that, John, actually. Bea and I could go and live in Ruislip.'

John holds on to the waist of his trousers with one hand. 'You're not taking my daughter anywhere. And anyway, you couldn't live with Kathleen and Tom.'

'I could. What's stopping me?'

'They wouldn't have you. Now fuck off downstairs and make yourself useful.'

Rose sinks more whisky macs until the ginger has run out. She is sick of the cloying sweetness coating her teeth anyway. She takes her whisky neat and nestles into the cosy fug of the cigarette smoke around her.

At some point in the early hours, she's not sure when, John appears in the kitchen. Perhaps she had fallen asleep at the table and he had woken her. His face thunderous, his lips curled back over his teeth. She stands to face him.

'What are you playing at?'

She thinks of Marco. 'It doesn't mean anything, John. It's just a bit of banter—'

'What have you done to my malt?' He smashes the glass he's been holding against the wall and puts the cut edge near her face. 'What d'you wanna do? Make me look cheap? Is that it?'

'I don't know—'

'Don't you ever pass off my single malt with cheap shit whisky.'

She says she doesn't know anything. Selfridges is ripping him off. There is a blurred movement in front of her face then his knuckles connect. He punches her cheek with a force that sends her head smashing against the doorframe.

'And don't ever think you can lie to me, Rose Fuller. I know you too well.' John shoves her away and leaves the kitchen.

Rose staggers upstairs and opens the door to her daughter's bedroom. Her face is numb and she's grateful the alcohol has dulled the pain. She looks at her daughter in the cot and her heart swells. Bea sleeps, breathing noiselessly, her little body soft and warm. Darling Bea. Clever Bea who knows her colours. She strokes the little girl's hair, the gentlest of touches, and wraps one of Bea's ringlets around her finger.

'I'll take you away, darling. I'll take you away from him. Don't you worry.' The action of bending down makes Rose's jaw throb. Blood and spittle leak onto the Beatrix Potter blanket. It looks as though Mr McGregor has shot Peter Rabbit in the head.

With surprising clarity considering the amount she's put away tonight, she realises that John is weak, not a successful businessman but a puppet with Marco pulling his strings. He's a villain just like the Laffertys but worse.

He works for the Mafia. He has learned something from them that wasn't there before. Women are not real people. They can be hired out like Rediffusion hire out television sets. When the TV goes wrong, Rediffusion will replace it with a new one, even if the owner has thumped the top of it to get it to work.

More seriously, John has fallen out of love with her and now it is a case of survival. He is only interested in two things: his precious daughter and making money. As long as Rose does her job taking care of Bea, she is safe. But step out of line, Rosie. Say you want a life of your own, Rosie, and you may end up in the canal after all.

Fourteen

Evie 2019

The boiler revs into action. While Bea organises the creamy pastries for afternoon tea, Evie slides a large chocolate box over to the sofa. It's an embossed affair, the brand name curvaceous and inviting, but the corners of the box have been nibbled by mice.

Sitting on top of postcards and photos of unknown people and events lost in time, Evie finds an official-looking brown envelope. Inside is her own birth certificate. She can't understand why she never took it from the house when she left home. She had needed it for applying to university, registering with a doctor and so forth, but she had always returned it to Bea. As if it wasn't hers to keep.

Her birth is registered at Kensington Town Hall. Ma's name in beautiful calligraphy is as clear as when it was first recorded and in the space for her father's name, the word "Unknown." She puts the document on the coffee table and as she leans forward, the brown envelope falls from her lap and some other papers reveal themselves.

A birth certificate, as crisp as the day it was issued. A baby boy called Gerard whose father is named as Andrew Eagan. Evie thinks it belongs to a cousin or a distant relative. But then she reads the mother's name. Rosemary Kathleen Fuller.

She stands, thinking to make her way to the kitchen to ask Bea for an explanation. But then stops. There is a letter stapled to the certificate. A letter from the Holy Trinity Church Adoption Board signed by Ma. She has given her consent to have the baby named on the certificate adopted. As she reads the letter, sees the date that tells her Gerard was born years before her own birth, Bea appears by the sofa carrying the tray, the teaspoons rattling as she places it on the table. Her hand is trembling.

Evie holds out the letter accusingly. 'Bea. A baby? Ma had another baby?'

'The father was a villain.' Bea holds her left hand and massages the trembling away. 'It wasn't John's baby. He'd practically abandoned us by the time Ma got pregnant again. Bea sits opposite and Evie knows she is reading her thoughts. 'What're you going to do? Set out on a mission to find him?'

'He's family.'

'Define family,' Bea scoffed. 'We are family. He can find us if he wants to.' She waves a dismissive hand at the papers.

'Perhaps she thought getting pregnant would make this boyfriend hang around. Like John did, with you,'

Evie says. She tamps down the wave of jealousy raising goose pimples on her arms. 'Gerard would be thirty-six today, four years older than me.' She slumps back in her seat. 'Well you've outdone yourself with this Unpleasantry.'

'Yes, I suppose so.'

'It's not an Unpleasantry, Bea. It's a cataclysmic point in Ma's life.' She sighs. 'It's quite a big deal. You didn't think to mention it to me at any time?' Evie sits hunched over her bump, waiting for a reply.

But Bea is silent. She picks up the papers and reads, but she hasn't got her glasses to hand and gives up. 'I'm telling you now, aren't I?'

'What is wrong with you? Ma had another baby. We have a sibling. God, Bea. It's like you don't feel anything.'

'I've feelings, Evie. I just keep them in perspective. No use crying over a person we have never met. What's the use to him or us?'

'Ma made a monumental choice here.' Evie points at the paperwork.

'And that's why she was such a wreck for years afterwards. Her drinking got really bad after the baby was adopted. Drinking was how she coped with everything: with John's fists; with the adoption and with me.'

Evie sat upright. 'What about me? She could've had me adopted. Like Gerard. Why keep me?' The enormity of what she was saying suddenly dawned on her and she raised her hands to cover her mouth.

'I insisted she keep you.'

'But Bea, what if—'

'That was never the case. You were never going to be adopted. We came to an agreement. I've told you before, how good you were, you never cried, you smiled at the least little thing. You were curious about everything. And I thought it would be good for Ma.'

'What if I had been a nightmare baby?' Bea is right. Memory tells Evie that when Ma was in a good place, she had fed her, dropped her off at school and taught her how to brush her teeth. Her memories of Ma when Bea went abroad were of treats: trips to the swings; white bread and jam and sleeping in Ma's bed.

But when Evie was very young, it seemed as though her mother was a shadowy figure, rarely seen. Ma would spend days and nights in her bedroom, curtains drawn and the door closed. Bea used to say that Ma was sick. 'What else have you been keeping from me?'

But Bea is busy clearing the plates and as the tea is cold and the pastries untouched, she takes the tray to the kitchen. There is another envelope in the box. It's a long thin one, the sort used for personal letters, no address or stamp so whatever was inside was never meant to be posted. When Evie peers inside, she is disappointed to find it empty.

The feeling that there is something else Bea is keeping from her is so strong, the baby inside her kicks in response to it. Evie searches inside the white envelope, hoping some flimsy document is stuck to its side. There is nothing. She turns the box over as if there are clues to be found on its base. But there is only a list of ingredients. The chocolates in this box were never fancy, they were a pretence. A vegetable fat and sugar conglomeration, the taste an illusion created by artificial flavours and colours. 'I'm fed up with secrets, Bea. You're still keeping things from me and…' Evie realises she is alone and moves down to the kitchen where Bea is repacking the cakes. 'You know, I won't be shocked if there are more skeletons in the cupboard.'

'No, I suppose you won't. The things you got up to when you were young.'

'No one gets shocked anymore. And these days all the embarrassing moments of life are captured on mobile phones.'

Bea returns to the lounge. Clumsily and with much effort, Bea hauls a large carboard box to the sofa. 'Here. Look at these.'

Evie empties the box: used plastic carrier bags from Kensington Market, tarnished metal chains with sun and moon symbols, incense burners, huge belt buckles, cassette tapes and a set of clothes.

Bea sneezes and picks up a leather necklace with a bell hanging from it.

'What's that old thing?' Evie asks.

'Hippy bell. I remember packing this lot away.'

Evie lifts a pile of neatly folded clothes and realises that the T-shirts and the jeans she's handling belonged to a man. She holds up a large brown T-shirt with a faded CND logo on the front. She places it over her knees and traces the cracks along the design.

'Did John go all pacifist, anti-nuclear?'

'John would have made nuclear weapons if he could've.'

'He disappeared, right? Did he go to India then, join a cult?'

'Could've gone anywhere. John left when I was fourteen.' Bea takes a deep breath and exhales loudly as if a pain that had been gnawing at her insides has finally been expelled. She unfolds the Levi's and places them over her knees. Then, smiling, rings the hippy bell as if summoning a spirit at a séance.

'Who do they belong to?' Evie picks up Gerard's adoption papers and reads the father's name again. 'Andrew Eagan?'

'No, Evie. Not that chancer.' Bea shivers. 'These things belonged to your dad.'

Part Two

Fifteen

Beatrice Mary O'Dowd
b. 1st September 1968

Bea 1983

The bloke called Andy sits on the couch surrounded by *Auto Trader* magazines. It's February and far too cold to drink anything but hot chocolate. Far too early for lager. He has a can by his side and now and again he reaches down and takes a gulp. Bea peers over the book she is reading. Andy has an enormous Adam's apple and she follows it as it slides up and down his neck. He's got dark rings around his eyes from staying out until the early hours. She heard him creep up the stairs around three.

'What's your problem?' he asks.

She's been staring again. She can't help it as to her, he is a Neanderthal living in the wrong era. 'I was wondering what you thought about the Liberal Party winning Bermondsey from Labour. D'you think the gay community will accept the result?'

'Huh?'

He has no idea what she's talking about.

Rose walks in. 'Here you are. It's so quiet I thought you'd gone out and left me.' Her face is dry and grey from the amount of booze she had consumed last night. She's looking from one to the other detecting the frosty atmosphere. 'Shall we go for a Wimpy? Treat ourselves?'

Bea holds her book to her face and shakes her head.

'Ah. Would love to, doll, but I've got a deal going down.' Andy's voice is deep and his eyes bulge as if he is permanently scared. He is going to sell a used car. This is his job. He knows nothing but car makes and engine sizes. 'Austin Metro's come on the market. One careful owner. I can name me price.'

Bea has had enough of Rose's boyfriends. They seem to come and go like the Jehovah's Witnesses that ring the bell on Sundays. She brought this one home from the Duke of York a few weeks ago. If he's not taking up the sofa, he's on the phone doing deals.

'Oh that's amazing, Andy. We should celebrate when you get back.' Rose is delighted and bends down to kiss his razored head.

Bea understands what she means by that: a session at the pub, then home, records on so loud the neighbour thuds the wall, more drink until they are both sparked out on the sofas.

'Don't know when I'll be back. I'll give you a bell later.'

'Can't you just tell me a time? I don't like waiting.'

'Then go out.' He slaps a tenner in her hand. 'Take Lady Penelope for a Wimpy. Don't wait up, doll.'

Once he's left the house, Bea relaxes. 'Why does he call me Lady Penelope?'

'It's your accent. He thinks you're posh.'

'Well I think he's a throwback cave dweller.'

'You need to be kinder to him.'

'That would freak him out.'

They layer up against the freezing February temperature as Rose decides on walking. The bus fare will eat into the tenner Andy has given them. 'See, he's not all bad.' Rose waves the note in Bea's direction before putting it in her purse.

'He drinks too much and you do too.'

'Cheeky cow. Don't speak to me like that.'

Bea remembers the promise of the Wimpy and drops the attitude.

'What if John catches him living here?' she asks.

'He won't. When was the last time you saw your dad?' Rose ties a scarf around Bea's neck but it's too tight and she bats her mother's fingers away to loosen it.

'Ages ago.' Bea remembers him looking in on her when she was in bed one night a couple of years ago. A dark bulky figure in the doorframe. She thought she had called his name but he didn't answer. Then he was gone. When she had come down to the kitchen the next day, her mother was sporting a livid black eye and sitting in front of a pile of cash on the table.

They open the door to leave but are stopped by the phone ringing. Rose answers it. She stutters when she speaks and tells whoever is on the phone she'll be right over. Her grey face has turned a sickly white and she whispers, 'Your grandma's passed away.'

Grandpa looks bewildered. He's not sure what to say or do. They stand in the hallway as he hasn't asked them to come in properly. He looks thinner than Bea remembers. His skin hangs in pale folds around his jaw like the old cardigan he has thrown over his vest.

'Let's go and sit down. I'll make you a cuppa.' Rose squeezes past him, heading for the kitchen and Tom follows like a lamb. There are grey marks along the wall that lead all the way to the kitchen. On their last visit, Bea noticed how her grandparents laid flat palms against the walls for support.

'She's gone, ain't she, Rosie? She's not coming back.'

'No, Dad. She's in a better place.'

'That mumbo jumbo. Never understood how she was taken in by that.'

'Look, if you want, I could stay over for a few days. Help you sort things out.'

'I don't know.'

'Can I stay too?' Bea says. But it's as if she's not in the room.

'I could look after you. Bea can stay at Evangeline's.'

'Your Aunt Vi's gonna help me with the funeral and that.'

'Oh. Right then.'

'Bloody weather,' he says. 'Killed her. Killed my Kath.' He blows his nose into a vast grey hankie.

Seeing Grandpa's wet eyes makes her stomach flip and her nose tingle. She has lost the comfort of Grandma's big cushioning bosom, the old Cockney songs she used to sing and the treats from the tin in the cupboard. That she will never see Grandma again brings on her tears. Rose fetches toilet paper. 'There, there, Bea. Let it out. You loved Grandma didn't you, darling?'

'Don't cry, kid,' Tom says. 'You'll set me off again.' Tom stares at the frost-webbed shrubs outside the window. A robin flits in and out of the leaves and the clock ticks.

A key turns in the lock and the gloom is shattered by Auntie Vi calling out. 'Only me. Are you decent?' She comes through to the kitchen and Vi spots Bea. She comments on how much she's grown since they last met. 'Who does she take after, Tom? Not my side. She's a tiny little thing, in't she.'

'I'd like to help with the funeral. Maybe I could choose Mum's outfit,' Rose says.

'It's sorted, love. I took her best outfit home and give it a good wash. Polished her shoes and everything.' She points down the hall. 'I've brought her stuff back from the hospital.' When Rose places a cup of tea in front of Vi, the old lady sniffs the air.

'You been to the pub, Rose?'

'I just had a glass of wine with lunch.'

Bea watches as Rose blinks away the lie.

'Now seriously, I want to do something for Mum. Perhaps I could organise the flowers,' Rose says.

'Co-op do all that for you these days. Marvellous, they are,' Tom says.

'But they won't be as nice. I could get a lovely wreath done. Fresh roses, chrysanthemums, lilies. There's a stall down the Bella. I'll pay.'

'You working?' Grandpa asks. His teary eyes have dried.

'I have savings.'

'Or John could pay. Couldn't he? He's got pots of money.' Bea smiles at her good idea.

Tom turns to Vi. 'I ask yer,' he says. 'You'd better be going, Rose. Before it gets dark. Too cold to be out at night.'

'Will you be alright?' Rose asks. Her voice is frail and Bea senses the rejection. She has been dismissed.

'I'll be fine, love. You get off home.' Tom stares out the window and Auntie Vi shuffles behind Rose and Bea to show them to the door. It's Vi who tells Rose she will ring her to tell her about the funeral arrangements and Bea doesn't understand why it's not the other way round.

On the train home, Bea sits with her head bowed. She shouldn't have mentioned John. She had just blurted it out wanting to be helpful. 'I didn't mean to upset Grandpa.'

'I know you didn't, love. He's upset about Grandma. That's all.' Rose wipes her nose on a crumpled tissue retrieved from her pocket.

'He doesn't like John, does he?'

'John once promised him something and didn't deliver.'

'What did he promise him?'

'A new flat in Evangeline's block.' Rose sniffs.

Bea tries to imagine what it would have been like living nearer her grandparents. They would have seen each other more often. She would have stayed at Grandma's instead of at Evangeline's flat when Rose wanted her out of the way. Would they have allowed Rose to have a string of boyfriends and drink so much? She didn't think so.

Grandpa disintegrates. He is taken to hospital not long after Grandma's funeral. The doctor says he's got pneumonia. When they visit, he is more often asleep than awake and he has no use for sustenance. Each slow breath struggles through a clot of mucus.

'Leave me alone with Grandpa.' Rose doesn't take her eyes off the old man's face.

'Why?'

'I need to say goodbye.'

Bea leaves the door open a fraction and eavesdrops on Rose. Her mother's head is bent low and she is whispering, but in the clinical surroundings her words are clear.

'Well, Dad, this is it. So I'm gonna be straight with you. You were cruel to Kath. And me. But it was worse for Mum. I honestly thought you'd be the one to go first. You and your temper, and your fists. She could've had some peace. It was you who kept us apart. We would have got on just fine without you. She would've loved having Bea around more often. But she went and that was that.'

Bea reddened. The cruelty recounted so matter-of-factly is unexpected and harsh.

Her mother continued, 'When she died, I wanted to give you a right telling-off about how shitty you were. Not to me but to Mum. I didn't do it, did I?' Rose sighs. 'Too busy with other things, hey.'

Bea ducks away just as Rose turns her head towards the door.

'Mum didn't deserve what you handed out. She didn't. She could be a bitch herself sometimes but I reckon it was cos you made her that way. I know, cos I reckon John's done the same to me over the years. Ha! You were right about him. Fancy that.'

Rose is crying now. Bea knows these tears are not for Grandpa but for Grandma. 'I know it's too late for you to say sorry for being handy with this.' Rose covers his hand with her own – an affectionate gesture without the accompanying words – 'I can forgive you for what you did to me, Dad. But I won't ever forgive you as long as I live, for what you did to Mum.'

Her mother's chair scrapes across the linoleum floor. 'C'mon, Bea. I'm done here.'

Sixteen

Bea 1983

Rose is pregnant. There is no excuse. Not these days. Bea sits on the edge of the bath and pours bleach down the toilet, careful not to splash her school uniform. Rose has probably been in bed all day. Leaving it only to bring up her guts. Most women have morning sickness in the morning, so Bea doesn't understand why her mother has it all day and that pregnancy renders her incapable of pulling the toilet chain.

'Bea? Is that you?'

Bea stands in the doorway of Rose's bedroom. 'Are you expecting anyone else?'

'Oh, thank Christ. Get me something to eat, would you? I'm starving.'

'There's nothing to eat, Rose. You haven't been to the shops.'

'You go, there's a good girl.'

Rose is a mess. Her hair clings to her head, sweaty and lank. The room is thick with the smell of unwashed bedlinen. Bea slams the door shut, saying nothing, feeling tainted by the stale air. Downstairs she takes some pound notes out of an old biscuit tin, picks up the shopping basket from the kitchen and slams the front door shut. It's really all she has by way of protest.

They sit opposite each other at the table and Rose eats ravenously, wearing a faded yellow housecoat. 'How was school today, Bea?'

'I got top marks in my English test. Teachers are saying I should set my sights on Oxford or Cambridge.' The part about the top marks is true.

'Oh, that's amazing. You'd suit Oxford rather than Cambridge, I think.'

'Really? How's that?'

'Oxford nurtures female talent. More than Cambridge apparently. I heard it on the radio.' Rose learns many things from the radio: how to change a wheel on a car, the reasons for the Korean war, why Margaret Thatcher isn't a feminist. It doesn't matter that Rose can't drive, has no clue where Korea is or ever voted in any election but it keeps her busy while Bea is at school. An upside of her obsession with the radio means they have something to talk about while Bea is:

A: waiting for her dinner, B: cooking the dinner, C: sitting in the maudlin atmosphere after one of Rose's bad break-ups.

Later, Bea studies for her O levels. There is no desk in her bedroom, but an old dressing table shaped like a kidney bean with a curtain that hides the shelves. It's where she keeps her notebooks. She has Sellotaped her study notes to the glass, organised thus: text notes for English; theories for Social Sciences; people in power for History; land formations for Geography; Maths formulae and life processes for Human Biology.

At fourteen, the mirror is no use to her. She doesn't share an interest in hairstyles or comparing lip gloss flavours with her friends. She likens herself to *Jane Eyre*. The eyes of a governess stare back at her through the gaps in the Sellotaped pages. According to her mother, her nose is too long, her chin too short, but thank God she has been blessed with Rose's slim frame.

Bea has no interest in boyfriends, no inclination to go out and snog. The thought of a boy kissing her leaves a nasty taste in her mouth, like chewing on raw meat. The thought of sex has her terrified and her mother's choice in boyfriends is testimony to the fact that all men are bastards as the feminist lobbyists declare.

'Bea. Bea!' Rose's holler comes from the kitchen. Why she can't manage to walk upstairs, knock on the door and speak in normal tones, Bea can't say. The radio is on as usual in the lounge, but Rose is in the kitchen sitting at the table reading a postcard. 'I forgot. It's from your dad. For you.' Rose rubs the skin of her chin and neck then proffers the postcard. 'I haven't seen him for months. What does he want?'

Bea leans against the worktop. The picture shows a coastline taken from the air. Out at sea there are sailing boats. People, miniscule and unrecognisable, are holidaying on the beach and quaint white cottages are stuck like cake decorations on clifftops.

The postcard starts with *Dear Beatrice* and asks after her health. *How are you?* He tells her the weather is very nice in Weymouth although they had rain for the first two days. He says he wants to see her about something important when he gets back and that he'll call at the house on Sunday afternoon. Bea takes that to mean after he has a roast dinner with his real family. Dad also says he wishes she were with him on holiday. *Wish you were here*, he writes. Bea doubts that very much.

'Camber Sands,' Rose says. 'Nineteen-seventy-six. We never had Weymouth. Too upmarket for us.' She takes a ravaged hanky from her pocket and blows her nose.

'I'll make us some tea and I tell you what, why don't I run you a nice hot bath?' She had bought her mother a bottle of Fenjal for her birthday from the money that John sent her. Upstairs, she pours a few drops into the gushing water and waits for the pungent herby odour to hit her senses. It masks the smell of the bleach and mould. Rose has recently dyed her hair to a colour called nutmeg and the smears of red paste are still visible around the sink. Bea wipes at the stains with a stiff grey cloth but they don't shift. She gives up and decides to wait until Saturday, the cleaning day.

She turns the postcard over in her hand. Her dad has good handwriting for a man. It slopes slightly forward and is elegant. She knows he does up houses and sells them or rents them out. Rose used to point to his properties. Their house is one of his doer-uppers, as Rose calls it. Poverty-stricken immigrants evicted from the rooms to make way for John's builders, so she says. No wonder Bea feels the presence of ghosts. Bea spots Rose through the gap between the door and its frame, an unsteady apparition ducking in and out of view, so she stuffs the postcard into the waistband of her skirt.

Rose has pulled her hair into a loose bun and her cigarette is held in yellow-stained fingers. 'Lovely.' She smiles and takes a deep breath to inhale all the warm Fenjal fragrance in the room. 'What you up to tonight?' Rose unwraps the housecoat and shivers in her pale cotton nightie.

'History. The death of the Tsar and his family.'

'Oh yes, there was something about that on the radio.' Rose uses the toilet, throwing the fag end into the bowl. 'There's a theory that one of the princesses survived the assassination. Anastasia, she's called. She's living in America.'

Bea explains that the Anastasia thing is a conspiracy and according to her teacher, there is a whole industry of so-called experts who make money out of people like Rose, gullible enough to believe the moon landing and Elvis Presley's death are both fake.

'You're so matter-of-fact, Bea. It wouldn't hurt to have a little fantasy in your life. I never thought I'd have a child with so little imagination.' Rose pulls the nightdress over her head.

'For goodness' sake. You could have waited til I was gone.' Bea turns and leaves the bathroom slamming the door as Rose giggles.

On Sunday, Bea dresses in jeans and a thick blue sweatshirt even though the day is turning out to be warm and sunny. Rose is up early and already in the kitchen. She's put on a yellow dress that clings to her figure. Her pregnancy is barely visible; she could be about to have her period. She has her back to her daughter and when she turns, Bea swallows hard.

Rose's make-up is too thick and her face is a white mask. Her red lipstick has bled and her eyes are hidden amongst thick black lashes. 'Sit down, love. I'm doing a fry-up.' She turns away and concentrates on the spitting fat in the pan. 'Put the toast on and while you're at it check the date on the eggs.'

'They're out of date. But we won't die,' Bea says.

'What time's your dad coming then?' Rose asks.

'He didn't say a time, just, after lunch.'

'Well, I could make him a second lunch with us. I've done that before.' She smiles and eats heartily. It's a good day. Rose out of bed and dressed before twelve and eating breakfast means she's looking after herself. The meal will sustain her, whatever the day brings.

Rose drops her cutlery and leaps up to check the fridge. She sighs as if relieved to see the food. There is a slab of gammon in there and a cabbage and some potatoes on the veg stand by the back door. 'Look at that. Your dad's favourite. When was the last time we all ate together?'

'Christmas Eve, three years ago. He arrived half-cut at six o'clock in the evening. We'd been waiting since twelve.'

'You've a photographic memory, you have.'

The clock ticks in the living room and in the kitchen the constant background buzz of the radio continues its calm bland monotone. Rose is out the back having a cigarette. The house smells of cabbage and salty bacon and the pot lid trips and shudders as the steam escapes. Bea sits on the sofa with her feet on the coffee table feeling a familiar electric current travel through her. Recently, the sizzle and crackle of an unseen energy has followed her around this room. She is convinced it's the ghosts of the previous tenants.

Sometimes, when she's alone, it's as though the molecules of a once-living being start coagulating into a ghostly figure. It's human-shaped and always in the same corner. Before the thing reveals itself, she usually flees, slamming the door behind her. It's not happening this morning though and she is slightly disappointed. Next time she will be braver and stay to see what happens.

She reads *Jane Eyre*. Mr Rivers has told Jane that she has actually been living with her cousins and has inherited great wealth. Bea throws the book on the table breaking the current. She is irritated by this fantastical good fortune in what is otherwise a very believable tale. Keys rattle in the front door and she stands like one of Pavlov's dogs.

Rose comes rushing in, panic in her panda eyes. 'You won't tell him, will you?' she gasps.

'Tell him what?'

Grabbing Bea by the collar, she spits the words out. 'If you tell him I'm pregnant, I'll have you sectioned.'

John calls from the hall. 'Bea?'

Bea pulls herself away, angry at her mother's empty threat. 'If anyone round here needs sectioning it's you.' Without a word, she passes her father and takes the path down to the gate with long strides. He makes her wait while he exchanges words with Rose. Then he is standing beside her jingling his car keys. He has an old brown jag which is parked on another street. He asks her if she wants to go for a spin. She shakes her head making her thick brown locks fall across her face.

'Suit yourself,' he says. He looks much older than he did the last time she saw him, as if he has aged ten years in three. He has more lines around his eyes and mouth. His nose is red and pockmarked. A dry mop of thin grey hair hides a bald spot, and he has an enormous round belly under his Arsenal shirt. He leads her to Powys Square garden. 'How you getting on?'

'Got top marks in my mocks.'

'That's grand,' he says. 'I gave Tim a tenner for every O level he passed.' His son Timothy is five years older than Bea. John talks as if she is familiar with his real children who she has never met and is never likely to. They sit on a bench in the shade of a privet hedge. Restless and shifting his weight, John runs a nervous hand across his mouth. 'I won't be seeing you from now on.'

'Okay.'

'I mean. I can't see you again. Or your mother.' He stretches his legs and crosses them at the ankle. 'I have a solicitor who has some papers for you. The deeds to the house. You can have them when you're older.'

'Okay.'

'You'll get a letter on your birthday. It means you will own the house. It'll keep a roof over your head.'

'What about Rose? Why don't you give her the house?' Bea has no idea what deeds are but she knows that having a roof over their heads is good.

'You know your mother.'

'Are you going to tell her, or shall I?'

'Rose isn't interested in small details.'

'So, you're not going to tell her that you won't be seeing her again?'

'No. You could tell her I'm moving to Australia.'

'Are you?'

'I might be. You'll understand one day. The way things work out… It's not always the way you want them to.' He scuffs the gravel path with his shoes. 'And you're not to get in contact with me. Or look for me. You understand that?'

'Yeah.'

'If anyone comes calling, you say you don't know where I am.'

'Well, I won't know, will I?'

'Tell your mum not to worry.'

She does no more than shrug and he rears up as if she's told him to fuck off.

'I've got problems, Bea. Money problems, business problems. You're lucky I'm not chucking you out and selling the house on.'

'Why don't you?'

'It's to do with stuff you don't understand.' He stands and paces back and forth. His stomach hangs over his waistband and his Arsenal shirt doesn't quite cover his belly. She wonders if he's popped around before he goes off to a match. He hoists his waistband up and returns, sitting so close to her she wriggles away.

'I've got exams. I've got to apply for university. I'll need money for that.'

'I'll drop some cash off before I go.'

'How much? Will it be enough to live on? We're on social security, you know. It's not very dignified.'

'For God's sake, what did I just tell you? You'll have the house, Rose.'

'I'm not Rose. It's Beatrice. The name's Beatrice.' She can't believe how calm she is.

'Sorry…' John puts his hands to his head.

'What did you used to say? Oh yeah, I'm just like your granny.'

'Beatrice, don't…' He stands again and Bea does the same, knowing he can't bear anyone being straight with him.

'What? Don't talk about the old cow? She was a swindler and you're just a crook, aren't you? Rose says you launder money for a drugs gang. Is that right? Is that the type of dad you are, because if so, I don't want to see you ever again.'

He slaps her face. 'I'm sorry. I love you, Bea.' He sobs fat tears in front of her. 'I'm trying to turn my life around, girl. It's not that easy. I've got to leave but I'll come back one day. Just for you, darling.'

'Why on earth would I believe that?' Bea runs back to the house. He doesn't call after her when the heavy park gate bangs shut behind her. She doesn't look back. It's only when she reaches her front door that Bea knows she's made it easy for him by running away. It was probably what he wanted all along. Sly old John, his grandma's heir.

Rose has been crying and her make-up is rendered down to a pink and grey smudge. Bea tells her that John took her for a Wimpy and they talked about her exams. 'He's going to give me a tenner for every exam I pass,' she says.

'He didn't come in. I thought he was going to come in.' Rose sighs. 'I said to him, come on in then, stay for lunch. But he said he couldn't. What's he playing at?'

The hob has been turned off under the bacon joint. The gaseous smell of over-cooked cabbage seeps out of the pot. 'I don't know. That war paint is pretty scary though.'

Rose wipes her eyes, smearing even more grey across her cheeks. 'He came all this way and he didn't even stay for a cup of tea.' She lights a cigarette. 'He brought me these.' A bunch of anaemic-looking pink chrysanthemums still wrapped in their plastic packaging lie on the table, the price still attached. 'You'd think he could afford flowers from a proper florist shop.' She points the cigarette at the drooping heads. 'He always sent bouquets and they always had red lilies and roses in them. So thoughtful.'

'You shouldn't be smoking,' Bea says.

'This is the last one. They make me feel sick anyway.'

'He has to go away for a while on business.'

Rose lights up another cigarette and Bea is about to admonish her but her mother is thoroughly deflated. A sad-eyed beagle in one of those animal cruelty posters.

Bea grabs *Jane Eyre* from the coffee table and runs up to her room. She's not sure she wants to read to the end of the story and will take it back to the library. Romantic nonsense all of it. The book is ruined for her now that Jane has overcome adversity with a big wedge of dosh. Miss

Eyre is too knowing for Bea's liking and she seems to get it all so right. Bea predicts Jane will marry Rochester and live on a country estate and have a London townhouse. She'll have a happily-ever-after marriage and nice, polite, pretty children. A nice happy-ever-after life so unlike real life it makes Bea feel *sick*.

The evening Rose's labour pains intensify and she's ready to drop she arranges for Bea to stay at Evangeline's. She's not allowed to go with her mother to the hospital because it may distress her when the nun from Holy Trinity comes for the baby.

As her mother roars with each surge of pain, Bea rings for a cab then makes another phone call to Holy Trinity to inform the nuns her mother is heading for the hospital. When the cab is out of sight, she walks up to Evangeline's flat.

It's familiar to Bea as her own home. There is the aroma of furniture polish which her mum's friend uses liberally on the dark brown dining set, the mirrors and the television. There is the metallic warm water smell of ironing and the multifarious fragrances coming from the rolls of cloth: the washing line smell of cotton; musky velvets and the chemical odour of nylon.

Evangeline is teaching Bea to sew. The light pours in from the windows and floods the old dining table where they work. Bea smiles as she irons the dress she has made. She's thrilled with it, a strappy summer dress, white with a blue floral print. The tricky bit was the gathering in the skirt. Evangeline swipes the tape measure from around her neck and inspects the spacing. 'You've done it, girl, they're all even. Try it on.'

Bea spins around and the skirt billows. When she stops, she doesn't see shy Bea whose school socks are so feeble they sink into her shoes. The potent magic of youth on the verge of adulthood stares out of the mirror at her. Her hair shines, her skin is taut and smooth and her breasts are pert. The full skirt of the dress accentuates her tiny waist. She sees her mother as she appears in old photos.

'Well done, Beatrice.' Evangeline smiles and begins to pack her workboxes.

'Thanks, Evangeline. It's beautiful.'

'It's you who are the beauty. That dress is gilding the lily.'

'I think I'm too skinny.'

'Hmm, true. Boys like a bit of fat on the bones.'

'Blah. Not interested in what they like. Much rather read a book.'

'Good for you. Too many women think they can't live without a man.'

Immediately Evangeline says this, Bea frowns and an image of her mother pushing the baby out fills her head. 'Rose is hopeless. These useless idiots she brings back to the house…' She changes back into her school uniform and carefully folds the dress so that it won't crease too much in her schoolbag.

Bea likes sewing. Every little task requires her undivided attention. Each mistake, and at first there were many, involves undoing the fault and restitching to make the dress perfect. She likes detail and sewing is all about fine detail. She packs away the scissors and winds bias binding around a card before placing a cover over the sewing machine.

Evangeline lowers the ironing board so that they can watch television without it getting in the way. 'Your Ma is too good,' she says. 'She takes them in like some people take in stray dogs.'

'Maybe we'll get a puppy when she comes home. Might save a lot of bother.'

Bea sleeps in the room where Evangeline keeps her stock of fabrics and haberdashery. It was once Sylvester and Linton's bedroom. She sleeps in one of the twin beds while the other has rolls of fabric laid out along its length. It's hard to imagine two grown men sleeping in this room with its rocket pattern curtains and duvet covers. Linton is at college but she's not sure what he's studying. He has a room in a house somewhere in South London. Evangeline doesn't see him as often as Sylvester.

Sylvester is tall and handsome. He could be a basketball player. He's an electrician and has a girlfriend called Letitia. They don't live far and Evangeline is expecting an announcement. She talks to Bea and Rose about grandchildren all the time and has knitted and sewn every spare moment to make sure the baby, when it comes, has a layette. An ottoman filled with tissue-wrapped clothes, lovingly crafted for her first grandchild, stands at the foot of the bed. Bea gets that everything in this flat, including the clothes for its children, are well loved.

Rose is giving birth and her baby will be taken away from her. Bea will never see it, never ask whether it's a boy or a girl, and it will have a separate life. There will be adoption papers which Rose will hide in one of her big old chocolate boxes. Bea closes her eyes tight to avoid imagining what is written on them. She shifts and turns in the bed unable to sleep and hopes that there is a nun with Rose at the point of delivery.

When she returns from hospital, Rose is quiet, staying in bed most of the time. Her milk dries up in her breasts and she takes aspirin to dull the ache. Bea can tell she is fighting the temptation to drink. She's fretful, licks her lips and makes countless cups of tea which are left to go cold.

One afternoon, Bea comes home to find her mother drunk. Her head rests on the arm of the sofa. There is an empty bottle of cider on the floor and the bottle of white wine standing on the coffee table is almost empty.

'Sit down, Bea Bea,' she slurs.

'I've got to get the tea on.'

'I'll get the tea on. Sit down.'

'You should go to bed. You've had a skinful.'

'What do you know?' She reaches for her glass and tries unsuccessfully to fill it with wine. The liquid spills onto the tinted glass. She mumbles, 'Oh for fuck's sake, Rose. Pull yourself together.'

Bea fetches a cloth and when she returns, her mother is sobbing dry tears.

'It was a boy,' she says. 'Gerard,' the nun called him. 'Beautiful-looking thing with a good pair of lungs.' She swipes her eyes with the heel of her hand. 'And a mop of black hair.'

'Don't, Rose, you don't have to tell me.' Bea remembers the father. Andy. It was early morning when the police raided the house. They dragged him down the path in his underwear, reading him his rights like the police do on TV.

'I wanted to keep it. But we can't afford it.' Rose swipes a hand across her mouth. 'S'right it should go to a good home.'

Bea watches her mother as she lifts herself unsteadily off the sofa and bends, using her hands to guide her along the little table. She reaches the door but there is nothing to hold on to after the safety of the doorframe. Before she gets to the stairs, she stumbles and falls. Bea listens as Rose fills the air with cursing. Then the thud of her feet and the eventual slamming of her bedroom door.

Sitting alone at the kitchen table eating cheese on toast, Bea makes the nuns right. They can sniff out a bad mother a mile off. They knew Rose wasn't up to raising a child so they must have suggested adoption. She also realises what John said was wrong. Her mother is good with small details. She had managed to make the baby sound like a used car.

Seventeen

Bea 1984

Kensington Market is a bazaar straight out of *Aladdin and the Forty Thieves:* a grand old building, floor upon creaking floor of hippy bells, bondage gear, dreamcatchers and incense. A twisting, moving maze lit by intermittent, blinding lamplight, the cables swinging in the dank musty air. And clothes moths. They flutter amongst the swirling motes and strike terror into the hearts of the vendors.

The people who run the stalls are strange creatures. Rose's old friend Sharon says they are the Avant Garde, the fashion rule breakers who form into distinct tribes: Hippies, New Romantics, Post Punks and Rockerbillies. Men and women in army gear or zoot suits, studded leather or floaty vintage. The whole place smells of patchouli oil fighting with the throat-catching, chemical tang of naphthalene-infused mothballs. There are tattooists, piercers and record sellers all adding to the fraternity of street credibility that is Kennie Market. The one thing they all have in common is that none of them would be seen dead in Next or *St Michael* clothes.

Rose has brought Bea along to the market to see if Sharon will give her a job. Since the baby was born, Rose has been working there herself on the odd day when Sharon has had to go on buying trips.

Her boss stands at the top of the stairs and waves at them. 'Look at you, Bea. How long has it been?'

'Years since I brought her here last. Mad, isn't it?' Rose says, handing Sharon a peppermint tea from the cafe in the basement.

Sharon has backcombed hair and wears thick eyeliner. Her face is heavily powdered and she's wearing a lace dress that could have been a wedding dress once. It has been taken up rather amateurishly to sit just above her knees. There is a vague resemblance to Miss Haversham. 'How old are you now?' Sharon asks.

'I'll be sixteen soon.' Bea had chosen a check shirt tucked into skinny jeans. The paleness of her skin is accentuated by a red lipstick. Her dyed black hair is a nod to the Banshees' Siouxsie Sioux. This is the limit of her rebellion.

'Wouldn't it be wonderful to be sixteen again, Rose?' Sharon says.

'God, if only.'

Sharon's boutique, Baby Jane, is at the top of the first flight of stairs where there is good passing trade. Clothes hang from rails taken from the shop Sharon used to run, and her dressing room is constructed out of scaffolding poles hung with luxurious red velvet. A slightly damaged mannequin stands at the entrance and Sharon drapes it with her best pieces. She is also called Baby Jane after Sharon's favourite film and is made up to look like the Bette Davis character.

Rose is a great sales assistant. Bea watches her while she waits for Sharon who is on the phone to one of her stockists. There's a woman in the changing room. She opens the curtain.

'Wow, that looks stunning,' Rose gasps.

'Do you think?' says the woman.

'Absolutely. It's your colour and the length's perfect. It just needs something…' At this point Rose is fetching accessories: a wide-brimmed hat, a shawl, scarf and a brooch. She's piling them on the woman as if she's the mannequin.

'I'm not sure…' says the woman.

'Perhaps we ditch the hat and wrap your hair in a silk scarf.' Rose reaches up to tie the scarf. 'That blue is a perfect match for your eyes.'

The woman looks at her eyes as if for the first time.

'For when you're in an open-topped sports car,' Rose explains. Then she puts the hat back on and the woman gasps. 'Gosh! How did you know? My boyfriend's taking me to Cornwall in the car.'

Neither too pushy or too disinterested, Rose has made a connection with the customer's lifestyle aspirations and the transaction is mutually beneficial. The woman pays and leaves promising to return.

'Your mamma can sell wool to sheep,' Sharon says.

'Rose tells me you can sew. What do you think of these?' Sharon opens the lid of a cardboard box and pulls out two white dresses from amongst a cloud of tulle and satin. The skirts are covered in crosses embossed with diamante. 'Confirmation dresses from Dublin,' she says. 'Can you put corsets on these? Give them a bit of slut appeal?'

Bea eyes the stitching on the seams, gauging how easily they could be adjusted. 'Yes, I suppose so. You could just get rid of the sleeves and yoke. Make it into a vest top.' Bea demonstrates the effect by tucking away the sleeves and lowering the collar on one particularly hideous dress. They agree on both a budget and a high-end corset version, then fix a price.

The reinventions fly off the rails. Kensington High Street is full of young girls wearing Bea's corsets and plunging vest-topped creations. Sharon adds twenty pounds to the price they had agreed upon and Bea makes a mental note to ask for forty pounds above her estimate next time.

Bea is lying on the sofa. She's taken up *Jane Eyre* again after seeing the old black-and-white movie.

Rose is getting ready for a night out. Bea can tell she's got a mood on as she's stabbing the powder compact as if she hates it. 'You've earned more in one week than I have all month,' she says.

'I don't work every week and I give you most of it. Anyway, we seem to be doing alright.'

'Good budgeting. That's what it's all about.' Rose dabs each cheek with a well-loaded brush.

'Budgeting with what? The pennies we get from Sharon?'

'I'm getting extra child benefit.' Rose repacks the large cosmetics bag and zips it up. 'Right, that's me done. There's a Fray Bentos pie in the cupboard. Save me some for when I get home.'

'How much does it cost to drink at the Duke of York?'

'Not as much as you think.'

'Maybe I'll join you, I could do with a treat.'

'Don't you fucking get any ideas. Little madam.' Rose screeches. 'Keep your nose out of my business.'

'I'm just saying—'

'Just remember who you're talking to.'

'So-rry.'

'And don't use that tone of voice with me.' Rose's face is flushed. 'I'm not one of your chums. I am the head of this household.'

'What does that make me? Your servant?'

Rose pulls the cushion Bea is propped up on and throws it across the room. 'Cheeky little bitch. Learn some manners.' She totters out of the room in heels made more unsteady by the wine she's been drinking.

It's a rare and joyous time when Bea is alone in the house at night. She fills the time by doing exactly as she pleases. She eats her dinner off one of the expensive plates they use for Christmas. She fills a crystal tumbler with Coke and sets *Jane Eyre* on the table by the side of her plate. Not everything in Jane's life is as hunky-dory as she thought.

Bea is over being envious of characters in novels as it's such a corrosive sin. There is nothing to redeem envy. At least with lust, avarice and greed you have a bit of earthly pleasure. Pride means you've actually achieved something in your life, unless of course it's false pride. Sloth allows you a day in bed and wrath basically means you care enough about something to blow your top about it. Envy does nothing but chip away at your soul. Each little dent leaves a hollowed-out cup where only poisonous resentment gathers.

Tonight, with Rose gone for a few hours, she bathes, dresses for bed in an oversized T-shirt and pyjama bottoms then wanders around the house trying to recapture that old electricity. She indulges herself by imagining ghosts appearing in the alcove. But the house remains still, the ghosts having stayed beyond the dark veil tonight. She is no longer afraid of ghosts. It's the living she fears the most.

Bea glances at the kitchen clock. It's half past eleven and she is about to turn the lights off and go to bed when she hears shouting from the street. Her mother is yelling. Bea runs to the door and sees her having a set-to with a man. He's young from what she can make out, dressed in a leather jacket and jeans. His head is shaven but his face is in shadow.

'I haven't got it. You must have dropped it when you dropped your trousers. I HAVEN'T GOT YOUR WALLET!' Rose yells.

Bea puts the front door on the latch and runs down the steps.

'Rose?'

'Go in, Beatrice. Go inside now.'

The man grabs Rose by the back of the neck and looks at Bea. He isn't as young as she thought.

'Your friend's nicked my wallet.'

There is no one on the street that she can run to and she feels absolutely useless. 'Mum?'

'It's your mother, is it? Bad luck, girl.'

Rose claws at the man's wrists and this seems to work as he swipes his hand away sharpish.

'Bitch. Give me—'

'Fuck off or I'll call the police. I haven't got your fucking wallet. Leave off me.' She belts him with her handbag which he grabs and empties onto the street. Bea can't help but notice the small square packets that scatter amongst her lipstick and fags. There is no wallet.

Then lights appear. White slits from the houses opposite and the flash of blue from a squad car. The man grapples with Rose and tries to search her coat pockets. When he hears the brief note of the siren, he scarpers, leaving a trail of expletives and threats in his wake. Bea steps forward to where Rose is crouched down gathering her stuff. Five-pound notes blow away on the eddying wind. 'Go inside, Bea. This is nothing to do with you.'

'Are you alright? Who was that man?'

Rose grabs hold of the neckline on Bea's T-shirt. Her breath comes warm and sour. 'Don't say anything.'

The police officer arrives and stands over Rose as she picks up her things. He is too close and as she rises, she brushes his leg. 'Good evening, Rosemary,' he says. 'Who might this beautiful young lady be?'

'This is my daughter.' Rose frowns. She seems just as

frightened of the policeman as she was of the thug that had her by the throat. 'Say hello to Sergeant Campbell, Bea.'

Bea greets Sergeant Campbell with the respect his office is due.

'And how old are you, Beatrice?'

'She's fourteen.' Rose steps in front of her and turns to face him square on. 'She's. *Fourteen.*'

Bea is about to correct her when the sergeant fixes her with a greedy stare.

'What a luscious age that is. Something for me to look forward to then.' The tip of his tongue glistening as it crawls across his teeth induces a creeping sensation of fear around her insides. 'Well, Beatrice, I need to have a few words with your mother, so best run inside.' He turns abruptly and gestures for the driver of the squad car to leave. The blue light flashes and the car disappears.

The warmth of the house contrasts with the cold night air. Goose pimples cover her arms. She pulls the lounge curtain back an inch and sees the sergeant and Rose walking away. They head towards St Stephen's Gardens and Bea has a terrible sense that something is wrong, that the police officer is not protecting Rose as he should. She stays at the window. A car passes by, then another. An old man in a raincoat comes into view, holding the lead of a small dog. She wonders whether he will walk the dog to St Stephen's Gardens. But they stop. The wind lifts the man's coat tails as the dog shits directly opposite her window. Then, ignoring the dog crap, the man walks back the way he came.

She is distracted by the man's disregard for the neighbourhood. Then Rose emerges alone into the light. She is wiping her face on her sleeves as if she's been crying. Bea lets the curtain drop and runs to her room. She knows where the extra money is coming from and feels sick.

Eighteen

Bea 1984

Bea isn't into sales like Rose. She just waits for people to buy things and takes the cash. She took the job description in its literal form and watches the stall. Rose hasn't worked for Sharon since the night she was accused of stealing the wallet so Bea has stepped in. The cash pays for the food and the gas bill.

A shoplifter, one of many, has come in. Wearing an oversized coat too hot for the unseasonably warm September weather, she stuffs clothes in the pockets. Bea has been told to stop them when they've left the stall. 'Excuse me but are you going to pay for those?'

The girl tuts and pulls a maxi dress from one pocket and a voile blouse from the other then drops them on the floor. 'Fascist,' she hisses. Stepping over the garments, she disappears into the maze of stalls on the first floor.

Bea swipes up the clothes, shakes them out and replaces them on the rails. She considers herself lucky today. Others, the more brazen veterans, laugh and walk out. She does nothing to stop them but if a neighbouring stallholder has witnessed the scene, they give the shoplifter what for. It all adds to the edgy ambience and medieval charm of the place. One of the owners from a neighbouring stall whistles at her.

'Looking divine today, Miss Beatrice,' he calls.

'Morning, Stan. How's your wife and kids?'

'Ball and chain round my neck, love. If I weren't spoken for, you wouldn't stand a chance.'

She tells him about the shoplifter and the message travels through the market as if all were bonded by some retail telepathy.

Then Graham from the record shop upstairs flies past the stall, making Baby Jane rock on her stand. He has swept-back hair and big blue eyes. He wears American baseball shirts, drainpipe jeans and Converse boots. He's into colours and wears china blue, bright red and orange with confidence, standing out effortlessly in a place where everyone tries very hard to be seen. He's taking the stairs two at a time.

In one bold move Bea leans over the balustrade. 'Hey. You going to the caff?'

'Yeah.' He stands on the stairs directly below her and looks up.

'Can you get me a coffee? I can't leave the stall.' She pulls a coin from her jeans.

He waves a hand. 'Don't worry. Take sugar?' When he returns, he leans an elbow on one of the rails. He tells her he works in his dad's record shop but he's looking for a permanent job and he lives in Kensal Rise.

She tells him she likes his clothes.

'You don't look so bad yourself. Want to go for a drink after work?'

'Just the one,' she says. 'I have to study.'

'I've blown that out.'

'I'm going to university.'

He raises his eyebrows. 'Good. That's good, innit?' He snaps at a clothes moth as it rises from out of the rail. 'Little buggers,' he says, squashing it between his thumb and forefinger.

One drink at the pub soon leads to gigs and discos. There are long walks home or trips on night buses. The kisses on her doorstep give them matching cold sores.

Today Graham meets her at her school gates and they take a bus up the Harrow Road to his house. There's no one home. He fetches two cans of Stella from the fridge and leads her up to his room. There's a double bed and a record player. On what she reckons was once used as a study desk, are piles of vinyl records. Rather than notes taped to his mirror he has band stickers, flyers for gigs and beer bottle labels.

'What do you fancy, The Cure? The Smiths?'

'I don't know. You choose.'

'You can't always let me choose. You should pick something you like.'

'I don't know what I like. I know I don't like the Rolling Stones.'

'I reckon you're a Kate Bush girl.' The jangling intro of *Love Cats* fills the room and Graham comes to sit next to her on the bed. He nuzzles her neck.

'What are Kate Bush girls like then?'

'Clever.' He cups her breast in his hand then moves down to her stomach. The old electricity begins to surge within her. She tastes acid on the back of her tongue then draws his head up to kiss his lips. 'They read a load of Jane Austen novels and wear Laura Ashley.'

'Thanks. I wouldn't be seen dead in Laura Ashley.' She laughs nervously.

He kisses her harder and she reciprocates. 'Graham. I don't mind, you know. We can do it.' Bea unbuttons her school shirt. They lie on the bed and she loses herself in the smoothness of his skin. He kisses her body. His whole being concentrating on the spot he moves to before finding another place: a nipple, a secret fold, a mound to fix onto.

'I've never...'

'I figured.'

With Christmas approaching Rose announces she would like to meet Graham. She suggests they organise a party and invites Nigel the new neighbour from next door, Evangeline's family and of course Graham. Bea agrees, thinking that the company will be a distraction from her mother should she get out of hand.

They pin paper garlands from one corner of the lounge to the other. The mantelpiece is decorated with green fir branches that Rose had scavenged after the Bella stalls had packed up for the day. The florist on the corner of Ladbroke Grove gave her mistletoe for free, she's one of their regulars after all. They argue over the decorations for their old Christmas tree which Rose has managed to pull out of the attic. Bea wanted something minimal – thick red ribbons tied in bows — but Rose goes all out for a laden tree, throwing everything she has accumulated over the years at the stiff plastic branches.

Bea has cooked a ham and there is a jar of piccalilli and bread. Rose managed to blag a deal on some cava from the man at the corner shop and Letitia pops round with a tray of jerk chicken and a tub full of rice and peas.

On the night of the party, the first Bea has ever experienced at the house, there is unfamiliar noise and excitement. Rose puts on a record and they both have a drink to calm their nerves.

'It's just like the old days,' Rose says. 'Only better.'

'What do you mean?'

'John used to throw parties for his business associates. All boozy, creeping-hands-everywhere parties. This is for us girls. It's much nicer. More refined.'

Evangeline, Letitia and Sylvester are the first to arrive. Evangeline's granddaughter Sarah is ten months old and adorable. She is dressed in her rompers ready for sleep when it comes. Sylvester carries her in and Rose then Bea makes a fuss of her before she settles on Evangeline's lap.

'Look at you both. You look like sisters.' Evangeline must be in her sixties by now, Bea guesses. There is a voluptuous roundness to her that makes Bea want to climb into her lap. She offers Evangeline a glass of cava.

'Not for me, darling. It gimme jip. Fetch me a stout, please.'

Letitia is in the kitchen and unwrapping silver foil to reveal the mountain of jerk chicken to be reheated under the grill. The rice and peas are tipped into a pot to heat through and a bowl of coleslaw is placed on the table. Bea pours Letitia a drink and they clink glasses to a merry Christmas. 'Who's in charge of the sounds round here?' Letitia says. Her hair is curled and the dress, a silver jacquard party dress, clings to her frame. She works at arm's length from the cooker to protect it. Bea puts on a Lover's Rock compilation.

Sylvester pours stout for himself and his mother and perches on one of the old dining room chairs.

Then Bea opens the door to Nigel. He is facing the street, as if looking out for a tardy companion. Short and tubby, with snowy-white hair, he is dressed like one of her teachers. 'I'm afraid I can't stay long. I have another engagement. Here, a little contribution.' Nigel holds out a bottle of red wine which Bea takes to the kitchen and puts straight in the fridge.

As she makes her way back to the lounge, the doorbell rings again and it's Graham. When he steps over the threshold, he kisses Bea on the cheek then steps back suddenly as Rose appears in the hallway.

'Graham. Nice to meet you finally.' Rose is beaming from ear to ear. It's as though she can already see the wedding photos on the mantelpiece. She is wearing a gorgeous dress in lime-green satin that drapes seductively over her breasts and hips. Bea in her black jeans and oversized blouse feels dowdy in comparison.

They gather on the sofas in the lounge. Rose sits next to Nigel who has his arms wrapped around his knees. Bea perches on the arm of the sofa next to Graham, watching her mother like she watches the shoplifters. Nigel says he is an import and export actuary. He is very impressed with Evangeline's occupation as a tailor but thinks Bea is right to continue with her studies, even though Evangeline tells him how talented she is.

'We love to hear your piano through the walls, Nigel. Do you play or do you have a special chum you're hiding from us?' Rose asks.

'No. I wish I had an Arrau or an Ashkenazy at my fingertips but sadly, mea culpa.'

'I can't understand a word of that but I'm sure Bea does.' Rose laughs.

Sylvester calls to Letitia to come and join them and when she enters, her cheeks are flushed from the grill pan. Sarah hauls herself off her grandma's lap and clambers over to her dad. As the music plays, she delights the crowd when she dances. 'Go on, Princess,' Sylvester says as he holds her arms. She sways, blessing everyone present with joyous baby moves.

Bea relaxes, refilling drinks and replenishing the bowls of crisps and nuts. She asks Graham to change the record and he puts on some obscure jazz that John used to play. He kneels at the old radiogram and browses through the collection. Sylvester joins him.

Nigel calls Kennie Market an insurance nightmare. 'A death trap that ought to be cleared,' he says.

'But it's where the young folk hang out,' Rose argues. 'Graham works at the market full-time with his dad. Carrying on the family business.' Graham nods and Rose puts her head on one side and smiles at him. 'How very traditional.' She raises the wine glass to her lips, misses her mouth and spills wine down her front. 'Oh silly me. It's that hole in my lip.' She laughs at her joke and pokes Nigel in the ribs with her elbow. He laughs along with her.

'So, Nigel, how are you liking the area?' Letitia asks.

'I love it. It's so charming and so cheap.'

'Cheap?' Rose raises an eyebrow.

'My friends thought I was insane moving here but you get an awful lot more house for your money than in Chelsea.'

'Yes, you do,' Rose agrees, draining her glass.

'I was put off by the crime at first although it's funny as I've grown to be quite enamoured of the edgy feel you get coming home at night.'

'Wait 'til Carnival. You might think differently,' Evangeline says, sipping her stout.

'I think the Carnival is a fabulous thing. And it's not a problem for me as I have a teeny-weeny bolt hole in the Dordogne.'

'Well, Nigel, if you ever need company in your teensy-weensy bottle hole, I'm sure we can all spare a few days for a trip to France.' Rose squeals as she realises her mispronunciation. She waves an arm and invites everyone to the kitchen to where the party food has been laid out on the Formica table. With the exception of Graham, the guests rise and follow her out. Bea notices the slight wobble as Rose leaves.

'I thought you said she was ill,' Graham whispers.

'She's trying to impress you.'

Graham looks around the room. Bea has spent hours cleaning and the shadows from the garlands hide the worst of the peeling wallpaper and soot.

'Nice house.'

'It's falling apart.'

'Do I get to see your room?' Graham places a hand on Bea's thigh.

'Not tonight I reckon.' They sneak a kiss and Bea tries hard to think up an excuse for them both to leave and go back to Graham's. She leans forward to kiss him again, emboldened by the sound of chatter in the other room.

After a while she hears Rose singing *Santa Baby*. It's too raucous for this early in the evening but she ignores it as she's enjoying Graham's lips. Then a chair scrapes the linoleum and a crash rings through the house. Bea leaps out of her seat to catch Nigel scampering up the steps from the kitchen, his white hair ruffled.

Letitia is running after him with a small foil parcel in her hand. 'Nigel. Take some jerk. There's plenty.'

Nigel turns. 'Thank you, Tish. That's very kind. Delicious. Delicious.'

'Don't mind Rose. She gets a bit excited. She's harmless.' Tish smiles. 'Merry Christmas.'

He turns to Bea. 'I'm afraid I have to be off.' He ties his scarf tightly around his neck. 'It's been fun. Thank you and merry Christmas to you all.' His smile is rigid.

In the kitchen, Rose is slumped at the table, visibly drunk.

'Don't take on so, Bea. It was an accident,' Evangeline says.

'What did she do?'

Sylvester grins, 'She got a bit flirty with old Nige.'

'Went bump an' grind. Frightened the old man half to death.' Tish laughs.

Evangeline grabs a broomstick and demonstrates Rose's lascivious moves. 'Santa Baby slip a sable under the tree, for me...'

Bea can't help but laugh along with the others.

'She tried to get on his lap when he was eatin' his chicken an' he just jumped out of his chair,' Tish says.

Graham is at the door. 'But he's bent as a nine-bob note.'

Bea is shocked. 'Graham! That's a terrible thing to say.'

Graham mumbles an apology as he takes a piece of chicken. 'Oh man, that is so good.'

'Thank you.' Tish beams.

'Now, Rose, don't be sitting on young Graham's knee,' Evangeline says.

'Oh my God, Graham. What must you think of me?' Rose says. 'It's antibiotics the doctor put me on. That's all.'

'Yeah, antibiotics,' Bea says. The guests take their chicken and fresh drinks into the lounge to carry on the party. Bea closes the kitchen door against the hubbub of friendly chatter and music. There is glass on the kitchen floor. When Bea fetches the dustpan from the understairs cupboard, the light catches on a cluster of empty wine bottles and lager tins. They clatter and fall at her feet.

Her mother sits with drooping eyelids, her head supported by one arm. Bea is overwhelmed by the feeling that she is responsible for this woman. Standing over her, she sees the years ahead as a lifetime of mopping up her mess, apologising for her, lying for her and despising her for allowing herself to sink so low.

Bea takes the bottle of red Nigel had brought to the party and sneaks upstairs. She places it carefully behind a set of files on the floor of her wardrobe and goes back to the party, leaving Rose to fend for herself.

On Christmas day, Rose opens a bottle of cava for breakfast. By lunchtime she's half-cut and forgets to use the colander to drain the sprouts she's cooked. They end up floating in the grey washing-up water. The meal is ruined anyway as the chicken is dry as dust and the potatoes are raw. After the Queen's speech, Bea tells her to go to bed.

'I'll go to bed when it suits me!' Rose yells.

'Fine. I'm going over to Graham's.'

Her mother follows her up the stairs, complaining about spending Christmas day on her own.

Bea opens her wardrobe in search of the bottle of red Nigel brought to the party. She knows exactly where she put it, her wardrobe is organised so that everything in it has its own space. But the bottle has gone.

'You bloody cow. You can't stop yourself, can you?'

'You're the cow. That was my wine.'

'Don't go poking about in my room ever again.'

'There's nothing interesting in here anyway,' Rose cries. 'Boring Bea.'

'Good. Then stay out.'

Rose frowns. 'It's Christmas. What we rowing for?'

But Bea has opened the bedroom door. 'Can you leave, please? I have to pack an overnight bag.'

'Bea? 'S'Christmas—'
'Get out of my room!'
'Sod you then!'

Bea stands on the step outside, waiting for her cab. The jacket she wears barely keeps the cold out. Like Evangeline's flat, Graham's house is modern and always warm. There's a tiny box room where his dad keeps his collection of vinyl records but which could be turned into a bedroom. She wonders whether she could move in with them. Whether Graham would want that. But first she must decide whether she has the guts to move out.

Nineteen

Bea 1985

Graham has taken great steps to avoid Bea at the market. She's had long enough to realise that he's a shit but it hurts to the point of feeling sick and crying herself to sleep at night. The hurt is double a normal break-up because Christmas night at Graham's house had been one of the best nights of her life.

Then the silence from Graham and worse, his lovely dad covering for him when she phones the house: Graham's out with mates; at his nan's; up at the record stall; taking the day off. And always at the back of her mind is that somehow, it's Rose's fault.

It's a cold dull February and this Saturday, no one seems to be buying. Customers come in, take a desultory look at the labels, then walk away. Even the shoplifters have taken the day off. She decides to rehang a rail of winter coats out of boredom. Concentrating on her task, she doesn't see Graham at first. He comes closer and she freezes.

He offers her a coffee but the smell makes her feel sick and she turns her back on him wanting to bury herself in the old tweeds and furs.

'What the fuck do you want?' Her voice trembles.

'Sorry.'

'So you should be.'

'I didn't get a chance to see you 'til now.'

'Fuck off! I rang and your dad lied for you. That was shit.' Bea realises she is hugging a coat to her chest and quickly hangs it up. 'But I got the message.' As her hands are free and need something to do, she turns to face him and takes one of the coffees. 'What is it?' she asks. 'Is it my intellect? My Kate Bushyness?'

'It was something you said at the party.'

'I didn't say anything. What did I say?' She tries to think but can't get beyond the fact that it had been fun. She had danced, sang along to Chas and Dave songs as best she could and laughed when they got ribbed for kissing under the mistletoe.

'You kept saying that you loved my family. You loved my aunts, my grandad, even my dad.'

'What does that matter? I was a bit drunk. It doesn't mean I actually do love your grandad.'

'I think you want something more serious. Like… long term.'

'And you don't?'

'You're studying. You'll be going to university. I don't figure in your plans.'

She tries to convince him she will come home, that it's not forever. But he strikes the killer blow. 'You'll meet other blokes. The sort who can talk about Jane Austen all day long.'

A drumbeat starts up from somewhere in the dark interior of the market but she doesn't know the song. She listens to it rather than to Graham who is telling her they can still be mates. She smiles and nods as she listens to the music; numbed and confused.

When she gets home that night there is a temptation to climb into bed and stay there. But she ignores it and concentrates on biology, the capillary action of the lungs. Every time her thoughts return to Graham's words, she begins the paragraph again, makes the same notes and draws the diagrams so that her notebook is filled with pulmonary arteries, ventricles and arrows. It doesn't make sense that her own difficulty breathing is not explained in her textbook.

But Graham is right. University must be life-changing for her and if that includes leaving Graham behind, well that's collateral damage. Except it hurts so badly she throws up her dinner. Sunday is the same. She wrenches the bed covers off, drinks tea and eats a handful of biscuits, longing to get back under the covers. But she works instead, wearing her nightdress and slippers, aware that there is a faint smell of unwashed skin about her.

It's late in the afternoon and Bea is tackling *Bleak House*. The bedroom door is open, and she can see Rose's reflection as she moves from the door to the top of the stairs. Rose is agitated, biting the skin around her thumbnail and picking at the landing's peeling wallpaper. Finally she stands framed by the doorway and yells. 'Can't you get your head out of that book? You got nothing to say that doesn't come from a book? What kind of an education is that?'

There is whining self-pity at teatime when Bea makes herself and Rose a sandwich. 'I gave up everything for you. A good man, a modelling career. I never go dancing no more.'

Bea escapes to her room. It is late and she has homework to complete for the next day. Rose slips into the room and sidles up to the dressing table. 'Bea? I'm sorry 'bout what I said. I didn't mean it.'

'It's okay.'

'Get me some wine and ciggies, please.' Rose drops a few coins on the dressing table. 'Be a good little Bea. Please.'

'I can't. I'm in the middle of something.'

Rose simpers. 'Clever old stick, with your studies. Go on, please, pet, just pop to the offie—'

'I've got this text to read. I can't understand it.'

'You're always busy. You've got no time for your ma.'

'Why can't you go? You haven't been out all day.'

Usually Bea snatches up the money, slams doors loudly then runs the errand. But not tonight. Tonight, the words jump about on the page. She has read and reread the chapters but the salient points evade her. And now it's ten o'clock and they are both in their nightgowns, both smelling ripe and her mother is demanding she fetch fags and booze.

'Go on, Bea. I'm not well.' Rose places a grubby palm on Bea's jotter.

'You're never well,' Bea mutters. It comes out curt and sharp and is compounded by a smack she gives her mother's hand to keep it off her work.

Rose pulls her hand away as if she's injured. 'Bloody little cow. I ought to give you a slap for that.' She picks up the money, coin by coin, accusing Bea of being an ungrateful madam. Grabbing the copy of *Bleak House*, she runs to her bedroom.

'Give that back. I need it.' Bea stands outside the locked bedroom door.

'Go away, ungrateful bitch.'

'I'll go to the shop for you, but please give me back the book.'

'Leave me alone. You make me sick. You've never appreciated anything I've done for you.'

Bea snaps and in a fit of fury, at her mother, at Graham and at her inability to concentrate, she hits the door with both palms and screams. 'It's not fair, I have exams. You selfish cow.'

'You've ruined my life.' Rose screeches. 'Why don't you just fuck off and die.'

Something thumps against the door and knowing that *Bleak House* is lying inches away and unobtainable, Bea sinks to the floor defeated. She laughs. It's not the first time her mother has asked her to leave the house and top herself.

In the past, Rose would utter the words then immediately run to her, lift her up and tell her she was sorry. Once under the covers and wrapped in her mother's arms, Rose would ask Bea whether she was a bad mother.

And Bea had always reassured her she was the best mother in the whole world.

There is a silence in which she is able to think clearly. Between them, Graham and her mother have destroyed her. Graham has revealed how feeble and needy she has become. Bea does love his family. The attention she got at Christmas had surpassed anything she had experienced with her own clan. She didn't love Graham but she liked the attention of that big loving family of his.

Something inside her shifts and hardens, as if a small marble egg has found a bed of dry straw in her chest. She whispers an answer to that question. 'Are you a bad mother? Yes. You are at the moment, Rose. You're a fucking nightmare.'

If it hadn't been so late, she would have taken herself off to Evangeline's place to get her homework done and to experience normality for a few hours. Instead, she returns to her desk and packs her schoolbag, smiling to herself as she practises her excuse. 'Sorry, Miss Evans, my boyfriend dumped me.' Her teachers would berate her for wasting her amazing academic skills on a boy. She tries again. 'Sorry, Miss Cartwright, I couldn't do my homework because my mother stole my book, No – 'Ate my book.' Like the dog in the joke.

In the kitchen next morning, there is evidence of a late-night visit to the off-licence. An ashtray full of dog-ends, an empty packet of fags and a glass covered in smudged fingerprints and lip scurf litter the table. She finds *Bleak House* by the telephone. She decides she needs a break from Rose and phones Evangeline to ask her if she can stay the night. Evangeline is delighted and says she should come straight from school.

After she has eaten the mountainous portion of sausages and eggs Evangeline has cooked and whizzed through her homework without a bother, Bea works on some alterations for Sharon. Then once these are packed away in black sacks, Evangeline teaches her something new.

Tonight, it's crochet. She wonders why this craft that she associates with old ladies should figure in her sewing tuition.

'You need all the crafts if you want to be a professional tailor,' Evangeline says after Bea has said that crochet is old-fashioned.

'I don't know whether I want to do this professionally. I want to study law or get a teaching job.'

There is an awkward silence. 'It's good to aim high, Beatrice. Always strive to better yourself,' Evangeline says.

Bea is mortified. She's insulted Evangeline in such a clumsy, stupid way. Bea's equally stupid fingers snag the wool. It twists into an ugly knot and rolls across the carpet. She raises her palm to her forehead and says sorry. Tears fall and she doesn't wipe them or try to sniff them back. 'I didn't mean…' Her voice is a thin continuous mewl as she drops to the floor to retrieve the ball of wool.

Evangeline kneels beside her and holds her tightly. She sinks into the older woman's chest. Eventually Evangeline coaxes her to stand. 'Come on, sweetheart, you need to help me up and you need your sleep.'

'I …I can finish the crochet.'

'No. You're working too hard. Sylvester was just the same when he was at college. you need to go a' bed.'

Bea sleeps the deep, dreamless sleep of an exhausted mind and in the morning she wakes to the comforting smell of toast drifting into the bedroom.

They sit together in the bright kitchen. There is a sewing pattern from another era sitting next to her plate. The small tears on the packet tell Bea it's been well used. She studies the illustration on the front. A girl who looks very much like Twiggy is wearing a crocheted suit. The jacket skims the midriff and the skirt skims the knee. It's a pattern from the nineteen-sixties.

'I made dozens of those. Cost me a few shillings to make and the clients loved them.'

'I don't really know what I want to do. But I do want to learn whatever you can teach me.'

'Things will get better for you very soon.'

'How?'

'You'll be leaving home for university. You won't be responsible for Rose.'

'I should go to university in London.'

'Your ma needs to get a lodger.'

'She won't be able to cope with that.'

'I've known your mother for a long time. She needs to be busy, something to focus her mind. That's what she needs. Now eat your breakfast before it gets cold.'

'There are rooms on the top floor that are never used.'

'There you are. Get a lodger, Bea. A nice young lady. Ask at the church if anyone wants some rooms.'

Bea can see the possibilities. There is plenty of space. The two of them have been haunting it for years. Bea wonders how they manage to get in each other's way. She hugs Evangeline and runs home. She can't believe she didn't think of this sooner. A proper income from renting out the top-floor rooms. She decides to call in sick and stay home from school. She knows her mother may take some persuading.

'Rose?' she calls but doesn't expect a reply. Breathless, she mounts the stairs.

The smell hits her. A mixture of alcohol and excrement. She retches, and her mouth fills with her breakfast toast. The bedroom door is ajar, and she immediately enters and pulls back the curtains. Her foot kicks an empty vodka bottle and it spins to a halt.

She turns the handle of the bathroom door but it's locked. The key is on the inside. Fear rises. There is no sound from within, no splashing of water over skin, no trickle of water from the wringing out of a facecloth. She knocks loudly, pulls at the door handle, kicks the door and kicks it again. Panic takes hold of her. 'Mum! Mum!' She moves backwards and kicks so hard the door flies open then bangs shut again.

Her mother is lying under the water. One arm, white and naked, sticks up in the air at a jaunty angle, like the mast of a cartoon ship. Bea grabs her by the shoulders, hauling her up.

Rose opens her eyes and the violent rasping of someone trying to breathe fills the bathroom. Bea jumps into the water and pushes her roughly so that she hangs over the side of the bath. She keeps on pushing until Rose, bucking like a line-caught mermaid topples out and onto the floor headfirst.

Bea slaps her back hard, runs to fetch a blanket from the linen cupboard and covers her up. The coughing subsides. 'Can you get up?'

Rose nods but they both know she can't. Her eyelids flutter as she lies on her side facing the gap at the bottom of the door. 'I didn't mean to…'

'I know. We do a lot of things we don't mean. Don't we?'

Bea calls Evangeline. It's an unlikely friendship, Bea thinks: an elderly Black woman, a widow according to Rose, a good Catholic all the live-long day and her mother a mess of a White woman who doesn't know the meaning of the word restraint. There must be something good in Rose that Evangeline recognises. Or are they a charitable case? The pair of them a cause worthy of the good woman's pity.

Bea listens in at the bedroom door as Evangeline tries to convince Rose to see a doctor. When she emerges from the darkened room, she tells Bea to phone an ambulance straight away if her mother does any such thing again. Before she leaves, Evangeline hugs Bea. 'Good luck for tomorrow, sweetheart.'

'What? What for?'

'It's your first English A level exam, remember?'

The rooms on the top floor are slowly taking the form of a cosy bedsit. Friends from Kennie Market help with moving the furniture. John's bar and neon sign are sold and Rose buys a bed. There's an electric hob, a Parker Knoll two-seater, a small kitchen table with a green Formica top and a couple of dining chairs from their own dining set. Sylvester tests the fuse board and all the electric sockets work.

It's as if Rose has stepped out into the sun for the first time in months. She drinks copious amounts of tea and asks Bea why they hadn't thought of this before. This question is repeated two or three times a day. Rose bathes, cooks and gets up early in the mornings. Best of all as far as Bea is concerned, she hasn't touched a drop of alcohol since the day of the bath incident. By the time it's finished, the top floor is bright and clean, sweet-smelling and comfortable. Good enough for a visiting Catholic virgin, Rose says.

Twenty

Bea 1986

Trevor is big, not just tall but broad with dark mid-length hair and a bushy moustache. Although the general impression is that he is handsome, his eyes are deep set, which adds a sense of mystery to him. Rose is wary at first, but when she sees the wad of cash he gives her for the deposit on the rooms, she soon comes round.

Bea had asked at the church about any nice young ladies they might know of who wanted to rent the rooms. She had also placed an ad in the corner shop window and asked the librarian but there was no interest from either quarter. It was just a happy coincidence that Rose was back working for Sharon on the day Trevor made a delivery to the market.

He works as a driver for a man who sells ex-army kit. Bomber jackets and khaki trousers, that sort of thing. Although their new lodger is built like a brick shithouse and looks as though he could give you a good thumping, he's a gentle soul and a confirmed vegetarian. He's into yoga and weed and the house is quiet out of respect for his chakras.

She can smell his fragrant herb each night when he's smoking in his rooms. Bea doesn't bother with it herself — it might affect her studies – but Trevor shares a spliff with Rose on occasion and it seems a preferable poison to alcohol. She's taken to wearing kaftans and flip-flops and is growing her hair long. It's beautiful. The colour is henna red and it's wavy with perfect curls that bob up and down when she's animated. Bea wakes her in the morning with a cup of tea and returns later to brush out her hair. The room is dark, and the languid small talk they share soon comes around to Trevor.

'Do you like him?' Rose asks.

'Yes. I like that he doesn't drink too much and he's quiet.'

'How old do you think he is?'

'How would I know?'

'Mid-twenties, I think. Hard to tell with hairy men.'

Bea laughs at this and Rose gives her the look that says don't be so clever.

'He's very spiritual for a northerner.' Rose yawns.

'What's being northern got to do with it?'

'Well, you think of the men down the mines, don't you? The strikers and the police lines. You don't associate yoga with miners.'

'Has he told you he was a miner?'

'No, but he's from Manchester way.'

'Why don't you ask him later?' Bea untangles a massive knot of hair.

'Ow. You're pulling too hard.' She grabs the brush.

'I don't get the veggie-but-wearing-leather thing though,' Bea says.

'Because the leather is a by-product of the meat industry, it's only fair to wear it. That way the whole animal gets used.' Rose attacks the knots with the brush.

'Okay, so what's with the not-eating-meat thing? What did he say about that?'

'Meat stays in the human gut for months after you've eaten it. Yuk. Can you imagine?'

'Hmm. Not sure he's as principled as we might think. Seems he's picking and choosing his philosophies.'

''Ark at you. Don't go questioning him about his philosophies or he'll philosophy off. Besides, I love that leather flying jacket he wears. Looks fabulous on him.'

Bea stares at her mother. In the dim light she looks young again. The lines from years of serious drinking are hidden and there is a lightness about her. She skips down the stairs instead of plods. She laughs. Not the usual sardonic laugh employed to mock, but a genuine chuckle.

It's not long before Rose has acquired a yoga mat. She joins Trevor in his rooms in the morning while Bea is alone in the kitchen. She has bought a Ravi Shankar CD and Bea leaves the house with the sound of the sitar and the smell of incense drifting behind her.

The whole house relaxes as if it's a ship that has just berthed in some peaceful harbour. Evangeline says God sent him in time for Bea's final A level exams. That she approves of him is further reassurance for Bea.

Despite the chaos of the last two years, Bea wins a scholarship at University College Sussex. The relief is immense in so many ways. Rose is in a good place and Evangeline was right. Bea will leave home free of responsibility for anyone else but herself. With exams over, she can relax at least for the summer. Trevor and Rose have been tackling the garden all spring and now she can join them.

One Sunday, as Trevor's veggie nut roast browns in the oven, Rose and Bea clear weeds. Trevor thins out the tangle of brambles and bushes, dressed in his steel toe-capped Doc Martens and khaki combat trousers. He's bare-chested and the sun has drawn straight lines that separate his tanned arms from his white shoulders.

'You'll get sunburn, Trevor.' Rose leans on her spade, sweating in the heat. Her mother is wearing a pink vest top and she's braless. The milky flesh of her breasts is exposed. Bea hisses at her to go and cover up.

Rose looks down at her boobs and snorts. 'He's not interested in an old cow like me.'

'I know. It's me who doesn't want to see your saggy tits.'

'Cheeky cow.' Rose glances at Trevor. He is oblivious to them when she pulls up her vest top and jiggles her boobs.

'Oh for... Grow up.'

They laugh and Trevor turns. 'What's funny?'

After lunch, they sit in stripy deckchairs they found leaning on a garden wall in Elgin Crescent. Trevor and Bea sip on beers and Rose has a cup of instant coffee.

Trevor pulls out his stash and starts to roll a joint.

'Some of them cars on this street…Each of them cars cost the same as a whole terrace of houses in Bradford.'

'Are you a communist, Trev?' Rose asks. 'You sound like you don't approve of monied people. I was listening to one of my programmes the other day and they said the communists have all given up on Russia.'

'Socialist. I'm a socialist in my blood and bones. Communism is too radical for me. Too…' He searches for the right word.

The birds sing and a gentle breeze lifts the cotton dress Bea is wearing and cools her skin. She shuts her eyes and waits for the word that will sum up exactly and pointedly their lodger's political stance on communism.

'…Angry.'

Bea smiles as Rose declares, 'That's hardly a political opinion, Trev.'

'No but it's my opinion and that's that.'

Bea catches the scent of an old honeysuckle shrub Trevor has disentangled from the brambles and the deeper, richer smell of newly turned soil. The row of deckchairs, her drying, salty skin and Rose and Trevor's idle chatter make her smile.

Later, they plant a rose that's been soaking in a bucket, then surround it with delphiniums for cutting. Bea sows a packet of sunflower seeds. Trevor wanted a raised bed for growing vegetables but Rose argued against it. 'Veg is cheap, Trevor. Good quality flowers are expensive. It will save me money.'

The trips to the Bella to buy the food shopping have become scavenging trips for furniture. They spot iron tables and chairs and garden pots with PLEASE TAKE ME signs attached. Trevor finds a small Buddha statue. He's quietly chuffed to bits and the statue takes pride of place on the third floor. Something about its closed eyes and enigmatic smile tells Bea it's a force for good.

It's not long before Rose and Trevor start a relationship. The top floor is silent once more save for the om shanti's during their yoga sessions. Bea and Trevor make awkward sidesteps to avoid each other on the landing outside the bathroom. Trevor is now committed to the house. He has cleared the wild buddleia and overgrown laurel bushes from the back windows, and light has entered the downstairs rooms. The once shiny wallpaper is dull. The paintwork is yellowed by years of heavy smoking.

Rose sugar soaps everything down and Trevor buys some knocked-off Laura Ashley paint from a man in the Alex. Altogether, there are six tins of various pastel colours and some white gloss for the woodwork. Mixing the paint results in a pretty shade of duck egg blue.

When the room is finished, it's as if the wind that was denied access to the house by the dense foliage outside has swirled around and blown all the cobwebs and dust away. One night in front of the television, with the smell of fresh paint still hanging in the air, Trevor offers to teach Bea to drive his van.

'Shouldn't she learn in a little car first?' Rose's legs are draped over his knees like a thin white blanket.

'It's only a minivan, not a transit. She'll be fine. Now go and make us some tea.'

Rose climbs off his lap and does as she's told without even thinking.

'Thanks, Trevor. Driving lessons cost an absolute fortune,' Bea says.

'I'd say you'll need to sign up for a few like, but only to get you through the test.' He shifts in amongst the cushions and stretches his legs and arms like an enormous cat. 'Happen you'll be able to help wi' me rounds,' he says, a yawn finishing the sentence.

There's always a catch, isn't there? No such thing as a free lunch. Still, his offer is generous, although slightly dodgy as it's a work van. This bloke with no connection to them whatsoever, no paternal obligations, no marital ties of any kind, is turning out to be their resident male hunter- gatherer. More importantly, he is good for Rose.

Trevor takes Bea out in the van every Saturday morning before going to work. Sometimes she drives him to the market and helps him unload the gear for his boss.

On the day of her test, they all meditate in front of the Buddha. Trevor has lit candles and she is filled with both calm and confidence as Rose and Trev join in every out breath and every in breath she takes. She passes first time so there is a rare celebration of an Indian takeaway. Trevor tells them about India.

'In Calcutta, they don't eat with a knife and fork.'

'They use a spoon then,' Rose says. 'Nothing wrong with that.'

'No. They use their fingers to scoop up dhal and rice.'

'That's disgusting. Where's their hands been? Don't you start getting ideas you can do that in my house.'

He just shakes his head. 'They have one hand for eating and one hand for cleaning their backsides.'

'Oh God, Trev, you're putting me off.' Rose opens her mouth as if she's gagging.

'You've been to Calcutta, I take it?' Bea asks.

'Nineteen seventy-nine. I was in the merchant navy. Nowt else to do except go down pit. So I went off to sea.'

Bea and Rose exchange a smile.

'Mind-blowing poverty. You've never seen anything like it in your life. Beggars so deformed you couldn't work out how they came out of the womb. Wild dogs roaming around biting the arse off of anything that moves. And cows. Skinny cows driven down the middle of the streets in between cars and bikes. You wouldn't believe the stink of the place.' There is a pause while he drops his spoon into his bowl of lentils. 'Unbelievable,' he says. 'I loved it.' Trevor stops eating and he is looking inwards at his memories.

They soften his features and Bea stares at him. If she looks long enough, maybe the images he is seeing will appear in the room. 'I want to go to India one day,' she says.

'No, Bea, you'd be sick all the live-long day, with your stomach,' Rose says.

The preparations for Bea's departure to Sussex make Rose fret. Trevor has agreed to drive her down to halls of residence which she's delighted about. But there is friction in the house.

Rose has started to take a glass of wine with her lunch. A trip to the pub after a shift at the market becomes a regular event. Then a stop at the off-licence on the way home and Bea hears the familiar rustle of carrier bags and the clinking of glass against tin. When he comes home from work, Rose bates Trevor. A bath towel left on the bedroom floor starts a war and God forbid if he forgets to pick up a bottle of vodka at the offie. That is nuclear fission.

It's Rose's raised voice that Nigel complains about because Trevor is quiet. He is all whisper and hiss. His tranquillity, which once seemed to both pacify her and lift her spirits, now winds her up. Bea is anxious to leave the house as she knows that what they had during the summer has all but evaporated like a rain puddle in the heat.

Trevor helps Bea load the van on the morning she leaves for Sussex. Rose says her goodbyes befuddled by a raging hangover. She grips the collar of Bea's leather jacket all the while pleading for Bea to come home at weekends. But both of them know she could never afford to do so. Eventually, Rose lets her go.

Trevor takes the passenger seat. Bea is used to the way the van pulls a little to the right. She is a confident driver, and they talk about getting her a car while she's down in Sussex. Trevor says he might know someone. Before they hit the M23, he takes the wheel. He drives fast and the little van rattles alarmingly.

'I'll miss you, Little Bea.'

'I won't be gone forever.'

'Ah, but you might get to like Brighton when you're down there. 'S a nice little place.'

'You didn't say you'd been to Brighton.'

'I'm like Johnny Cash,' he says. 'I've been everywhere, man.' Trevor fetches a spliff out of the top pocket of his jacket. He asks Bea to light it up for him while he tells her about Brighton. She selects a cassette from the glove compartment – a compilation of reggae tunes someone has put together for him – and inserts it into the tape deck. The van is soon filled with the sweet, heady smell of weed and after a while she can almost feel the buzz coming off him. She reaches over and takes the spliff from between his fingers and steals a draw.

Twenty-One

Evie 2019

Bea fetches two glasses. Evie is only allowed wine once a week and thinks this Saturday night is as auspicious as it can get. She's just learned who her father is. What did she know? Trevor lived on the top floor as a lodger until he moved in with Ma. He was vegetarian and practised yoga. There are no photos of him, Bea says. Evie finds this incredible, but she holds back from firing questions at her sister. It's as if Bea is controlling a steady drip feed of her past and she doesn't want to stop the flow.

The pizza is delivered, and they eat. Evie hadn't realised how hungry she was. The wine tastes like Italy in a bottle and probably costs as much as an air ticket to Milan. She takes the pizza box through to the kitchen and eats the leftover vegetables and bits of crust. She snaffles a little cake.

Bea is packing away Trevor's things. She folds the jeans and the T-shirt and leaves them on a chair.

'I thought you might want them. You know, they might have some DNA on them.'

'I'm not planning a criminal investigation. I just need his surname.'

'I don't know it.'

'You must know. He lived here. He taught you to drive.'

'He had lots of surnames. All on envelopes or packages. I couldn't tell you which one was the real one.'

'What about his birth date?' Evie asks. 'Did you ever celebrate his birthday? Or did he tell you it?'

Bea shrugs, 'I was at uni, remember.' She takes the empty wine glasses out of the lounge then calls from the kitchen, 'I'll get you a hot water bottle. You must be exhausted.'

Evie surveys the boxes, the suitcases and the pile of disinterred belongings. Surely there is something here that reveals Trevor's real identity. Perhaps these are the palatable truths, the rest being the Unpleasantries. He was a drifter, working for cash in hand as a driver. Although Bea said he was a good sort, Evie can't help thinking there's a fair chance he has a criminal record by now, if he's still alive.

Bea returns with the hot water bottle and Evie clamps it to her chest. The heating had gone off an hour ago and the old house has returned to its natural state of chilly. 'You should do something about those windows, Bea. They need double glazing.'

'Go to bed. You'll soon warm up.'

'What about you?'

'I'll tidy up down here first.'

'You won't throw anything away? I think there might be some more info about Trevor.'

'Perhaps. If it's here, we'll find it.'

The bulb has gone in the bedside lamp and the harsh ceiling light is blinding. Evie crosses her old bedroom in the dark. The furniture appears as her eyes adjust and she follows a familiar path to bed. Bea has left a nightdress for her. As she throws it over her head, her phone lights up and it's Max texting goodnight. She reciprocates.

When she closes her eyes, the boxes and flimsy cardboard files are projected in nebulous images on her eyelids. She can't help thinking about what Trevor is doing now. First, she imagines him with a couple of kids, living up north somewhere. He's badly dressed in tracksuit and trainers, middle-aged and bald. His kids are pale interpretations of him. There isn't enough money in the household and his wife scolds him about this. He just goes to the pub and drinks his universal credit while his kids set fire to cars. She apologises to Trevor and his imaginary family, raising her hands in prayer. He is, after all, her father.

She shifts in the bed to get comfortable. Warmed by her own breathing and the extra blankets Bea has slung on top of the duvet, she pushes the negative images out. Now he's a yoga teacher in Thailand or better still, in a community centre in his home town, giving free yoga lessons to the sort of children she just accused him of rearing. He is a local hero, changing lives for the better.

In the morning, she rises and despite the extra weight she's carrying, she suddenly feels small and light, like one of the hippos performing ballet in that ancient Disney cartoon. Her room is in darkness but the outlines of the furniture are familiar. The mix of IKEA flatpack drawers and shelves and the robust walnut wardrobe drag her back to the days when her surroundings didn't matter. What did she care if the furniture was mismatched back then? Her interests and the interests of her friends extended to clothes, toys and her CD collection. Then make-up and boys replaced the toys. She dresses as the central heating fires up.

Evie tiptoes downstairs with the intention of searching the boxes without Bea. She imagines there's a photograph of Trevor hidden somewhere, or maybe a parking ticket with his full name on. What she does find is nothing to do with Trevor but with Ma and Bea.

There are paper wallets from the chemist filled with photographs of Bea as a baby. The negatives fall out of slits in the folds and land in Evie's lap. She holds some of them up to the light and sees the shadowy images. There are padded albums too, the tacky plastic that holds each photograph yellowing with age. Grandma and Grandpa stand in a sunny garden with Bea as a toddler. They are all smiling at the camera. As she hears the gush of water from the bathroom upstairs, an irrational feeling of being the ugly daughter, the one least loved, bubbles up and she clutches at her bump. Where are the copious photo albums of her as a baby?

Bea stands behind Evie peering over her shoulder. 'Not another baby pic. Coffee?'

'Decaf?'

'Hah, no chance.'

Bea looks gorgeous. Her hair is pulled up in a perfectly smooth chignon and she is wearing a product that makes her cheekbones shine. Evie experiences a great sense of relief at her sister's healthy appearance, pushing the bubble of jealousy out of her head.

Max arrives. He is dishevelled and unshaven. He brings treats and so is forgiven for turning up looking like he's spent all night watching Netflix. There are Danish pastries and proper coffee. Evie has found it necessary to turn her knickers inside out as Max has forgotten to bring her any. He has brought some leggings and one of her favourite baggy sweatshirts.

'I thought I told you to bring something smart,' Evie moaned when he handed her the bag of clothes. 'We're not going to the garden centre.'

'Sorry. I was up until three.'

'Whatever for?' Bea asks.

'Papers for the case. There's a lot to get through.' Max sits heavily on the sofa.

'You're going to have to take care of yourself, Max. Evie will need you competent when the baby comes along.'

'Mum's coming down to stay for the first couple of weeks.' He yawns and rubs his stubbly chin.

'You never mentioned that.' Bea's tone is curt.

'Well Max is really busy and you're working, and Judith is a retired G.P, so it made sense…' Evie reddens.

'Yes of course it does.' Bea stands and brushes imaginary pastry crumbs from her clothes. There is a slight shake to her hand, an involuntary tremor. 'I wouldn't be much use anyway.'

'No, Bea. Don't talk like that.' Evie struggles to sit upright. 'Of course we want your help.'

Bea's face takes on a peevishness that reminds Evie of Ma. 'You're going to be an amazing auntie.' Evie looks at Max.

He is wide awake now, realising what he's done. 'We want you to be indulgent, naughty Auntie Bea to Mum's stern Grandmother.'

'Yes, that's it. We talked about it. Didn't we, Max? You're glamorous, jet-setting Auntie Bea. Judith is…' Evie can't think of how to both demote Judith and at the same time make her out to be a saint. 'Medically trained,' she says.

Bea relaxes and sits down again. 'I've made some baby clothes. I do have my uses.' She fiddles with a large ring on her left hand, twisting it and drawing her thumb over the flat cream stone at its centre. The action seems to soothe her.

'What's all this?' Max stares at the boxes and suitcases.

'I've put together a family archive,' Bea declares. 'I know how important it is to know your roots. I'm revealing our roots to Evie.'

Evie tells Max about Trevor: the naval connection, his driving job and the false names.

'Classic. The lodger's daughter. He sounds like a rogue. Love it. Your ma could have kept benefit statements or parking fines.'

'Possibly. Ma was a hoarder,' Bea sighs.

Evie sends Max upstairs to get some rest. With him gone, she settles once more into the treasure hunt. As she sorts through a pile of official-looking documents, she comes across her garden diaries. Evie flicks through the notebooks, four in total: *Summer, Autumn, Winter and Spring* By Evie Fuller, written in a neat schoolgirl script. Dried flowers: rosebuds, lavender, dianthus and more are held static under sticky-back plastic.

It was impossible to dry the sunflowers towering above the back wall so Evie had drawn them. Bea had ordered a *Reader's Digest* book on gardening. When Ma was alive, they hadn't bought a single seed packet or bulb without consulting it.

The garden diaries bring back good memories and Bea is as delighted as Evie. She is keen to see *Winter* in which Evie had drawn the funeral wreath for Ma's burial. It had included some leaves of the honesty plant, blue hydrangea and cerise stonecrop. They had made the wreath together.

'It was your dad, you know.'

'My dad what?'

'Trevor cleared the garden.'

'You used to send me out in all weathers to draw these plants.'

'Ma loved flowers. She used to say they were more reliable than men and they smelled better too.'

'Did you really like him?'

'Trevor? Yes. He was good for us. Good for Ma. But she had to go and spoil it, as usual.'

'How? What did she do?'

'She accused him of having an affair.'

'And was he?'

'I don't know. He could have been, but she was

drinking heavily. Here look, you should see this while Max is upstairs.'

'What do you mean?'

'You might need time to let it sink in before sharing it with him.' Bea flips through a bunch of papers until she pulls out a large envelope. 'I'd gone down to Sussex by this time.'

At first, Evie thought Max was right. She would learn Trevor's details in an official document and the mystery would be solved. But that didn't make sense as Bea would know his surname. Confused but hungry for information about her father, she takes out the papers within. There, in black and white, dated and rubber stamped, was a summons served by the Metropolitan Police.

Twenty-Two

Rose 1987

Rose shivers as she stands looking out of the kitchen window. January has brought sharp winds. She has left the deckchairs out for too long in the rain and they're streaked with black mould and bird shit. The canvasses snap violently in the wind. Back and forth they fly as if they are trying to escape from her garden.

There are fag ends in the plant pots by the kitchen door and the raised beds have been demoted to cat litter trays. Each bed holds a few brown stems and seed heads too sodden from rain to be of any use as a dried arrangement.

Rose fetches a bottle of wine from the fridge and pours it into a pint glass. It's been a long morning. She was woken at three by the front door closing. Trevor left early for one of his trips and she couldn't get back to sleep. False dawn they call it. Something about blood sugar levels dropping. Or rising. She could never remember which. So she had got up and had a drink. Well, what else could she do?

The phone rings and it makes her jump, slopping wine on her slippers. It's Bea. She knows it's her daughter because every Wednesday, Bea's tuition ends just before twelve.

After the greetings Bea asks about Kensington Market. 'Are you getting any work?'

'No, love, Sharon's struggling.'

'Shame,' Bea says. And something else that Rose didn't catch.

'These new customers, they're not fussed about the vintage stuff.'

'How's Trevor?' Bea asks.

'Alright. He's got plenty of work. I don't see much of him. He's fetching God Save the Queen T-shirts from a bloke in Southampton today.' Rose is sure that's what he said last night or it could have been the night before. She takes a glug of wine. 'They buy any old tat now. Giant safety pins and Johnny Lydon masks. What the fuck for? Ten years out of date.'

Bea says something else but Rose doesn't understand. And anyway she has been waiting to tell Bea the news. 'He's not sleeping with me, darlin'. I don't know what's going on.'

'Is it so he doesn't disturb you when he gets in late?'

'Yeah maybe. Or he's seeing someone else. Some old slapper up north. I miss him, Bea. It's so lonely here. I miss you, Bea. When are you coming home, love?'

Bea has to go. There's a hurried goodbye, the pips interrupt her and the phone goes dead. She tuts when she realises she hadn't asked Bea about her studies.

It's like that these days. People will tell her things and whatever they say is gone within seconds. She's like a goldfish swimming in soapy water. The old house has lost a daughter: the busy sewing machine has been silenced; books have disappeared from the shelves; Bea's clothes are missing from the laundry basket and the crater on the sofa that Bea made with her tiny arse has flattened out. Rose fetches one of Bea's old study books. Not to read it, that's beyond her, but to read her daughter's margin notes. 'I miss you little Bea Bea,' she says.

By evening she has listened to four hours of radio and caught the six o'clock news on the television. She's waiting for Trevor to arrive home. He will bring food, wine for her and dope for himself. As long as she doesn't get a phone call from him to say he won't be home, she's fine. She passes out eventually, her head on the arm of the sofa, her wine glass perched on a little side table within easy reach.

Rose is jolted awake when the fist that has been supporting her head slips and knocks the glass over. It shatters on the wooden floor. The light and noise from a late-night music show on television helps her focus as she tries to remember where she is. She wipes dribble from her cheek and lifts her head to find herself alone.

There's no sound of Trevor's boots on the stairs, or a can being opened in the kitchen. Only the rhythmic beat of a drum solo. Ignoring the broken glass, she hauls herself up kicking over an empty wine bottle and bashing her knee on the edge of the coffee table. Then she hears a key turning in the latch and staggers to the hall.

'Where the bloody hell have you been?'

Trevor pockets his keys in his leather flying jacket and shuts the door. 'I was down Basing Street. What's the to-do?'

'You're always down Basing Street. Who's down Basing Street?' Rose folds her arms and stands with legs apart, her slippers with the low heel making her unstable.

'Don't give me grief. I went to get some weed.'

'Who is she?' Rose sees lipstick on his T-shirt. She's convinced he's just had sex.

He shrugs off the jacket and hangs it on the hook. 'Don't be daft. Go to bed. You're pissed.'

'I'm not going to bed until you tell me who she is.'

'What the fuck are you going on about, woman? You need your head testing.' Trevor raises his forefinger and stabs at his temple. He pushes her aside, but Rose grabs his shirt.

He throws her off. 'Go to bed. You're drunk.'

'Who is she?'

'Go. To. Bed. Rose.' Trevor spins her around to face the stairs and pushes her towards them, but she ducks away and, unbalanced on her stupid slippers, opens the front door.

'Get out.' Her voice reverberates in the cold stillness of the street. 'Get out. You're all the same. You talk your way in, then can't keep your cocks in your trousers.' She imagines a pile of cheap jeans in the back of the van and some country bitch lying on them with her legs around his hips. She tells him he's a selfish git and a lazy sod. She's done everything for him, but he treats her like shit.

Trevor reaches for his jacket and leaves. 'Suit yourself,' he mutters as he passes her.

Rose shouts after him. 'You're not going anywhere until I get my rent money.'

'Rent money?' Trevor opens his arms wide. 'I don't pay rent.'

'Yeah, and don't I know it? You owe me money.'

'I bloody well pay for everything. Get back inside the house.' Trevor looks left and right. It's pub closing time. There are coppers everywhere and she knows he's frightened of making a scene. He's got a bag of weed on him. She opens the little gate at the front of the house and steps out onto the street. 'No, Trevor. You've had a roof over your head thanks to me, and you ain't paid for it. So, come on.' Rose holds out a hand. The streetlamp shines on her palm. 'You've got money for a slapper and spliff, you can pay your rent money.'

Trevor raises his voice for the first time and it's a deep guttural bark that splits the night air and makes her jump. 'I'm not giving you owt, you stupid cow. I've paid me way. You're mental. Go inside.'

Rose is confused. Is she mad? Her feet are icy and there is no grip on her slippers. 'For fuck's sake.' Her ankle gives way and she is about to fall but Trevor keeps her upright. 'Get off me.' She is screaming now, rigid in Trevor's big hands. 'Help. Someone. Help! Rape!'

'Rose. Shut the fuck up.' He shakes her, and her head clears for a moment. She sees the street alive with the silhouettes of people spilling out of the pub. A couple of police officers appear in front of her. They look so young she can't believe they're real.

She laughs. The set-to with Trevor quite forgotten

at the sight of the two young lads in uniform. 'Are you strippergrams? My God what a couple of lovely boys. Are you going to get your kit off then? You're a bit early for me birthday, lads.'

Trevor has released her from his grip. She pulls her cardigan around her. The police officers look from her to Trevor, who is standing behind her. 'Sorry, officers…' Trevor says.

'They're not real police, Trev. They do a striptease for people on their birthdays. She turns to look at him and catches him signalling to the lads. He is raising a hand to his mouth as if raising a glass. 'You bastard. Don't make this about me. It's you they'll be after.'

Rose swings a fist at Trevor, but the arm stops in mid-flight as someone has a hold on her. She raises her other fist and it connects with the face of the younger of the two police officers. His helmet falls off his head and rolls into the gutter.

As someone is telling her that what she says might be used in court, she is pinned against the door of a squad car and her hands are wrenched behind her back. A blue light flashes and blinds her. She is cuffed. A hand is placed on the top of her head and it feels as if the vertebrae in her neck are about to concertina downwards. She is shoved into the back seat. Outside her house, Nigel is talking to Trevor.

'Don't listen to that old faggot,' she cries. But Nigel doesn't hear as Trevor is gently guiding him back to his house. She wants to tell the officer in the driving seat that Trevor's got dope on him but some unwritten rule stops her.

Shop-Bought Flowers

There is an underlying smell of stale vomit and urine in the car and a sharp synthetic tang of air freshener assaults her nose. She sneezes and her spittle hits the window. Tears fall but she has no control over where, and then, through the misted glass, she sees Trevor disappear behind her front door. Both officers are in the car. She yells at them. 'You cunts. You wait 'til I tell Sergeant Campbell.' One of the officers reaches over his seat and slaps her face with the back of his hand.

Rose is released on bail the next day and returns to the house, retrieving the spare keys from under a pot that holds a neglected wisteria. In the lounge, the broken glass has been cleared up and through the party wall she can hear Nigel playing the piano. She is reminded of last night and whispers a pathetic sorry, her lips close to the wall.

Trevor has packed a bag and gone, leaving behind the stone Buddha and his dirty laundry. Rose sighs, walks down to the kitchen and switches on *Woman's Hour*. The calming voices are reassuring and slowly the chaos of last night seeps away. She badly needs a drink and pulls the lid off the biscuit tin. Trevor has left two crisp twenty-pound notes. She takes one of them straight round to the off-licence to buy a bottle of vodka and a packet of Embassy Number Five.

Twenty-Three

Rose 1987

Evie Frances Fuller sleeps in the Moses basket on the kitchen table. She's four weeks old and there hasn't been a murmur out of her all morning. Rose hasn't dressed yet. It's still early and she hasn't finished her wine.

Evie is Trevor's baby, there's no doubt. She has his big open face, so unlike Bea's. She can't help but love the little thing. It would be inhuman to take out all the ills Trevor brought to the house on this baby. What a fucking year. She'll be glad to see the back of it. 'December soon. Good riddance to bad rubbish,' she says.

Bea has got herself a sewing job. It's a shame she couldn't finish her degree, but it was her choice. Ever since her daughter's return from Sussex, Rose has been unwell. She blames Trevor for everything but still cries for him. She misses him but she hates him more. She has every right to.

She empties the remains of the bottle into her wine glass and looks at the clock. It's nearly eleven and she's worried whether there's another bottle in the fridge. She doesn't like warm white wine – it's undrinkable – she scampers over to the fridge and sighs. There are two bottles standing to attention ready to serve. She thinks she'll take this glass easy, sip it slowly and luxuriate in the fuzzy feeling that is beginning to diminish the memories of Trevor.

Rose doesn't really have much of a clue when she's supposed to feed the baby. Time seems to stand still one minute and then a whole morning has gone by without her knowing how that happened. Bea is always cross when Rose doesn't do the right thing. Her daughter has become a bit of a bitch, truth be told: don't give her gripe water in her bottle; don't lie her down on the carpet and make sure her nappy is changed before her feed. She makes Rose jump, she's so sharp with her tongue.

'Do you want a feed, Little One? Ma'll just have another drinky, then she'll make your bottle.' Rose pours a glass of wine which sploshes on her knuckles. She runs her tongue over her hand before she fills her mouth, swilling the liquid around her teeth. She sighs then holds a fist to her chest as the reflux burns. 'Right, let's do you now.'

The baby wakes and cries an insistent, braying cry impossible for her to ignore. She slaps an empty pan on the stove and turns the gas on under it. She switches on the kettle, meaning to boil the water to heat up Evie's milk. It's quicker to boil the water in the kettle then pour it in the pan. Only the kettle has no water in it, and it squeals as if it's in pain. The baby cries louder and Rose is confused. She fills the kettle. The dry element makes the water spit and crackle. She takes a swig from her glass to calm her nerves.

The baby is screaming, the kettle is boiling. Pick up the baby or put the boiling water from the kettle in the pan? The baby or the kettle? The kettle or the baby? There's a smell of burning.

Both. She can do both. She leans over the Moses basket and draws the baby up. The smell of scorching metal makes her gag. She holds Evie tightly but the insistent howling means she can't think straight. 'Shut up, Evie. Shut your cakehole for a minute.'

Evie shifts in her arms and a continuous amplified howling fills the kitchen. Rose reaches for the kettle, steam issuing, the water inside bubbling furiously. The doorbell rings and Rose ignores it, concentrating on getting the boiling water into the pan. The baby bangs its little head on Rose's shoulder, too young to hold it up. All the while she howls. The doorbell rings again. The pan slips off the ring as she pours water from the kettle into it. Boiling water splashes over the hob, putting out the gas flame. The insistence of the ringing bell adds to the mayhem.

Rose is glad to leave the kitchen and the smell of gas behind her. She carries the baby to the door. Evangeline is standing there in a lovely coat. Rose is about to say how nice Evangeline looks but her visitor has run into the kitchen without even saying hello.

'Ow! Jesus Christ and all the saints!' Evangeline screams as she runs cold water over her hand. 'Rose, what have you been doing? You can't be drinking with your baby. You can't be setting fire to the place.' Evangeline wraps a wet tea towel around her hand.

'Have you hurt yourself?' Rose jiggles the baby, who squeals.

'I've burnt me hand, Rose. I'm just glad it was me.' Evangeline tends to her hand while Rose watches. 'Take the baby into the lounge.'

The baby is wet. Rose feels it on her stomach. Again, she is unsure what to do. Does she change the baby or wait for the bottle? Evangeline hands her the warmed milk, but when Rose places the teat on the baby's lips, Evie howls and refuses to drink. 'She's wet. I have to change her. She's a fussy li'l thing.' Rose reaches out to put the bottle on the coffee table, but it falls short and rolls onto the floor. 'I can't. I can't.' Rose sobs. Her hands knead the baby blanket Evie is wrapped in.

Evangeline lifts Evie out of Rose's arms. 'Go to bed, Rose.'

'Why does everybody keep telling me to go to bed? I don't want to go to bed. I want to look after my girls.' But she is talking to herself as Evangeline has taken the baby into the kitchen. An overwhelming tiredness, bone-deep, wells up inside her. She's tired of looking after Evie, she's tired of the secrets and lies.

Eventually Evangeline returns to the living room carrying the Moses basket. 'Evie is sleeping. I fed her and I've changed her nappy. Why don't you get some sleep too?' She's whispering so she doesn't wake the baby.

Her friend's face is lined but the skin in between shines with love and good moisturiser. Rose is quite jealous of

Evangeline's skin. But how could she tell her friend this without sounding stupid? She cries and all she can manage is an incoherent thank you.

'You can sleep, and I can stay until Bea gets back from work.'

'You go, Evangeline. I can wait for Bea. She'll be back soon.'

'Bea won't be back from work for hours.'

'I didn't know.'

'I know, darling. Do you know what? I reckon it will be good for baby if I take her for a walk—'

'I can take her for a walk.'

'You've had a drink, my love. You can't be taking the baby for a walk today.'

Rose lowers her eyes.

'You know. There's a group that meets at Holy Trinity,' Evangeline says. 'People talk about their drinking. How it takes over. Becomes more important than their own children.'

Rose hears herself trying to say that Bea and Evie mean the world to her, but she can't get the words out in the right order. Eventually, Evangeline leaves, taking the baby with her and Rose is alone. She grabs her wine and takes herself up to bed. It's better to sleep off the booze before Bea comes home. She'll only moan. Rose decides she will have a day off from drinking tomorrow. She will drink the herbal teas that Bea buys. Disgusting though they are.

She wakes and noises from downstairs tell her that Bea is home from work. This is always the worst part of the day.

Coming round, slightly less drunk than she was before she went to bed, knowing she is in trouble. Her throat and chest burn with the pain of reflux and she lifts herself up. Did God send Evangeline? Rose is certain Evangeline has a direct line to the Almighty. She's probably a genuine guardian angel. Rose's guilt washes over her and she is determined to ring Evangeline and apologise as soon as she's properly sober.

She thinks about going downstairs. It's hard to face Bea these days. Don't do this. Don't do that. Don't swear. Rose had even lost her name. Bea insists that Evie should grow up just like other little girls so her name is now Ma. Bea wanted to call her Mum, but she wasn't having any of that. Rose was given the choice: Ma or Mum and under duress she had chosen Ma. Rose splashes her face with cold water before tiptoeing downstairs.

Evie has just been fed and Bea is holding her. The little head is trying to lift off Bea's shoulder. 'How are you feeling?' Bea asks.

'I'm not very well. Think I'm coming down with flu.' Rose sits at the kitchen table and fidgets with the edge of the tablecloth.

'I had to collect Evie from Evangeline's.'

'She took her for a walk. I said I wasn't feeling well.'

'R... Ma.'

Huh. Good She's having trouble remembering the new rule about the name. Rose fetches a glass of water, trying hard to stop her hands from shaking. She takes her fags from her pocket then glances up at Bea and puts them back.

'You need to get help. Evangeline says there's a group.'

'I know. A group that will help with my drinking.' Rose laughs a rolling chesty laugh. 'I don't need help. I'm very good at it.' She looks at Bea and sighs. Like Evangeline, Bea is blessed with good skin. Rose places a flat palm on her own flaccid cheek.

She's only thirty-seven but she feels older. Sometimes she looks in the mirror and sees her mother staring back at her. On bad days she sees her father. She's more mishandled than Miss Selfridge. She laughs at her own joke.

'What's funny?' Bea asks.

There's a mood on her, Rose can tell. 'What?' Rose is sure she is going to get a telling-off.

'Ma. You need help with your drinking.'

'I'm fine. I only had a little one to calm my stomach.'

'But Ma…'

Bea. Beautiful Bea is sad and worried. Rose wishes John were here. He would tell her not to spoil her pretty face with a frown. Rose coughs. 'See, I'm coming down with something, darling.'

'I'm going to ask if Tish can look after Evie.'

'Letitia? She'll want money. We haven't got any.'

'She's a registered childminder. She'll take care of Evie.'

'We can't pay her.' Rose was suddenly angry. 'She's mine. I can look after her.' She stabs her chest with her thumb. 'Evie is mine. Remember.'

'But you're not well.'

Rose watches as Bea walks towards the door. 'Do you want me to leave?'

'Where would you go, Ma?'
'I mean I can go to my room.'
Bea sighs and takes Evie upstairs.

Twenty-Four

Evie 2019

Evie senses that Bea is finally opening up about the past. Max is still asleep upstairs and she fears that when he joins them, her sister will lock all the memories away. There was something that had stopped Ma drinking, Evie was aware of a sort of before and after time that coincided with the start of a school term.

She has early memories: Ma in the bathroom being sick with her head in the toilet bowl; the thud of Ma falling over and of bruises on her arms as she prepared the tea. She remembers being woken by the sound of raucous singing. And then there was a smell. A smell she associates today with cockroaches.

'Do you think that the day in Kensington Gardens we talked about last week—'

'The Serpentine?'

'Yes, do you think that…because somehow it feels significant. I seem to think it is anyway.'

'Yes actually.' Bea smooths the hem of the tunic she's wearing. 'It was my day off. It was the summer holidays. You were about to start in reception at school.'

'We went to the Italian gardens. I remember there were hundreds of pigeons and we got spattered in smelly fountain water,' Evie says.

'We had a picnic of Dairylea cheese triangles and ham sandwiches.'

'How can you remember that?'

'Because I remember every detail of that day. We were near the Peter Pan statue by the water.' Bea reminded her of how the picnic blanket had blown away and how Evie had chased after it. Ma had sat with her hands in her raincoat pockets as if she was searching for her keys, ready to go home.

Bea closes her eyes. 'You were wearing blue striped dungarees.'

'I loved those.'

'And you wouldn't put your cardigan on.'

'I wanted to play hide-and-seek.'

'You wouldn't let up. I decided on a lesson in delayed gratification.' Bea stops. All the muscles in her face go slack. 'I wish I hadn't.'

'You went to get ice creams. I asked Ma to play hide-and-seek with me and she turned her back on me. I thought she was counting.'

'You ran off,' Bea whispers.

'I ran off *to hide*.'

Bea tells Evie how they had searched along the path frantic with worry. Others joined in. A young couple, hearing them shouting Evie's name, started shouting too. A man, whose dog ate the ice creams Bea had thrown to the ground, searched in the bushes by the water's edge.

Bea is unlocking a memory Evie has kept buried. Her sister's voice is the key winding up a musical trinket box. The forgotten moment is about to be revealed and before Bea reveals it, before all the musical notes have joined together to make the tune, Evie has recalled it herself.

Bea continues. 'Then someone screamed, and when I looked back the man with the dog was lifting you out of the water.'

Evie is silent. Then she gasps. 'I'd forgotten.'

'You could have drowned.'

'No, Bea. I couldn't have. It's shallow. I remember seeing you and Ma running. I saw you through the branches.' Had she rejected the danger as too painful to recall or was it that she hadn't felt that danger at all?

'You were filthy, covered in mud and blanket weed. You could have—'

'No, Bea. I wouldn't have drowned. I walked the railings and got behind them. I must have slipped on the way out.'

'But that's not what we thought at the time.'

Evie nods. She recalls the vivid image of Ma and Bea running towards her. Only now she realises it isn't branches she's looking through. It's strands of wet hair.

She finally understands her mother's frequent absences before that day. 'She stopped drinking, didn't she?'

'You could've drowned.'

'But I didn't and Ma sobered up.'

'It was a turning point, not immediately. But it frightened her so badly she tried harder.'

Max appears and settles down next to her. He folds his arms and there is a belligerent mood on him. 'What's the matter with you?' Evie asks.

He looks at Bea. 'How come you never told Evie about Trevor before now?'

'It was never the right time, and anyway Ma had affairs. I was never sure if Trevor was the father.'

'Come on. I'm not sure you've been straight with us. I mean…you must have known it was Trevor, just by Evie's looks. She doesn't look much like you or your Ma from what I can tell.'

'Max, leave it.' Evie is watching her sister as Max attacks her. Bea's face darkens. She has gathered up all the memories and locked them inside the trinket box.

'Are you calling me a liar?' Bea's voice is measured. 'I know you think we're not good enough for you. But let me tell you something. Evie has no need of you. She has a home here whenever she wants it.'

'What are you saying, Bea? Stop it.' Evie slides to the edge of the sofa.

'She doesn't need you, Max. She has a perfectly respectable family of her own. Remember that when you're crowing about your great-grandfather the thirteenth Duke of Nothing-Doing.'

Max nods. 'Fine. She doesn't need me. She *wants* to be with me. Right?' They are both staring at her. 'For fuck's sake. Are we okay or has your sister poisoned you against me? It would be good to know now.' Max stands with his hands on his hips.

'Apologise, you moron. You've upset Bea and now I'm angry with you.'

'Evie doesn't need this, does she, Max? You thought you were being smart, but it's in bad taste.'

'Well? Is it true? Is there a reason you don't want Evie to know his surname? Do you want her to find him or not? Why show her all this shit?' Max waves a dismissive hand at the boxes and suitcases.

'That is enough!' Evie stands and faces him. 'You have no idea what you're talking about. And this isn't shit. This is my family's past.' She stabs a finger at the boxes. 'It's actually nothing to do with you, Max, it's between me and my sister. So fuck off.'

Max opens his mouth to speak but Bea interrupts.

'Don't upset yourself, Evie.' Bea is calmness personified. An empress suppressing an irksome dog. She comes over and runs a hand along Evie's lower back, and it soothes her. 'Evie doesn't want to see us arguing, Max. Just leave it be.'

'Do you know what I think?' Max leans forward.

'We're not interested in what you think,' Evie says.

'I think you're really good at avoiding the truth. You want to tell Evie about her dad but you can't. For whatever reason, you won't let her in on the big family secret. That's what I think.'

'Are you finished?' Bea's voice is flat.

'And it's not good for her. Knowing there's something wrong but not being allowed to deal with it.'

'I can decide what's good for me, thanks,' Evie says.

Bea stares at Max as if dismissing him. He tuts, raises his eyes to the ceiling and skulks out of the room.

Evie has one last question for her sister. 'Was he at the cemetery the day we were laying flowers?'

'Trevor? You think the old man assaulting women was Trevor?'

'No. I'm... It's just weird how he stared at me. How he ran when he saw us together.'

Bea fetches a newspaper from a pile of recycling. 'Here. Read.'

The picture in the newspaper was of an elderly man with an unshaven face and straggly white hair. The report said he had been caught when one of the groundsmen saw him following a woman. When he was approached, he tried to run but was outpaced by the younger man.

'Trevor would never...' Bea said.

'How do you know?'

Max sticks his head around the door. 'It's one already. The table's booked for one-thirty. Get a move on, you two.'

The lunch turns out to be a successful diversion from the tension at the house. The air is cleared over the starters, the explanations from the combatants accepted over the main dish and by dessert everyone is calm and talking about the forthcoming birth. As far as Evie is concerned, breaking bread is the best way to sort out disputes. It's a practice she intends to continue.

After an amicable coffee at the house, Evie collects her things then selects a few items from the boxes: a photo of her christening; a group photograph taken at Linton's wedding, the tarnished hippy bell and the charge sheet. For research, she explains. From one of the make-up bags she takes a powder compact. It's an embossed silver thing, that feels solid in the palm of her hand. She sees Ma's eyes looking back at her through the mirror when she opens the lid. Max is wrong about the family likeness.

Bea gives her an old copy of *Vogue* which shows a picture of a dress which Evie, according to Bea, helped to create. The model is captured in a moment where she seems to be floating on air. The cerulean skirt billows and twists around her and sparkling crystals, sewn into a cascade of sunflowers, dazzle the eye. On either side of the catwalk the great and good of the fashion world are giving the dress and its creator a standing ovation. The man accompanying the model is Bea's boss, the internationally acclaimed designer Derek Croft. Standing in the shadowy background she can just make out a slight serious-looking woman. Bea.

Twenty-Five

Bea 1990

Bea drops Evie off at Sylvester and Tish's place before going to work. The arrangement has benefitted everyone. Evie thrives under her care. Bea assumes that Tish is glad of the extra money and Ma is freed up from the responsibility of looking after Evie. Most importantly, Bea can keep her job.

She is assistant to a former art student who made his name designing a dress for Princess Diana for which he has received an enterprise grant. St Martins trained, he is intense and gifted. Derek Croft is in awe of her skills, and she is equally impressed by his art school training and his new decade prescience.

She works in a long, brightly lit studio above the cafes and clothes shops of Mayfair. There are professional sewing machines integrated into workbenches, two cutting tables and floor to ceiling shelving containing haberdashery and fabrics. The walls are London brick, painted white to reflect all the light from the Crittall windows. From these windows, Bea can peer into the opposite building which houses the workshops of shoemakers and diamond cutters.

Three dressmakers' dummies stand in front of the windows. They are silhouetted observers of Derek Croft's fabulousness. He is dubbed "The Fabric Engineer" by the fashion press. His designs incorporate structures not seen since the Tudors: bustles, ruffs and farthingale hoops. Bea is fascinated by the way Derek intuitively knows how to transform the drape of a skirt. How pleats and hemlines can be manipulated to transform the ordinary into the extraordinary. Evangelina taught her how to sew but her new boss teaches her how to create.

They are working on a spectacular piece of eveningwear. The significance of the new decade is not lost on Derek. There is pressure on the house they work for to be the first among equals, to come up with something utterly new and exciting. His inspiration is sunflower fields in Provence and he is engineering an enormous sunflower head. Fabric is pleated around padded wire and tacked. The intention is to secure the enormous gravity-defying flower to the shoulder of a silk evening gown.

They work for hours but the sunflower refuses to sit on the shoulder at the desired angle. It flops forward and is frustratingly limp. Bea makes a sponge mount to give rigidity but still the flower refuses to search for the sun. It is late in the day, the atmosphere intense and Derek is becoming more agitated with each failure. Then, when there is some semblance of success, the weight causes the fine fabric of the bodice to ruck.

'Oh for God's sake you useless, skinny cow, get out of my gown.' Derek addresses the dummy waving his arms and legs as if he is trying to shoo a herd of cattle off his land. 'Bea. Bea? Get the dress off this bitch.'

She moves away from the tantrum and extracts a few coins out of her purse to buy tea. Derek needs a moment alone so the trip serves two purposes. She leaves the open purse on the cutting table and by the time she gets back to the studio he is breathing steadily, sitting cross-legged on the table.

'Here.' Bea holds out a cup.

'Thank you, Beatrice.'

She fetches some toilet paper, and he blows his nose fulsomely.

'Better now?'

He reaches over, puts his arms around her neck and like a child he tells her he loves her. It is only when she pulls away that she sees the photograph in his hand. It's from her purse.

'It fell out on the floor. Who is it?' he asks. 'Is it your sister?'

Bea laughs. 'It's my mother. That's Kensington Market.'

Ma is wearing a vibrant green maxi dress and her red hair is long and wavy. Derek says it reminds him of a Pre-Raphaelite painting. 'She could be a model. She could model for us.'

'That was taken years ago.' Bea snatches the photo from him. 'You'll sort it, Derek. You'll get the dress right.'

'Thank you for having faith. Are you out tonight, my darling?' he asks.

'No. Are you?'

'You never come out. Why don't you come to the club tonight? You might meet someone.' He talks as if he is taking pity on her.

She blows on her tea. 'I don't think so, Derek. Gotta get Evie home.'

'Yes, but you could meet me there afterwards. I have a new date. He's really sexy—'

'My mum's not well.'

'Oh. I'm sorry, love. Nothing serious, is it?'

'She's an alcoholic.' Bea blushes. She's never told anyone. Never said the word out loud. But then no one has ever asked until now.

'Oh, Bea. Poor love. You must be frazzled by it all.'

'Yeah, that's a good way to put it.'

'Addiction's a bitch. It ruins your looks and your mum's so pretty,' Derek shakes his head. 'Sorry. That sounded so shallow. If there's anything I can do.'

It's her turn to throw her arms around his neck. The relief of saying that forbidden word with all its implications overwhelms her. 'You've already helped.'

Bea parks Evie's buggy in the hall and takes groceries into the kitchen telling Evie to go up and get Ma. She unpacks the bags and opens the back door to let much needed fresh air in.

Ma sits herself down at the kitchen table. 'Close that bloody door, Bea. We'll all be dead of pneumonia.' Her voice has the dry nasal twang of the alcoholic. She's lost a front tooth after a fall and is worrying the gap with her tongue. Evie clambers up onto Ma's lap. 'You're a right princess, you are. Chair's not good enough for your bum. You've got to have a lap.' Ma pulls Evie in and squeezes her. She snivels, mawkish in her drunken fug.

'Ma, pull yourself together.'

'I can't help it. I love my little Evie.'

After they have eaten, Ma offers to clear up the dishes, but Bea sorts it. 'Evie, go and get your colouring book.' The little girl wriggles off her seat.

'Did you go to the church, Ma?'

'Mass is Sundays, Bea.'

'To sign up to the meetings?'

'Oh that. I went, and they said I wasn't too bad, I don't need to go.'

'That's not how it works.'

'How do you know how it works? You've been, have you?'

Ma's indignation rises to meet hers. Before they clash, Evie returns. She hoists herself up at the table and the atmosphere in the kitchen softens. Tish had bought her a colouring book for her last birthday and she opens it. There is a whole field of nodding flowers. Bea watches mesmerised as Evie takes a yellow pencil for the petals and a brown one for the seed heads and turns them into sunflowers.

Seeing Evie's picture coming to life as she applies the colour, Bea runs out to phone Derek. He's out of course so she leaves a message on his answerphone telling him she needs to work at home. She tells Evie to go into the lounge and the sound of the *Magic Roundabout* theme tune floats towards the kitchen. Ma drops her head and brushes a skeletal hand over her skull.

'We're going to church tomorrow,' Bea says. 'You're going to the meeting.'

Ma makes a whistling sound, the gap in her teeth acting as a wind tunnel in her mouth. 'I will not.'

Bea leans in close and her mother's rancid breath revolts her. She whispers. 'Remember the summer holidays? The Serpentine?'

'That's not fair...' Rose shakes her head.

'She thought you were counting—'

'I was telling her to wait—'

'You turned your back on her to drink vodka. Evie nearly drowned.'

Rose sniffs back tears. 'Sod it.'

'We're going tomorrow.'

Bea drops Evie off at Letitia's then instead of taking the Tube to Bond Street, goes straight home. She opens her sewing boxes and sits in her room. The old dressing table now stands next to the door and a white linoleum desk has replaced it by the window. She cuts petal templates and circles from card. She cuts fabric to size. Each circle has a set of tiny seed heads made from glass beads. She crochets a grid pattern using silk ribbon and the flower heads are attached.

Bea draws the dress, aware the sketch doesn't have Derek's mastery, and adds a cascade of sunflowers. It's more naturalistic than the single monstrous flower head Derek had intended but the effect is similar. When she looks at her watch, she swears and runs down to the kitchen.

She pours a single shot of vodka, baulking from the

smell, then runs back upstairs to knock at her mother's door. Ma stands clinging to the doorframe, sweating and shaking. She takes the proffered vodka and knocks it back like cough syrup.

Later, Ma sits in the kitchen wearing the navy polyester suit she wore for her court case. Her legs are so thin the fabric pools on the chair. She clutches her handbag to her chest and sucks a mint, her jaw a slowly tumbling machine wearing away at the sugary coating.

It's too cold for Bea to stand outside the Holy Trinity church hall and she's not allowed in. She walks up and down the street to keep warm, convinced Ma will try to sneak out. She glances over at The Swan pub on the corner. Her feet are icy and her gloves have lost their insulating properties but she is warmed by thoughts of their future.

She imagines Ma looking after Evie, taking her to school on time every morning and picking her up in the afternoon. In her daydream, the dry mottled skin of her mother's face is replaced with a tanned glow and her teeth are repaired. Bea will pay for them to be veneered. Derek might help with that if he is sincere. Which he tends to be. Bea summons up an image of Rose as she was when Trevor lived at Falmouth Road. She's bronzed from a summer spent in the garden, supple and clear-eyed and choosing flowers for cutting. This is the version of Ma she wants back. Bea needs the thin squalid imposter that haunts the house smelling of stale booze to disappear and her mother returned to her.

Her throat aches from suppressing tears when the church door opens. A young man in a three-quarter-length coat steps outside, draws his collar up and walks around the corner and out of sight. An older man, legs bowed with rickets, places a cap on his bald head and lumbers away in the direction of the pub. The church door remains open for a few seconds, a black empty hole, before Bea detects movement from within.

An old woman emerges. She is clinging to the door and a nun she doesn't recognise is helping her across the threshold. They stand close together as if they are colluding. Then the old woman straightens up and looks at Bea. It's Ma.

'Whose coat have you got on?'

'Sister Mary's. She said I could borrow it. My jacket's too thin for this cold.'

'That was kind. You'll have to return it tomorrow.'

'Oh. Shit.' Ma raises a hand to her forehead. The nun had got one over on Rose by tricking her into returning to church. 'I fell for that one. Hook, line and sinker.'

Derek is thrilled. He doesn't show it, but Bea reads the signals, his eyes running over every inch of the sketch, the pinching of his lower lip. He sits cross-legged on the cutting table as he studies the prototype flowers on their crochet grids. He pulls at a petal and prods the seed heads before glancing at the sketch again. 'This is crap.'

'No it isn't. Don't be so rude. A field of sunflower heads on the shoulder then you could have a big sunflower-shaped hat. A nod to fifties Dior.'

He looks at her through narrowed eyes. 'It's far from perfect but I can work with this. Your Nobel Prize is in the post, darling.'

They work together to attach the pattern to rayon, working both ends of the table. The scissors fly through cloth, she applies pins and he tacks as fast as she can pin. Strips of rayon float across the room, pirouetting and sliding to the floor. Derek kneels on the table to work on the bodice. He stops. 'Corset. It must have corsetry.' Then Derek insists she teach him how to crochet using silk chiffon.

Bea runs the voluminous skirt through the professional machine. It takes her hours and by the time she's almost finished her body aches. She looks up at the clock and realises she's late. Derek insists she stays to finish the dress and indeed, she would like nothing more than to see it on the mannequin. She could phone Ma and ask her to go to Letitia's to pick up Evie. Yesterday had been cathartic. An awakening. Ma had gone to bed early and this morning, there was no sign of her getting up in the night. No dirty glass or empty bottles. She phones home.

'Ma?'

'Bea?'

'How are you?'

'I'm doing fine. If you're asking if I've had a drink, no, I haven't. I went to church. Returned the coat.'

'That's good.'

'I thought so too.'

Bea explains she needs to work late and asks her if she could pick up Evie from Letitia's. Rose says yes in a heartbeat. 'What do you want for your tea?' Ma asks.

She can't remember the last time Ma shopped for anything other than booze and fags.

'Whatever you like, Ma. I'll eat whatever you like.'

Bea phones Letitia to say that Ma will pick up Evie. She tells her to ring if there is a problem.

'What kind of problem?' Letitia sounds worried. 'Shall I call Evangeline?'

'Ignore me, Tish. Head's all over the place with work.'

The dress, with its voluminous panels, is draped over Derek's arms. He has drawn the blinds at the window. Together they haul the folds of rayon over the mannequin. Derek uses chalk to draw lines for a boned corset and Bea pins the fabric for threading the bones. He tacks on a hidden peplum and creates an idealised version of the feminine – long legs, full hips, cinched waist and voluptuous breasts. In a last flourish, he attaches the riotous field of sunflowers. The glass beads throw pinpoints of light across the room as they work the final seams. There is no rucking as the weight is evenly distributed. It's an evening gown for a guest at the Mad Hatter's tea party, the mannequin a glorious queen commanding the room.

'It's stunning. It's like nothing I've ever seen,' Bea says.

'That's the idea,' Derek whispers. 'It's all my favourite women. Queen Elizabeth the First, Greta Garbo and Grace Jones. It's what I meant to say all along.' He throws a calico sheet over the prototype dress. 'Make sure no one comes in who we don't know. Anyone making deliveries. They're to leave them at the door. Do you understand? Don't describe this design to anyone. Don't sketch it on a napkin when you're sitting in Mickey D's having a Happy Meal with Sis.'

'She doesn't eat—'

'I mean it, Bea. You know I love you, but if you tell a soul what we've done here, you're sacked.'

'The silk should be blue, like a Van Gogh sky,' Bea says evenly.

'Your input is noted. Good job, Bea. Good job.' He is as exhausted as she is.

The shops on Oxford Street are rolling down the shutters as Bea reaches the Tube. She doesn't want to go home as she's filled with an unquenchable energy. She can make a claim on the dress and one day she will tell Evie how her little colouring book and pencils inspired a great designer. She'll tell Evangeline that, through passing on her formidable skills, she has taught one of England's greatest designers how to crochet.

There is a pub that Derek introduced her to and for a moment she is tempted to turn around, walk down Marylebone Lane and have a drink, just the one, a rare one these days. It won't take long. She turns, bumping the shoulder of a passer-by who tuts at her. The urge to treat herself evaporates and she runs down the steps of the Tube.

Twenty-Six

Rose 1991

Rose is running to pick up Evie. The gates are already open and some of Evie's classmates are walking towards her with their parents. They nod and smile as she dodges their buggies and makes her way to the classroom door.

Breathless, Rose apologises and takes Evie by the hand. The journey home is much calmer. They agree on fish fingers and chips for dinner after Rose makes Evie promise not to tell Bea. 'You know what she's like, darling. She'll make me go out and buy carrots or something disgusting.'

'Carrots are nice,' Evie says.

'S'pose they're alright as long as they're in shepherd's pie.'

Rose stoops to unbutton the toggles on Evie's bright red duffel coat.

'Miss Thompson says I look like Paddington Bear,' Evie says.

'Miss Thompson doesn't know her arse from her elbow. Paddington's coat is blue.'

As soon as Evie is free, she runs into the living room and switches on the television. Rose calls after her, telling her to take off her shoes. While the oil is heating up in the fryer, she opens the kitchen door and has a cigarette. There is the promise of an Indian summer ahead but a fresh breeze means she must lean against the door to make sure it doesn't bang shut.

There's no smoking in the house as it's bad for Evie. There's no alcohol in the house as it's bad for Rose. She's a member of the Temperance Society and her lateness is due to the fact that Rose is celebrating one year without a drink. The little badge they gave her sits in its velvet box ready for when Bea gets home. The slice of M&S sponge cake Sister Mary provided to go with the tea is repeating on her. This time last year she had given up drink altogether because last year Evie had almost drowned in the Serpentine lake.

One year and not so much as a cider lolly later, she feels more alive than she's done in decades. She stubs her cigarette out in a flowerpot and lowers raw potato chips into the frying pan. They sizzle and spit as she watches them turn brown. 'Evie! Come and get it!'

Evie wriggles onto the kitchen chair and attacks her food, burning her tongue on a hot chip and having to drown her mouth in water.

'No rush, madam. They won't run off your plate.' Rose makes a pot of camomile tea and inhales deeply. It reminds her of Trevor and she passes a flat palm across her stomach to calm the butterflies that have taken up residence there lately. Bea says he was good for them, but Rose has so many gaps to fill in and they never speak about him. After tonight's little celebration of sobriety— a pinning on of the badge and some herby tea— she will ask Bea about the time he lived with them. Bea remembers everything.

Evie is in bed asleep by the time Bea gets home. 'How was work?' Rose stands by the sink.

'We're busy. I'm going to Paris with Derek next month.'

'What for?'

'A show. It's for a private audience of the über-rich. A magazine is paying for it all.'

'There'll be decent freebies then,' Rose says. She ladles out lentils flavoured with Swiss bouillon and butters a mound of white bread.

'I'll get a goodie bag for you. What about your day? The big One.'

'Yeah, had a bit of cake, got a badge.' Rose shrugs as if coming off alcohol was nothing. As if every morning she got up and didn't crave a shot of vodka. That sometimes during the day she could smell wine as if it were in a glass at her lips. Bea is still wary of her relapsing as she is herself. She can never keep secrets from her daughter. She's been told that children of alcoholics are hypersensitive to their parents' moods. They develop survival strategies and know when to approach and when to back off.

'I want to say sorry for—'

'Don't be silly. You were ill. People don't apologise for having the flu.'

'No. I s'pose. This reminds me of Trevor,' Rose says, sipping the soup.

'He would put a rake of potatoes in it too.'

'Did he ever speak to you about me?'

'He used to ask me what to get you for your birthday and Christmas.'

Rose drops her spoon. 'It's just, I think. What happened…'

'Don't think about the past, Ma. Things are fine now. Evie is thriving, I'm pulling in good money and you're well.'

'I know. We're all good. All fine. But I have these blank spaces. I need to know if it was my fault. Or was he just like all the other freeloaders and chancers? Was he always going to—'

'Yes, Ma.'

'What? Which is it?'

'He was a user, an opportunist.'

'And I didn't drive away a good 'un?'

'No Ma. You didn't.'

'And. What happened—'

'Don't, Ma. Please don't.'

'We need to talk about it, love. Evie's getting a big girl.'

'No. Let's talk about it another time. We're in a good place. Let it be.'

Rose is frustrated. Have they been talking about the same thing? Why can't she make Bea listen? She sighs, too exhausted with the effort to stay sober to raise her voice and have it out with her daughter. 'I'm such an idiot. How is it you're so nice to me?'

'You're my mum.'

'Don't call me that, Beatrice. Ma's bad enough.'

Rose and Bea settle in for a night of television: *Coronation Street*, a programme about building your own home and the news. Fed up hearing about the unemployment figures, Margaret Thatcher and the woes of the car industry, Rose gets up to go to bed. But the first item on the London news sends her back to her seat.

A body has been discovered in Paddington. A recently bulldozed building has revealed the remains of a white male, about forty years old at the time of death according to the police. The man had been hanged from a girder which must have collapsed, as it had fallen onto the body. There is speculation that it was a gangland crime and the corpse has lain in the derelict warehouse for the best part of a decade.

'What is it?' Bea looks concerned.

'Nothing. It's just made me think of something someone said once. Years ago. Doesn't matter.' Rose switches off the television. 'Bedtime.'

Rose is awake into the early hours. Her head is filled with the memory of a day long ago when she had stood watching Rob and Colin Lafferty's funeral. She had been carrying Bea at the time. Bea had been about fourteen or was it fifteen when John disappeared. She raises her fists to her temples and presses hard. The problem with being sober is that she cares about not remembering the past.

She remembers the guy called Marco and how John's people stood around at the parties, nervous in their shirts and ties. They had every right to be scared after Marco had sent his men out to kill the Laffertys. And John.

Napoleon syndrome they called it on *Woman's Hour*. Small-man complex. Greedy, cowardly John, who hadn't even defended her against the drunk in the pub that night in the Alex. He only hit women.

She lifts herself up onto her elbows as it occurs to her that the arrest of the Mafia was national news and she had kept articles about it. Eyes heavy with lack of sleep, Rose tiptoes downstairs before the house is awake. She opens the sideboard cupboard and retrieves a stack of yellowed newspaper cuttings.

Sitting on the floor, she thumbs through them until she finds what she's looking for. In column inches she reads about the Laffertys' murder, the closure of the Self-Serve after the licence is revoked, the corrupt coppers in the pay of the Mafia and the raids on brothels and clubs by Scotland Yard. She keeps the flimsy sheets on her lap while she replaces the unwanted papers in the low cupboard.

Suddenly the light goes on and Bea's voice hisses. 'Ma? No.' Bea flies to her side and kneels next to her.

'It's okay. I'm not drinking. Look. I think it's your father. John is the man whose body has turned up in Paddington.'

Bea frowns and Rose tries again. 'The Maltesers he worked for got sent down in eighty-three. The police were corrupt. John does a runner because Campbell, that's him…' She points to a grainy image of a heavily decorated police officer '…Can't protect him no more. Won't protect him cos he's gone up the ranks.' Rose is whispering, mindful that Evie might walk in on them. John took you for a Wimpy just before he disappeared.'

'He didn't. I lied to you to make you feel better. And he didn't give me a tenner for passing my exams.'

'He was devoted to you.'

'He left us. Anything could have happened to us but he didn't care. He only cared about himself.'

Her daughter is right. John had played Bea off against her in a sick and twisted mind game. One in which Rose was made to feel jealous of the infant. But Rose, sober, rational Rose, even now admits she has feelings for John. He was good to her for a time and she pities him. She isn't hardened by what life has thrown at her like her daughter is.

Rose sends Bea back to bed then returns the cuttings to the cupboard and rummages some more. She finds a small black address book, a Christmas present from Kath going back to her teenage years and in it is the phone number of Carol Lafferty.

Carol has asked Rose to meet her at a nursing home out in the suburbs. Rose had dreaded the initial phone call but there was no hesitancy on Carol's part. She sits waiting for her old friend on a bench in the grounds reading a glossy brochure given to her at reception. St Bridgette's Sanatorium was once a stately home that was requisitioned in World War Two then gifted to the Catholic Church as a home for the mentally unstable.

Carol approaches. She's put on a lot of weight. Her body tilts left to right across the grass to where Rose is sitting. She's wearing a smart wool coat and her hair is a glossy chestnut brown. She smiles as Rose rises from her seat.

They hug. Two old friends, long parted.

'Before you say anything, love, I want to say sorry.' Carol's voice is thick, deeper than Rose remembers. Up close her skin is smooth and well cared for. They are both forty but Rose feels older, as though her time on the planet has accelerated and Carol is still a teenager.

'You still smoke, Carol?' They sit on the bench and light up, their hands acting in well-rehearsed synchronicity. They could be sixteen again. Rose reminds her of when they were teenagers. How they used to say that Rose would be Carol's bridesmaid and Carol would be Rose's. How they would live next door to each other and have holidays together. They would be godmothers to each other's kids.

Carol laughs. 'You wouldn't have wanted to marry into my lot, Rose. They led me and Mum a right dance, they did.'

'What about Paul?'

'He's here. Thought you might like to see him.'

'Yeah, I would. I got questions about John O'Dowd.'

'I thought as much.' Carol lifts herself off the bench. 'Good to clear the air, hey?' As they walk towards the broad steps up to the entrance, Carol tells Rose about the night Paul had learned of John's whereabouts. 'It was like he'd won the pools. Hopping around the front room, laughing, kissing me, Mum and the dog.'

Rose remembered that braying, mocking laugh. 'How'd he find him?'

'He'd got a bunch of IRA men onto it. In those days they'd do anything for money. They found him in a hostel in Cricklewood. They found him on account of his using the name Tom Fuller.' Carol tells Rose that a few nights later, Paul had returned home and collapsed on the kitchen floor. 'He was having a fit or something. He'd had a bash to the head, see. The doctors couldn't believe it. Told us by rights he should be dead.'

Rose looks away and gulps as if the air is sweeter and more breathable at the top of the steps. The trees that line the garden are sprinkled with new leaves. The land beyond is hidden save for a lone tower block. 'I never got a chance to tell you I was sorry for your loss.'

'They were too cocky. Silly sods thought they were the kings of Ladbroke Grove. And those Maltese friends of yours were vicious. Proper Mafia they was.'

'Did Paul say what he did with the body?'

'Rose—'

'Was it Paddington Basin? There's a body been found there—'

'Rose—'

'And they were *not* my friends, Carol.' Rose's eyes sting. 'I hated every last one of them.'

'I know, darlin'. We was just caught up in it. An accident of birth as far as I was concerned.'

'I had to get away from me dad. John was good to me. Once.' They stub out their cigarettes and throw them in the litter bin by the entrance.

Rose and Carol are led up a steep flight of stairs into a dimly lit corridor lined with locked doors. The attendant unlocks one of them. Rose clutches the strap of her handbag, moving her fingers along the soft leather as she follows Carol into the tiny cell-like room. She clocks the red panic button and keeps it in her peripheral vision.

The window looks out onto the grounds but it has bars across it that cast shadows on the bed and the chair. The bed is pushed up against the wall and in an armchair staring up at the window, sits Paul Lafferty. A plume of smoke rises from a cigarette in a tin ashtray on his lap. His white vest sags, revealing grey chest hairs and flaccid pale skin. He has lost the muscular tone that had once made him physically threatening.

'Hello, Paul,' Carol says. 'I brought you a visitor.'

Paul turns his head and looks directly at Rose. A livid scar running from the middle of his forehead and down his left cheek comes to a scabby end at his jawline.

Rose sits on a plastic chair while Carol unpacks a small blue carrier bag. There is a bar of chocolate, fags, shaving foam and the newspaper. She puts them all on a little table by the bed as she talks. First she lists the items, then tells Paul their mum is having trouble with her legs. She describes her day at work and the state of the potholes on her journey to the home. 'Remember Rose Fuller, Paul? She really fancied you.'

'Carol! No I never. Don't be listening to her, Paul. She's just kidding.'

Paul brays. 'Did you fancy me?' His grin reveals brown teeth, his eyes are liquid.

She flinches just as she did all those years ago when he had spat at her feet. 'Do you remember John? He was my boyfriend.'

'Fuller.' Paul stares at her. 'Little Rosie Fuller lives in that dump of a basement.'

'Carol tells me you found John when he went missing.'

Paul turns to look at the window. He seems to disappear into the smoke from his cigarette. 'Did he do that to you?'

'Yes, he fucking did.' Paul wags a slow finger at her. 'Never play on building sites, kids.'

Rose can't speak. She runs her fingers the length of the strap on her handbag, up then down then back again.

'Paddington Basin? Was it up by the canal?' Carol this time, much calmer than Rose as if asking him which branch of Marks and Spencer he got his vests from.

'Yeah. Took him down there in the boot of the Audi.'

'What happened, love?' Carol's voice softens, like she is speaking to a child.

'Bloody girder fell on me head.' Spittle runs down Paul's chin. He grimaces as if reliving the moment his face was cracked open by falling ironwork. 'Worth it though. For Rob and Col.' He turns towards Rose again and drops his head to one side as if his neck is unable to support it. The medicine-dulled eyes are at a level with hers. Paul raises his left fist above his head as if he were holding a rope. His tongue lolls and Rose thinks he is coughing. But he's not. He's pretending to choke and his torso jerks while he pulls the imaginary rope upwards. Suddenly, the macabre mime is over and he sits upright. 'Still fancy me, Rosie?'

She understands the little play and gasps at the cruelty. Kath and Tom used to say the Laffertys weren't so bad. A little dealing here, a gentlemen's nightclub there. But they were just as bad as the Maltese gang John worked for. Paul Lafferty had hanged John O'Dowd from a girder but it had fallen and hit him, breaking his skull. He was lucky to be alive. If you could call this living.

Carol and Rose stand on the path leading to the car park. The fresh breeze is cleansing after the dense atmosphere of Paul's room. They smoke.

'You won't tell anyone, will you? That'd kill me mum,' Carol says.

'No. God no. I couldn't tell Bea. She'd be off down the cop shop making a statement.'

'What will you tell her?'

'I'll just say he was deranged. Waste 'a time.' Rose shivered.

'Yeah, that's what I'll say to Mum.'

Part Three

Twenty-Seven

Bea 2019

Bea waves as Evie and Max drive away. It's a cold, dark afternoon, so she puts the heating on earlier than usual. It's not that she's miserly, but the old house takes ages to warm up and she only uses one room at a time. This is the final treat at the end of a lovely weekend. She is making an Aran cardigan for the baby in a sturdy cream wool. The knitting needles click out their familiar rhythm.

She quite enjoyed the little spat with Max. It certainly charged the atmosphere and brought a bit of noise into the old house. She is fond of him but he can be such an idiot. He's a man living on a single plane, an inhabitant of a flat, calm world, ordered in the traditional sequence of events. He's a beneficiary of a good education, gainful employment, a happy marriage and fatherhood. He, being a steady sort, will probably make a good daddy. And he, being the dogged sort, will probably be in love with Evie forever.

Max reminds her of Trevor in one way. They both allowed the wind to blow them in any direction and take the path of least resistance. But Max will almost certainly live by the consequences of his actions. He will fix his mistakes as he did today. The apology at lunch was sincere. Whereas Trevor just turned his back and walked away when everything got messy.

With a convulsive spasm, her hand trembles, causing her fingers to clamp the knitting needle in a rigid grip. The tingle becomes a quiver and she holds her breath because she knows what's coming. Her left hand begins to shake.

The panic is rising and she drops the knitting. Bea takes hold of her left hand with her right and digs her nails into the flesh causing tiny spots of blood to appear. Her whole body tenses up and her heels lift from the floor involuntarily, toes pressing into wood. Her chest is tight and she fights for breath. Then a terrible cramp rips through her left calf and her body jerks. The muscles are steel rigs, the pain is intense, and Bea moans as she lowers her feet. Her body shaking, she gasps with the effort to rid herself of the cramp.

Closing her eyes, she thinks of Evie as a baby. Of Ma in the garden and of Evangeline. Then the heel is down, the muscles relax and the pain disappears as suddenly as it arrived. Bea slumps in the seat and her breathing becomes regular again.

Her hair has come loose from her chignon and she lets it fall. She walks off the cramp and washes the bloodstained hand before picking up the wool. Its soft pliable form dispels the panic and she instructs her body to relax, breathe, sink into the cushions.

The first time she had a panic-attack was when Evie announced she was pregnant. There were hugs and congratulations, plans were made for the layette and the christening and everything was fine up until the point Evie had asked Bea to be godmother. They were having a pub lunch out by the river and Bea had left early making her excuses. She drove home in a state of high anxiety and, once the door of the house had been slammed shut, she succumbed. That first time she thought she was going to die.

Bea picks up her needles. Looking at the instructions for the cardigan, she realises she's made a mistake. It's quite near the beginning and it's a shame as her work must be unravelled to fix it. There are many rows to unpick to make it perfect.

Twenty-Eight

Bea 1995

The slight irritations of life seem to have come to the forefront at Falmouth Road: finding the shampoo bottle empty whilst she's in the bath; a split fingernail catching in her hair; flying ants and tomato blight all conspire to spoil what is by any measure, good times. When she thinks of the past and compares it to the present, she can do nothing but bless the days.

It's the end of August. Evie will be going back to school after a summer of holidays and school clubs. She's thriving, deemed bright by her teachers, popular with the other children in her class and curious about everything. A conglomeration of both her parents' talents and looks.

Ma is out. She has taken a sewing kit down to a lock-up garage in Latimer Road and is helping Evangeline with last-minute adjustments to costumes for Carnival. She's been involved with the preparations for years now.

It keeps her busy but it means the gardening is Bea and Evie's responsibility.

The tomato plants are blighted. They are an irritation, an eyesore and a mark of failure. Bea dons gloves and grabs a fork and is deep into the task of removing them when Nigel peers over the garden wall.

'Tomato blight?'

'I don't know why I bother. We prefer a cutting garden.'

'But home-grown tomatoes taste so much better than anything you can buy in the shops.'

'Only if they're edible, Nige.' Bea throws the diseased plants into a small compost bin and clears up as Nigel comments on the weather. Diplomatic relations have improved since Ma got sober. Bea invites him in for tea and they agree to sit in the garden taking advantage of the summer sun. 'I wish I'd stuck to flowers. They last much longer and go right through the year,' Bea says.

'You have the best garden on the street, you know.' Nigel tells her that there's a duchess living two doors down. She invited him over for a little piano recital one evening and there wasn't much happening in her backyard.

'You mean the old lady with the cats? She's a real duchess?' Bea has had little to do with the recent blow-ins on the street. Their lives are a mystery to her.

'I was asked over for drinks at the big house on the corner once. I got the impression they thought I was someone famous. Their faces when I said I was in import export. Such a sight.' Nigel giggles. 'I was completely ignored after that, so I hoovered the canapés.'

Bea laughs. 'I know what you mean. Whenever Derek

visits, he can't step out the front door without some passer-by giving him a business card. We use the rat run through the estate to get to the Bella.'

Nigel tells her he is leaving. Retiring to his place in France and selling up. She almost chokes on her tea when he tells her the price he has agreed on the house. He leaves, telling her she can have his piano. 'I know a young Vietnamese girl. Very talented in her own right but needs the money,' Nigel says. 'Evie could have lessons.' He promises to keep in touch and Bea hopes he will.

Later, Ma arrives home. There is a letter for her on the telephone table. She follows Bea into the kitchen and opens it. Another rejection letter. Gaps in her employment details, her criminal record, which Ma insists she must declare on her application forms, all lead to her receiving polite letters wishing her luck in her future career. She runs a hand through her hair. 'Fuck's sake, they don't even want me in Boots.'

'Here, stop that. They don't know what they're missing.' Bea smiles. 'You don't need to work, Ma. I'm working and you've got Evie to take care of. What's the problem?'

'Days can be very long. It's very tempting…'

'I have to go to Paris again. I can't get out of it.'

'I'll be fine, love. I won't—'

'I know. I know. You've done so well.'

Ma fetches a sturdy box that once contained chocolates. It's from a time before Bea was born. From a time she believes when her dad loved her mum and bought her nice things. The box is full of Ma's paperwork. A bulging lid rammed down onto rejection letters and application forms, benefit statements and television licences going back years.

'Why do you keep the rejections? Isn't it depressing?'

'I need to keep them as evidence for Unemployment Benefit. Once upon a time you could get a council house by turning up and telling a sob story. Now they need a paper trail for forty quid a week.'

Bea travels to Paris on the new Eurostar. Despite the diversion of work, there is a moment when she is aware of the weight of the water above her. A panic rises. The image of water pouring down through the roof of the tunnel and dripping through the carriage sends a shiver down her spine.

She glances at the passengers across the aisle and they are concentrating very hard on their files. Then she realises that travelling miles under water is no different to travelling miles above the ground in the air. They are twin elements. Both could cause catastrophe and death is possible in both situations. The moment passes.

Paris is beautiful at this time of year. The season brings mellow autumnal colours to the streets and she catches the smell of chestnuts roasting as she leaves the underground. It reminds her of Portobello.

The private show takes place in a run-down church off Boulevard-St-Germain. The models, in their flamboyant glossy couture, look extraordinary against the backdrop of graffitied walls and black mould. The stone statues of Mary and St Christopher look down with disdain at the near nakedness of the women and the brazen young boys backstage. Bea sees Derek and knows he is finding his

Zen. He is carefully arranging flowers in the cracked font as people move across the space; models, hair and make-up, lighting crew and photographers are all working like ants. They seem reluctant to raise their voices, avoiding the echoes that rebound from the vaulted ceiling.

Bea moves into work mode as soon as she arrives. 'Derek, it's impossible. I don't have enough people to cope. We need to get another pair of hands or drop a set.' She ticks off a list.

'Whatever you say. Just remember the profit margins are almost zero.'

'You're not a charity. Get a new business manager.'

'Would you like to do it? I've never seen anyone work a clipboard like you.' Derek picks up scissors to snip the ties from a bunch of white lilies. 'Welcome to Paris, Bea.'

'I'm not the accountant, Derek. And am I going to be the only one stitching the models into their clothes?'

'Don't be so uptight, darling. We're in Paris. I'm out to get laid after the show. How about you?'

A DJ appears with his decks and sets up too close to the stage. He blocks the view for the cameras.

'Hey! Get out of there.' Derek marches across the gritty floor. 'You can't put your kit there, love.'

'*Tu ne peux pas rester là,*' Bea says.

'Vamoose,' Derek offers, shooing him away.

The young man gestures towards the chapel door. '*Mais je suis reservé.*' There is a stream of incomprehensible French before Bea realises the misunderstanding.

'He thinks you're asking him to leave.' She turns to the

young man and gestures like an air steward showing the passengers the exit doors. She points first to the kit then to where he should move. '*Désolé. Par ici, s'il vous plaît.*'

The boy gathers his decks and speakers, wires trailing across the aisle, and the mood calms as he fills the chapel with the Pet Shop Boys.

'Crisis averted. Give the lad a Kate Moss baseball cap and we're good to go,' Derek sighs as he returns to the flowers. His whole demeanour adjusts to the task as he arranges the lilies and gladioli using oasis foam to keep them upright. Satisfied with the overall display, Derek wipes his hands on a towel.

As the day unfolds, backstage becomes more and more frenetic. Catastrophes need to be averted: people on edge require their egos to be boosted and pills are administered where necessary. The show is due to begin at eight p.m. and Bea hasn't stopped. Finally, moments before the show, she flops into a chair next to Derek to catch her breath.

'You do love this job, don't you?' Derek asks.

Bea does love the job, mostly. It had rescued her. 'Why do you ask?'

'I've been asked to relocate to Paris. The money men want more shows, more events like this. I'm thinking about it.'

'What's that got to do with me?'

'I'm asking you if you want to come with. It's one of the conditions I've asked for. That you get to come along.' Derek stares at her expectantly.

'No, Derek. I can't come with you. It's impossible.'

'Will you think about it?' Derek sighs heavily. But she

has no time to explain. Someone is signalling frantically for them to come backstage and they must go and avert another catastrophe before the show begins.

Derek doesn't go out afterwards. He joins Bea on her return journey to London. 'There would be more money. A relocation package. You know. Set you and Rose up in an apartment. Li'l sis can go to school here. It's good for children to learn another language.'

'Please stop.' Bea is tearful. She hasn't had a break all day. Her bones ache from the sheer physicality of her job. 'To tell you the truth, doing the shows is the worst part.' She wipes a tear from her cheek.

'Bea? What's up?'

'It's all veneer, isn't it? The shows I mean. Not the clothes. The clothes are works of art but there's no glamour in sewing kids into catwalk couture. I can't count the times I've held scarves around the neck of a model while she hurls her guts up into her handbag.'

Bea is saddened and angered by the young models who have succumbed. Bulimia, anorexia and heroin addiction are a dark, frightening presence in her world. 'Sometimes, Derek. Sometimes, I want to rip the clothes off them and tell them to go home. Go back to their parents, get some help.' She realises the real reason she can't bear backstage is the lifetime's worth of addiction she's dealt with at home.

The press praise Derek's genius. He wins a medal from the Queen in her Birthday Honours list for his services to the fashion industry. Rose has squirrelled away a copy of *Vogue*. There is a photo of the Paris show where Bea can be seen in the background. Ma loves the shot, says Bea looks serious, intelligent, beautiful against the skinny ghosts that surround her daughter. 'Heroin chic, they're calling it on *Woman's Hour*. Makes me sick,' Ma says as she stores the *Vogue* magazine in one of her boxes.

Derek announces he has turned down the job offer. And Bea is delighted. She wants nothing more than life to carry on as it has done since Ma got sober.

The welcome interlude of calm and normality at Falmouth Road comes to an end when one night, a woman calls unannounced. She is probably in her sixties, older than Ma by ten years at least. She's smartly dressed and has a wrinkled brown face and neck as if she has spent too much time in the sun. Her raincoat is a decent cut, as is her hair. She announces herself as Moira O'Dowd. With barely a blink of an eye, Bea leads her father's wife to the lounge and offers her a seat, switching on the lamp against the dusk.

'What's she doing here?' Rose whispers. She is stacking plates on the draining board.

'She wants to talk to you.'

'What's she got to say to me except she hates me, and I ruined her life?'

'She won't say that. And anyway, she doesn't look like a woman living a ruined life. She's probably come here to thank you.'

'Tell her I can't see her. Tell her I'm ill or something. I can't, Bea. I can't…' Ma twists a tea towel around and around as if she were wringing it out. Her knuckles are white.

'Come on. I'll be with you. You've got to be a little bit curious.'

Moira O'Dowd sits tall and stiff on the edge of the sofa. She is partly in shadow, her face lit by the hefty brass lamp. 'I have something for you, Rose,' she says without a trace of malice.

Ma seems small, swallowed up by the opposite sofa. Homely in her track pants and cardigan.

'What?' Bea asks. She doesn't hide the truculent tone. She thinks the woman has a damn cheek being here.

'I'm leaving England. Moving abroad.'

'Why are you here? There's nothing for you here,' Ma says.

'I told you, Rosemary, I have something for you. My husband John was declared dead, you know. Or maybe you don't? I'm sorry.' Moira looks from one to the other. 'He's been missing for over six years. So the law declared him deceased. The legal wrangling over his estate went on and on. You've no idea how complicated these things are.' Moira doesn't sound anything like a grieving widow. More like a homeowner having improvements done. 'I had his safe opened and found these.'

Moira hands Ma a long velvet jewellery case and a pink envelope. She avoids looking at them. Instead, she plunges them down the side of the sofa as if the box contained heroin.

Moira smiles and shakes her head. 'I suppose there really is nothing more to say is there? I've not come here expecting an apology if that's what you're thinking.'

'I've no intention of apologising,' Ma says softly. 'For anything.'

'He was selfish and dangerous and we're all better off without him,' Bea says.

Moira moves her head into the lamplight. It catches the saliva glistening like slug trails around the inside of her mouth. 'You should have more manners.'

'You were curious, weren't you? Wanted to see my mother. The house.' Bea presses her knees into the hard edge of the coffee table.

'I know this house. John was going to move us all here. But I didn't think much of the area.'

'A bit too cosmopolitan for you?' Bea asks.

'I won't deny it. I like my coffee *con leche*.'

Ma sits upright, straightening out her back, matching the older woman's height. 'I'm sorry for my daughter's rudeness, but I won't tolerate bigotry in this house.'

It seems to Bea as if Ma is acting like a potential employee. She is hesitant and nervous. When she admonished Moira for her comment, there was a hint of deference.

'I suppose Tommy handled John's will,' Bea says.

'You know Beresford?' Moira fixes a cast-iron glare on Bea. 'Did you work on John together to get this house?'

It's obvious why Moira has come. It's nothing to do with old gifts. She wants the house.

'He used to say she was like his old granny,' Ma says softly.

'God help us.' Moira smiles at this and there is a moment when Bea senses an affinity between the two women. She wonders what would happen if she left the room. Would they bond over her namesake?

Moira stands and smoothing the skirt of the raincoat,

she looks down from left to right as if checking she has everything before boarding a flight. Bea does this herself at airports and in hotel lobbies. She leaves. There is a sweet fragrance that lingers on. Ma runs a hand across her stomach.

'He smelled of that perfume when he came over. I used to ask him about it and he'd say he was showing a client around a house. He was such a liar.'

Ma turns off the lamp that had lit Moira so unflatteringly. They open the box together. Inside is a string of emeralds and diamonds, brilliant in the dim light of the living room. The card has a pink crib on the front. It reads:

On the birth of our daughter Beatrice Mary O'Dowd.
Well done, Rose. Love John.

Twenty-Nine

Bea and Rose 1996

It's Saturday. The piano lesson has ended. Evie's teacher is preparing her for the grade one exam and informs Bea her progress is good and that she will pass.

She leaves and the greetings and goodbyes are all whispered, as Ma is upstairs in her room. Bea has made bread and soup. She tells Evie to take the bread out in five minutes and to watch the soup, while she goes up to persuade Ma to join them for lunch.

As she mounts the stairs, she involuntarily sniffs the air for the smell of alcohol and listens out for Ma's troublesome hacking cough. She is relieved the air smells of bath foam and the bedroom is silent. 'I've made soup,' Bea says, opening the curtains to allow daylight into the room. The rain slides down the window to obscure the street outside.

Ma lies on her back, her eyes fixed on the ceiling. 'I don't feel like eating.' Her voice is cloaked in accumulated spit.

'Smell that bread. How can you resist?' Bea sits by her.

Ma is a ghost who has forgotten to go back to the grave during the day. Her unwashed hair is spread in greasy strands where she has pulled it up away from her neck. 'It's been like this since that bitch visited.' Bea sighs.

'It's nothing to do with her. I have a cough is all.'

'I'm going to smother my bread in butter today. It's a smother-your-bread-in-butter day if ever there was one.' Bea smiles. It is a wasted smile as Ma doesn't see it. The rain has turned to hail and it's clattering on the windowpane.

'Go downstairs and eat with Evie,' Ma says. Her eyes are closed against the light from the window.

'No. I've baked bread. I've made soup for you.'

'I can't stomach your wholemeal bread nonsense. Please leave me alone.' She swallows. Her lips are paper dry and there is a strong smell of nicotine that seems to rise off the pillow.

'Let me ring the doctor for you, Ma.'

'Don't call me Ma. You never called me that before Evie came along.' Ma's words are so bitter they cut through the mucus.

'It was for Evie's sake.'

'I can't go on, Bea. It's too much for me.'

'Don't speak like that. You can get better. You need to get the right treatment, that's all.'

'What if I don't want to?'

'I need you.'

Her mother rolls her eyes. 'Just the same selfish madam. If it's what Bea wants, Bea's gotta have it.'

Bea is taken aback by the spite in Ma's voice. She

remembers John saying those words, had worked out a long time ago he used them to get at her mother. Callous and intended to cause damage, those words and a thousand others like them were the fragile glass filaments that formed Bea and Rose's relationship.

'Are you giving up on us, Ma?'

'Giving up? I gave up the day you came home from Sussex.' Ma coughs and Bea watches as a tear trickles down to stain the white pillowcase. 'Don't mind me. I talk nothing but shit these days.'

'Come down to eat with us. Please.'

Ma turns away. 'I love you, Bea.'

'I love you too, Rose.'

Bea leaves the bedroom door slightly ajar. She is shaking as she descends the stairs, wishing Ma would throw the covers back and scamper down to eat with them as she used to do before Moira's visit. Just as she did when times were normal and ordinary.

Bea slumps down on the middle stair. If Ma keeps on refusing to see the doctor, she will never get better. She will die. No one, not the nuns at Holy Trinity or Evangeline, have been able to persuade her. And neither has Bea.

Bea returns to Evie, who has allowed the soup to bubble angrily.

'Evie, for God's sake.' She moves the pan off the stove. 'I can't trust you with anything.'

'But I took the bread out and—'

'Watch both. The bread *and* the soup.'

'Sorry, I didn't mean to—'

Bea spots the crust of bread and the butter knife

with its yellow blob on the blade. 'You're eating the bread already.'

'I was testing it.'

'Testing it? You're a greedy guts.' Bea turns away from her. 'You're just like Ma, can't tell the truth even if it would save your life.'

'Why are you being so mean to me?' Evie shouts and doesn't wait for an answer. As she storms out of the kitchen, she passes close to Bea and the air between them is filled with a familiar static.

***

Thank goodness for Evie. She has become Rose's shield against Bea's onslaughts. She's tall like her father, with big bones. Rose takes comfort in Evie's physical presence as if she were a strong boy. Sometimes Evie stands up to Bea.

It's early evening. Rose is sitting up in bed and smoking her last cigarette when Evie arrives at the door with a tray. She's still in her school uniform and coat. Rose had heard the noises from the kitchen as Evie made a sandwich. Ham with salad cream in white sliced bread. None of that wholegrain nonsense. As it's Evie, Rose takes a bite and chews, long and slow.

'Evie, you need to do me a favour.'

'What's that, Ma?' Evie opens a packet of crisps. She pours half of the contents onto Rose's plate and eats the rest.

Rose leans forward and whispers. 'I need you to get me some fags.'

'I can't get fags. I'm too young.'

'I'll give you a couple of quid for going.'

Evie sucks the salt off her fingers. 'I can't, Ma. Bea will kill me. Sorry.'

Rose crashes back onto the headboard. The tray slips and Evie just manages to keep it from falling to the floor. 'It's like I'm a prisoner in my own home.'

'I can't get you fags, Ma. Bea says they are really bad for you. They're making you really ill.'

'It's not the cigarettes making me ill. It's Bea.' Rose's chest heaves with the effort to catch her breath.

'Why don't you go and see the doctor?' She licks each greasy finger and sits back down on the bed. 'Bea says—'

'Bea says this, and Bea says that. Sod Bea.' She lifts herself up and her excitement brings a rumbling in her throat. 'I need to tell you something about your sister—'

She stops when she realises there is no point without the evidence. Bea has instilled in Evie that same instinct for proof that Bea has perfected over the years. Evie would want evidence. Bea would lie without it and Rose would look a fool. Evie is expectant but the moment is lost. 'Your sister used to wet the bed,' she says at last.

Evie cocks her head to one side and rolls her eyes and Rose is reminded of Trevor. It was the look he used when she'd said something crackpot and stupid. 'Don't tell her I told you.'

'I won't.' Evie slides off the bed scooping up the tea tray.

The door bangs shut, and Rose is alone. Bea will be home in an hour. There's no point searching her room. She will wait until tomorrow and get up after the girls have left.

'God, what a bloody mess,' she mutters. She blames Moira O'Dowd. It's Moira who has ruined everything. She brought emeralds into the house. They are known to be unlucky. The stones seem to contain globules of poison. It was a deliberate act of revenge. They were probably stolen, knowing John. A toxic gift made to wreak havoc on her and her house.

The night of Moira's visit, Rose had sat in front of her knowing what had happened to John and unable to speak. Not even to offer condolences to his widow. His wife and children would never know what she knew about John's death. And there's the problem. There are too many secrets and keeping them is unbearable.

Rose wipes her watery eyes. A coughing fit brings her head down over the side of the bed. Her ribs ache and her throat feels as if it were cut. This is what you get when you've done things that go against God. Evangeline would understand. God watches. God judges. She should go to confession. Rose lowers her head onto her pillow and cries herself to sleep.

She is woken by the sound of her bedroom door shutting. Either Bea or Evie has left a breakfast tray on the bedside table. Evie, she thinks. Bea would have snuck in and left the room in silence. The house is empty. Rose pulls on a pair of towelling shorts and a sweatshirt. Stiff from lying in bed a whole day and a night, she stumbles like a newly born foal finding its feet. She swills the warm milky tea to rid her mouth of the scurf that clings to her teeth.

Bea's bedroom smells of expensive lotion. The

sun pours in and bathes every surface with soft light. Although the furniture is old and worn in places, it is cared for and the wood is polished so that it creates pools of sunshine. The old childhood bed has been replaced with a white metal double one covered in a soft white counterpane. There is a camelia motif on a rug by the bed. A pair of satin slippers are placed on the rug. Rose imagines Bea slipping her delicate feet straight into them as she gets out of bed.

She remembers carrying the rug upstairs with Bea when the room still smelled of new paint. It was one they had found rolled up outside a house in Elgin Crescent bearing a "Take Me" sign. Was it after or before Trevor? She can't quite remember.

Rose begins her search, dragging her own chair into Bea's room to stand on, fearing that her footprints will give her away. She starts with the top of the wardrobe where she finds a thin layer of dust and a wide-brimmed sunhat. Inside, there's a high shelf where Bea keeps her winter hats and gloves. Then the bottom of the wardrobe where a couple of overnight bags stand ready for her trips to Europe.

These yield nothing more than used travel tickets, a hand mirror and small packs of tissues. She runs a hand along the shelves of the old kidney-shaped dressing table, catching the rose-patterned curtain so that it wraps around her wrist. Nothing interesting there.

She's craving a cigarette but ignores the dryness in her throat and fumbles around. She lifts the mattress, though this causes her some distress and starts a coughing fit that leaves her on her hands and knees. She scans the carpet for spittle.

In a drawer, she finds an out-of-date pack of contraceptive pills. Rose imagines Bea having a frank discussion with Evie about periods, sex and boys. Bea would have a set of leaflets from the health centre. She squeezes a pill out of its bubble, and it lies in her palm. Had she talked about contraception when Bea was a teenager? Was she the most unqualified mum in the world when it came to handing out advice about boys?

Rose makes herself a tea and thinks about going to the corner shop to buy cigarettes but can't be bothered to get dressed. Instead she starts the process of searching the drawers and cupboards of the sideboard. She holds little hope of finding anything in the rooms they share.

The kitchen drawers yield nothing of value, so she returns to the front room to watch daytime television. It's impossible to concentrate on the good-looking fella in the sharp suit talking about fox hunting and the topic fails to motivate her. She thinks about buying cigarettes again then switches on the radio, using it as background noise while she rips out the contents of the sideboard once more. She wasn't thorough enough the first time.

Rose hears a key in the door and Evie appears. She is busy tucking away the old gas bills and TV licences in the big sideboard. The door won't shut, and Evie drops her rucksack and kneels down beside her.

'What are you looking for?' Evie pushes the contents back into the cupboard.

'It's for you. Something you should see, but I can't

find it so never mind. I'll do the tea.' Rose stands and immediately keels over, dizzy from a rush of blood to her head.

Evie has arranged Rose so that she is lying on her side where she fell. She is under a thick blanket and its weight bears down on her bones. Her face feels the chill of autumn seeping through the floorboards. The back of the sofa takes a few seconds to come into focus and black dots swim in her vision. Evie must be talking to Bea on the phone.

'Don't tell her nothing. Don't fuss. I'm fine. Get off that phone…' Rose's voice comes in shards, broken by the weakness of her lungs. She tries to move but her head spins. Before she loses consciousness completely she realises Evie isn't talking to Bea. She's calling an ambulance.

Thirty

Evie 1997

Princess Diana's face has been on every newspaper front cover and there are pages and pages devoted to her. Evie gets it. She was young, beautiful and died in a horrible car crash.

The Prime Minister had referred to her as the People's Princess the other day and every second person on the news speaks reverentially about how they were permitted to stand in the sunshine of her saintly presence. Can anyone living be that perfect? Evie doubts it.

She has spent the last year watching her mother disappear. Ma is a scarecrow in a pale blue gown, attached to a tube. Bea explains the bag on the end of the tube is feeding her a drug called morphine. Evie imagines it as a coldness hitting her veins and making her insides shiver. She thinks of ice lollies that numb her brain and wonders if morphine being dripped into Ma's body feels the same. Does Ma think she's eating an ice lolly? That would be good.

She has learned not to flinch when she holds Ma's hand, and she believes that Ma must know she's holding it, because sometimes she squeezes her fingers. There is this tiny flicker of hope every time the muscles contract. But she keeps overhearing Bea saying it's nearly time. She had said it to the doctor on the phone and whispered it to the community nurse.

It is Saturday. There are no piano lessons scheduled for the indefinite future and Sylvester and Tish are bringing Evangeline over for a visit today. Evie stands watching the kettle, waiting for it to boil. The old lady walks with a stick now, but she's always smart. She has a pale blue coat and a wool scarf and claret-coloured hat.

Sylvester ruffles Evie's hair. 'Mum's wearing her West Ham strip today. What d'you reckon?'

'It looks nice and cheerful,' Evie says.

'Spare pillowcases. You can never have enough.' Tish is talking in whispers to Bea.

'How is it today?' Sylvester asks.

Evie wonders what *it* is. Her teachers are always saying you have to be more specific with your nouns.

'Much the same,' Bea says as if she fully understands.

'And how's things with you? No Sarah today?' Bea asks.

Sylvester explains she's out with a couple of friends. Then Bea asks Evangeline how she is and it seems like any ordinary day.

'Legs aren't what they used to be but everything is okay upstairs.' Evangeline points to her temple and smiles.

'We're trying to convince her to come and live with us,' Trish says.

But Evangeline shakes her head. 'As long as I have the Lord and the lift, I'm fine where I am.' Evangeline's eyes disappear into her crinkly skin when she giggles. Bea smiles but it's like her smile muscles are disconnected from the rest of her face.

Tish and Sylvester announce that they are on the way to the big Sainsbury's in Ladbroke Grove. 'Everyone goes there now,' Tish says. 'You can park at Sainsbury's and load the car up. Can't do that down the Bella.'

'And you can get everything in one place,' Sylvester says.

'You like Portobello Road, don't you, Evie?' Evangeline looks at her goddaughter.

Evie nods.

'You'll be able to go on your own soon.' Sylvester chips in. 'It's a rite of passage. Strolling down the Bella with your mates and checking out the record stalls and all the cool clothes.'

'And buying watermelon in the summer. That's what we did,' Tish says.

'Next summer, you and Sarah can go off on your own,' Bea says as the company around the table rises. Sylvester and Tish leave and Bea takes Evangeline into the back lounge. This is where the paramedics have set up a hospital bed for Ma.

Evie doesn't know whether she is invited so sits herself down on the stairs, fists under her chin and waits. After a while, Evangeline emerges. 'What're you doing, sweetheart?'

'Nothing. I mean I'm deciding what to do.'

Evangeline holds the banister as if it's propping her up.

'You know about Heaven, right?'

Evie nods.

'Rose will find a place in Heaven. I know that is a true thing.'

'How?'

'She is kind.'

'Like Princess Diana?' Evie asks.

'Like Princess Di. The first time I met Rose, I was struggling, and she was kind to me. She was kind to my boys. Your Ma went down the wrong path sometimes in her life, but she came back right in the end. As sure as there is the big Sainsbury's in Ladbroke Grove, there is a Heaven where your Ma will live when she's left you.'

Evie gulps. She hasn't really thought about Heaven, or the angels that will take Ma there. 'Will she have a garden and her Rolling Stones records?'

'Yes, she will.' Evangeline shifts her weight from one leg to the other. 'She once told me she wanted to be a shop manager. She can have her own place up there.'

'Will there be cigarettes?'

'If there are cigarettes, they will be the kind she can smoke without making her ill. You see, it's her own special heaven.'

'Will Saint Peter let her in the pearly gates, though?' Evie's scripture tumbles into her head.

'As sure as that revolving door at Sainsbury's will whoosh Tish and Sylvester inside. Come, darling.' Evangeline turns awkwardly and re-enters the lounge to sit beside Ma. Evie follows. But for Evangeline's soft prayers, the house is silent.

Evie stands behind the old lady. She sees the slight mound Ma makes under the bedspread. Her godmother's blue-coated back looks solid and reassuring, as if it's a wall protecting her mother from the disease that's killing her. Evie searches for angels at each corner of the bed but there are none, just the drip with the lolly juice.

Evangeline stops praying and holds Ma's hand. There is the sound of a soft whistle from Ma's lips, the one Evie listened to during the hospital visits. Only this time it's louder; there are no beeps or buzzes to drown it out. A mouse's whistle. No, quieter. The sound you would hear if garden spiders could talk. Sylvester and Tish come to pick up Evangeline and it's just Bea and Evie and Ma once again.

The house seems to bend inwards on itself. Everything appears softened. The walls, the doorframes, the floors are all made of wool. Inanimate objects whisper instructions: the curtains tell Bea when they need to be drawn; the kettle tells Evie when to fill it and the post slips onto the doormat and it tells her to pick the letters up. It's as if the house knows what to do and this reassures Evie as she has no idea what will happen at the end or when it will end.

Bea lights perfumed sticks and waves them about. The smoke rises and weaves its fragrant way around the living room. Evie leans on the doorframe when Bea lifts Ma's hand and runs a sponge from armpit to fingertip. It is as if she is watching a ballet with just two principal dancers. She can't hear what Bea is saying and thinks it's not her business. It's secret talk.

A priest comes to the house. He stands tall and black at the foot of the hospital bed and murmurs a prayer. Evie stands close to Bea and grips her hand. He makes the sign of the cross and Bea does the same. Unlike the priest her 'Amen' is uttered through streaming tears. Evie listens out for the spiders talking. But there is silence.

Ma dies and Evie looks up to follow the angels guiding her soul to Heaven. Somewhere beyond the dark clouds, St Peter unlocks the big iron gates. Or are they revolving doors these days, like the ones at the big Sainsbury's?

'I am not wearing that thing.' Evie stands in front of her sister, her coat buttoned up to the neck.

Bea is holding out a pink woollen beret. It doesn't go with her smart black coat. 'It's freezing cold. You'll need it.'

'It's a baby's hat. I am not wearing it.'

'You have to wear it. It's respectful.'

'I'm not wearing it,' Evie scowls, pursing her lips.

'Bloody wear the thing or you're not coming!' Bea screams.

Some relatives Evie has never met arrive at the cemetery. A grey-haired lady in a heavy black coat is introduced. She is Great-Aunt Vi and she is with her son, Kevin. He stands tall and alone in a grey suit and bulky jacket. It has a logo on the breast pocket that says Dunlop. He has driven Vi from West London. Neither are wearing hats. Vi greets Evangeline, who she remembers from Evie's christening, apparently. Evangeline wears a black hat with a net that covers her eyes. She looks very respectful.

Ma's friend Carol and her husband talk in low whispers to Vi then Carol leaves her husband's side to come and hold Bea's hand. 'She was a one, your mum,' Carol says, her eyes watery and soft. 'We was always getting up to mischief when we were young. I'm so sorry, love.'

'I'd love to hear about that sometime.' Bea smiles.

Evie has met Carol at the house a couple of times. One time, she brought a packet of Opal Fruits and lined up the sweets so that each flavour was shared equally. Carol had said it was what she used to do with Ma when they were young.

Sylvester and Tish are here, and they've brought Sarah, who is glum in her black coat. Evie wonders if she looks the same as her friend or whether her outwards are as confused as her inwards. Tish and Sarah are wearing hats and so is Derek, Bea's boss. He's here with his friend, a man in a smart overcoat and a hat.

Evangeline's other son, Linton, has driven all the way from Bristol and Evie joins the Stanleys as Bea moves amongst the static groups of mourners. They hold out their arms as she approaches, ready with their quiet condolences. Evie's face is cold, and her hands are numb inside her gloves. She is glad of the woollen beret after all. She hadn't meant to shout.

The sheltered walkway that leads to the chapel of rest is long and narrow. There is a patchwork rug of wreaths and bouquets lining the marble wall. Some are beautiful, seasonal in their muted colours of orange and blue, wrapped in paper and tied with twine.

Some are shop-bought, probably from Sainsbury's and Evie is fascinated by the bright gaudy colours and the snap of the plastic wrapping. Bea doesn't like supermarket flowers. There is not enough thought given to buying a ready-prepared bunch, she says. Much better to work with a florist to choose the best blooms for the occasion. The wreath she had made with Bea out of their own flowers is nowhere to be seen. Someone pats her arm. She looks up and Bea is there. Her sister's face muscles are coordinated into a genuine smile. Evie hears the opening bars of *Ava Maria* and is led through to the chapel of rest. Their wreath has been placed on Ma's coffin.

During the internment, the wind blows strands of her hair out of the hat, she tries to tuck them back under, but her gloves are too cumbersome. She can't take them off as she must throw dirt on the coffin. Bea holds one hand as she scoops up soil from the graveside with her other and throws it. Vi throws in a single cigarette, declaring it a family tradition. Bea mutters, 'For God's sake.'

There is a sort of theatre interval between the ceremony and the cars arriving to take them back to the house. Bea leads her to where a vaguely familiar figure is standing.

'Evie, you remember Sharon?' Bea says.

'Dear Bea, and this is little Evie all grown up.' Sharon places a gloved hand under Evie's chin as if inspecting her teeth. 'You've got that same cheeky look your mother had when I first met her.' Evie remembered her stiff blonde hairdo and bright red lips. Now she looks like a farmer's wife in a nursery book, plump and red-cheeked, wrapped in a black woollen shawl over her wax coat. It turns out she is a farmer. 'We're in Nottinghamshire, pigs and dairy. You must come and visit.'

'We'd love to,' Bea says.

There is an old man who leans on a walking stick with such force Evie thinks it will break under him and he will fall to the ground. Bea fails to mention his name. This is odd as she is normally so diligent about introductions. He removes his hat and bows slightly. The hand clutching the cane is bright red. He has beady eyes in a hamster face.

'My condolences, Beatrice,' he says.

'Thanks, Mr Beresford. You'd be welcome at the house.'

'I'm so sorry. I can't do that. But, dear Bea, I wanted to tell you that your mother was a splendid person. A truly funny and kind lady.'

Evie watches the old man walk a tremulous path across the car park towards a big black car. A smartly dressed man helps him to sit in the back seat then drives him away. Evie thinks the old man hasn't got long to live. But he has already lived longer than Ma and that's just unfair.

As she is led to the car that will take them home, the other guests disperse. Car doors slam and the gravel crunches underfoot. Vi is offered a seat in their car but declines, preferring to stay with her son. Evangeline joins them instead.

Evie looks through the window and traces the little path that leads up to where Ma rests. The crooked steps disappear into glossy evergreen bushes. The mound where her mother is interred is no longer visible and she leans into the glass, desperate to hide her face.

Evangeline offers a clean white handkerchief. 'Let it out, Evie. Let it all out, my darling.'

At the wake, Evie serves tea in the best cups. Kevin accepts his with enthusiasm, as if relieved he has something to hold. Vi admires Bea's elegant black dress. 'So, you work in fashion, Beatrice. That must be very interesting. You must get good discounts on clothes.'

'I make my clothes, mostly,' Bea explains.

'Your mother was going to be a model at one stage. She was beautiful. You've got her looks.'

Evie notices the old woman glance over in her direction before addressing Bea again. Vi had the briefest frown on her face, a quizzical wrinkling of the forehead. Evie ignores her and walks around the room, offering up a plate of sliced ginger cake.

'Will you manage money-wise? You'll be needing a few bob to get by, I expect,' Vi says.

'We'll manage. But thank you.'

'Oh, I wasn't offering, darling. Don't get me wrong. If you was short, I could help you out with a couple of quid now and again But that's all.'

'Sorry, I thought—'

Bea's embarrassment seems to radiate towards her like a laser beam. Evie can feel it inside her chest. Her own face is warm on her sister's behalf. Vi never came near when Ma was in hospital. Never offered to sit with her to give them a break. Only Evangeline and Tish had insisted that Bea get fresh air or that Evie needed to get out of the house. Even Sarah came to say goodbye. But not Ma's aunt. Not her flesh and blood.

Bea brushes past her catching her arm. 'Evie, get Vi another tea, would you?'

Bea moves away and the shadow she had created disappears. Vi sits in full sun, all leathery wrinkles and quivering jowls. Evie has a picture in her mind of Ma on a good day. Like Princess Diana, Ma will never grow old.

Thirty-One

Evie January 2020

Scarlet arrives. Pink and warm with fingers curling and uncurling to touch the air. Max cries and Evie is euphoric. The midwife takes a photograph of all three of them which Max immediately posts online. When they get home, Max's mother, Judith, and Bea are waiting. Evie brings Scarlet over the threshold and they both applaud as if they are extras in a production of Handel. The Queen of Sheba has just arrived.

'You'll have to bring her to London, so I can show her off to Evangeline and Derek,' Bea says. Evie can't remember her sister ever smiling so broadly and for so long as when she holds the baby. She has to prize Scarlet away from Bea to put her in the crib.

'Where is the name from?' Bea asks. 'Is it from your side, Judith?'

'No. I thought it was from yours.'

'It's completely uninherited,' Max says. 'We couldn't risk offending anyone, so we went for something new to the family.'

'It's not that at all, Max. Don't listen to him.' Evie looks at both her relatives. 'We just liked the name, and by coincidence, she does have the reddest hair I've ever seen.'

They discuss the inheritance of the red gene. A red-haired baby born in the depth of winter makes the name seem so perfect. Bea asks about the baby's middle name.

'We thought Mary,' Max says. 'There's lots of Marys on my side.'

'I'm a Mary. That's my middle name.' Bea sits bolt upright.

'Mary it is then.'

They all raise a glass to Scarlet Mary Ryan.

Bea has brought flowers from the little stall by the station. A flamboyant arrangement of pink and cream tied with an enormous ribbon. Evie imagines she has supervised the florist, as the arrangement is so perfect. She brings news of Evangeline. She's left her flat and has moved into a ground-floor block where a warden is on hand in case of emergency.

'Is it a nursing home?' Judith asks.

'No, sheltered accommodation, they call it. Please don't mention nursing homes when you see her.' This last plea directed at Evie.

'Did Evangeline know Trevor?'

Bea's mouth moves but she doesn't speak. Max's glass is midway to his mouth.

Judith is curious. 'Who? Did I miss something?'

'I mean, did Evangeline know my dad before I was born?'

'Evie is looking for her father,' Max explains.

'Evangeline met him a couple of times. She liked him.' Bea wears her composure like sugar coating and Evie knows the question has thrown her. 'The last I heard he was working on a farm near Dorchester,' Bea says.

'How would you know that? I thought you hardly knew him at all.'

Judith and Max head for the kitchen as if they had simultaneously heard the oven timer bleep.

'Of course I *knew* him. I didn't know him *well*. Is this really the time?'

'So was it Ma who told you he left for Dorchester?'

Bea took a sip of wine. 'She must have done. Why the interrogation?' Her voice is shrill.

'It's funny. In between breastfeeding and sleeping I've been thinking of him. I mean, ever since the birth. Wondering what he's like. How he would feel if he knew he had a grandchild.'

'I told you…'

'But you haven't, Bea. That's the thing.' Max and Judith return and Evie decides she has tormented Bea enough. Her sister's back is straight, her face pale under the sheen of foundation. Evie's intention was to warn Bea, not frighten her. The subject of Trevor is not resolved.

The podcasts she listens to tell her giving birth clouds judgement. New mothers experience a cerebral meltdown while base instincts take over. But Evie feels it's the opposite. There is a steely resolve to get things straight, even if it means upsetting her sister.

When she leaves, Bea hugs Evie as if someone has died rather than given birth and Evie senses her despondency. She expected irritation, anger even, but not this overwhelming sense of resignation.

'You'll come to London soon?' Bea asks.

'Yes, we'll visit Evangeline.'

'And we'll talk about Trevor.'

The task of getting Scarlet ready for the trip to London is like a military operation. She requires an all-in-one winter outfit and a bag packed with the equipment needed for feeding, cleaning and diversion. Fixing the car seat and fastening her in is a new skill. They set off with Evie wondering whether she should have done a local drive first instead of the motorway and London.

In the lounge at Falmouth Road, the boxes and suitcases are much reduced by Bea's culling and are tucked away in a corner. Evie's old Moses basket has been placed on the coffee table and as she lowers Scarlet into it, the wicker sides seem to wrap themselves around her like swaddling.

Scarlet wakes and Bea holds her. There is a light that seems to encircle them, and it brings a sudden unexpected lump to Evie's throat. She chides herself for being mean to Bea. They hold a seamless conversation while Bea feeds Scarlet, burps her and changes her nappy. Then Evie takes photos to show Max and Judith. She asks about Bea's condition.

'I've learned some coping strategies, I have medication, a diet plan. Doctor Khan has been fabulous and they have ruled out the major causes. Some people just get the shakes apparently. It can run in families.' Bea says she wondered if that old witch she was named after shook. It would be sod's law if so but she has no way of confirming this. Bea peers over the side of the basket to watch the baby as she sleeps.

'What does Doctor Khan think, then?' Evie asks.

Bea settles back onto the opposite sofa. 'He asked me if I have any anxieties.'

'And do you?'

'Yes. I do.' Bea clears her throat. 'I need to show you something. Please don't be angry with me.' Bea presents her with a white envelope. Evie has no reason to think this, but she knows it's the empty one she found before. Inside is a small round-edged photograph. Faded colours stand out against a white sky in the background.

'It was what Ma was looking for all those years ago.' Bea's voice is shaky.

At first, Evie doesn't understand. Then she remembers the day Ma collapsed. Evie scrutinises the old photograph. Two people are smiling directly at the camera. There's a tall man holding a baby standing next to Bea. He is broad-chested and the baby is a tiny bundle of white linen against him. Her sister is holding on to one of his arms, her face locked forever in a beaming smile. It's the smile that Bea reserves for Scarlet. Evie's stomach turns over and she feels sick.

'Scarlet looks like him,' Bea says.

'Scarlet looks like Max.' Evie's eyes are fixed on her sister in the photo.

'That's your father, Trevor Williams.' Bea sits with her hands clasped, completely still.

The two people in the picture are standing in a car park. It's a blustery day and strands of their hair are held ransom in the wind. There is a sign in the background that reads *Brighton and H*. The rest is hidden from view by Trevor's broad frame.

'So Ma is taking the photo?' Evie knows the answer but the need to delay the truth is overwhelming.

'She was here in London when this photo was taken.'

Evie looks up and snorts loudly, an involuntary noise in place of coherent speech. She lowers her eyes, stares harder, her brain reluctant to make the connection between the words she's hearing, what she's seeing and what Bea has told her about Trevor.

Evie's belly is flaccid from recent birth, a small bulge remains hidden under baggy clothes. Although the photograph is old and faded, Bea's stomach, peeping out from under the cardigan she is wearing, is the same, a hollow mound that once contained a baby.

In this picture Evie is the baby. In this picture Bea is the mother.

'You give me this now? You keep this from me until now?' The bile rises in her throat. She drops the photo on the coffee table as if it burns. She grabs the baby bag, reaches for Scarlet and attempts to leave. But she hasn't wrapped the baby up for the weather outside. 'Williams?'

She puts Scarlet back into the crib, picks her up, puts her down again while she scrabbles for the baby's outdoor clothes. 'Trevor W... You...'

She picks up one thing and drops another, unable to think straight enough to complete this one simple task.

'Lies. Lies. Lies.' Defeated, she sits down. 'Why all the lies? And… and…why have you waited until now? It's not as if being an unmarried mother was scandalous. I'm not a bastard child born in the sixties.'

Bea raises an eyebrow at this, but otherwise her face is placid.

'I'm sorry,' Evie says, wiping her tears. 'You told me Trevor was Ma's boyfriend.'

'I thought I was doing the right thing. I think I have done the right thing. Look at you. Look at your lovely husband and beautiful Scarlet.'

'Look at who I thought was *my sister*.' Evie shoves the photograph at Bea. It skims across the table and lands at her feet. Scarlet begins to cry.

Evie hunts for a lost mitten.

'You can't drive in this state. Let me call Max.'

'I will call Max. You stay away from me. I don't want to talk to you, and I don't want to see you.'

'That's ludicrous—'

'Ludicrous? What's ludicrous is that you've waited until now to tell me I'm…' She couldn't bring herself to say it. The truth was incomprehensible.

'You should do what you think best.' Bea looks down and straightens the pleats in the skirt she's wearing. Her hands are steady as they run the length of her lap.

'What have you done to us, Bea?'

'Your father wanted nothing to do with you before you were even born.'

'It's not about Trevor. Is it?' As fast as it appeared, the anger drops away. Evie finds the mitten behind a cushion and holds it balled up in her fist while Bea continues fiddling with her skirt. 'Stop that. Look at me.' Evie struggles to get off the sofa. It's old and has no support left in it. 'It's not about Trevor, Bea. It's about you. And Ma. And me.'

Evie walks out holding Scarlet close. She stands in the kitchen to put space between them. The house falls silent but for the tick of the kitchen clock. Evie reaches for her phone to call Max but drops it back in her pocket. What can she say that will make any sense?

It feels cold in the kitchen compared to the lounge and she can smell hyacinths. Evie glances around and sees them on the windowsill above the sink. Blue, fully-formed bell flowers standing neat and compact in their bowl, the ones she bought Bea when she returned the emeralds. She remembers the shop, how overpriced they were but how she knew Bea would love them. That was before she knew Bea was ill. Before she knew about Ma's drinking, the police record and the adopted half-brother.

Evie shudders. Bea has lied to her all her life. Ma must have been complicit in the deception. But how complicit? Ma was always so weak. She always deferred to Bea's intelligence. Her reasoning. She cradles Scarlet in her arms. Evie wants the photograph, but it is on the floor in the room where Bea sits. She needs to see it again to convince herself this whole thing is real.

She returns to the living room. 'Whose idea was it?' Evie asks.

'Ma's.'

'Why would she do that? Why would you agree to it?'

'I was vulnerable. Ma was a nightmare. She said it would be more respectable as Trevor was her boyfriend. So, if there was a new baby in the house, it had to be her baby.'

'But you and Trevor?'

'It was a very bad decision to fall for him, but I did.'

'Couldn't she have adopted me?'

'She thought she wouldn't be allowed. She'd assaulted a police officer, remember.'

Evie sighs. 'Who knows? Apart from us, who else knows?' The house falls back into silence.

Bea looks at a spot of brown damp on the ceiling, placing her hands in her lap. 'Apart from the maternity unit, no one. No that's not true. Evangeline knows. I think. But being Evangeline, she never pried. There's an… implicit acceptance.'

'You should come out with it. Tell her she was right and while you're at it you could apologise for lying to her as well.'

'You're right. I will.' Bea leans forward and places the photograph in front of Evie.

'How could you live with yourself? My christening. For God's sake, Bea. My wedding.'

Evie draws a breath, her heart thumping. 'Were *you* going to put me up for adoption?'

'No. Never. You must believe that. You have every right to be angry. Ma was angry. But we thought it was for the best at the time. I always thought there would be a moment to explain.'

'So, what makes this the right moment?'

'You're a mother yourself now. I thought you might understand.'

'Perhaps your understanding of being a mother is slightly perverse.'

Evie ties the found mitten to the baby's wrists and gives up looking for the second one. She wriggles Scarlet's legs into her outdoor clothes, ready for the journey home.

Bea picks up the missing mitten and gives it to Evie. The moment their fingers touch, Evie is transported back in time. A time of overwhelming confusion and sadness. The old resentment of being the unloved child and the injustice of being ten and losing Ma, swept over her in that touch. It's as if she has lost her all over again.

'You should go to confession, Bea. It may save your soul.'

Thirty-Two

Bea 1986

Brighton is the best thing about Sussex. It's like London but with a seafront. She blags her way into a job at the Golden Hind, a throbbing plane-hangar of a bar at the Kemptown end. It's seedy, very rowdy but the tips are good compared to the smaller places. Along with a young gay crowd who come for the disco, there are older regulars who flee before the music starts.

One night, just as the doors open, Trevor walks in. Unshaven and wearing the fighter pilot jacket. Rose is right. He does look fabulous in it. Bea is serving one of the pre-disco regulars, and she freezes with the pint hovering between them.

'You alright, love?' The customer looks concerned.

'Bea?' Trevor stares at her.

The old man leans over and grins. 'No wonder you're all a-quiver.' He takes his pint and returns to his seat.

Trevor leans his elbows on the counter, and she smells the warm musk he has collected from the drive down from London. She explains she's working part-time.

'Rose didn't mention it.'

'I've only just started. Don't want to tell her in case I mess up.' His teeth are white and straight. She'd never noticed before.

'You. Mess up? Not likely.'

'Don't tell her. Just in case.'

'When's your break?'

They stand amongst the casks out the back and Trevor lights up a joint. He passes it and she hesitates before taking a puff.

'How's the English going?' he asks on an exhale.

'It's okay, a bit boring.'

He offers the joint again.

'It's wasted on me, Trev.' She declines it with a raised palm.

'You should travel, Bea. You should get out before you realise you're gaining Jack shit from it.'

'I can't give up. I don't do giving up.'

'S'pose it's early days yet. But mind, you only live once. That's what I always say.' He leans back against the wall and stuffs the fingertips of one hand into his jeans pocket. His shoulders are hunched up against a sharp wind that eddies around their heads.

'Think on't, Bea. Don't hang around if it's not for you.'

'I was talking about the spliff, Trev. Anyway, that's not my philosophy, moving on when things aren't working. More your style than mine.'

'Choose Life.' Trevor says this just as a Wham song belts out of the speakers.

'It's actually Katherine Hamnett. She designed the tees as an anti-drugs reference.'

'Buddhist. Buddhists agin' damaging the universe.'

'Is that right? You know so much about stuff, Trev.'

'I know a little bit about nowt in particular. Don't ask me to explain the meaning o' life.' Inside, the place is filling up. The music pounds bluntly through the brick wall they are leaning against. Dancers will congregate on a square of lino in front of the DJ, oblivious to everything other than the fact it's Friday night.

Bea realises she is in exactly the right place at the right time. It comes on the wave of electronic beats from the sound system. Base driven and intense. 'How long are you in town for?'

'Overnight. Back to London tomorrow.' Trevor stubs out the joint on the wall and is careful to pocket it rather than leave it lying around for the fuzz to sniff out. Bea tiptoes and kisses his cheek.

He tenses for a split second then relaxes, drawing her into him. His cheek brushes her nose before finding her lips. The rush, the sheer pleasure from his breath, his body, the moistness of his kiss is exactly how she dreamed it would be.

He stays in a bedsit on Charlotte Street. It's owned by the man who sells the second-hand clothes to Trevor's boss. There are racks of them and boxes of shoes and accessories. It reminds her of Kennie Market with a sea view. The window looks out on a triangular spit of water between the rooftops.

Bea wakes early in the morning and kneels on the pillow to stare out at the sherbet lemon sunshine dappling the sea. Trevor sleeps beside her and as she bends down to nuzzle him awake with her nose and lips, she believes she will never be this happy again. The single fly in the ointment, the pin that has the potential to burst her party balloon, the dark cloud that hovers above the little bedsit, is Rose.

It's easy to lie to Rose. Whatever time of day Bea phones, Rose is usually drunk and incoherent. 'I don't half mish you, Bea,' Rose drawls. 'It's not the same without you.' She starts to cry, and Bea listens to the muted voices on Rose's radio as she waits for her mother to calm down. Bea throws coins in the slot. It's eating into her wages but she thinks it's worth it.

'I miss you too, Rose. But I'll be home for the holidays although I might not be able to stay too long as I'm working now.'

'What d'ye mean, working? You're at college. You can't be working too.'

'I can. We all do. I've a few shifts at a pub in town and it pays for stuff.'

'I think Trev's got the hump with me.'

Bea freezes. 'Why would you think that?'

'He says he can't sleep with me anymore. Sleeps up in his old rooms again. On his own.'

'Well. Trevor's always liked his own space.'

'That's what he says, but I've got good at knowing when I'm being lied to over the years.' The clunk of a glass being lowered without control onto the telephone table travels down the wires. 'And he's young. Isn't he? I'm probably too old for him.' The sound of the pips when the money runs out brings relief.

She imagines Trevor arriving home after his trips and how Rose will drive him mad with accusations. On the upside, if there is one, she is cheered by the fact that he no longer sleeps with Rose. Shagging his girlfriend's daughter, that red top headline in the *News of the World*, is mortifying by anyone's standard. Not sleeping with said girlfriend makes it less shameful. Bea has no intention of returning home in the summer.

The pub is busy with tourists and there are more shifts. She could do with the money and it's good to keep busy. She tells her mother she can't come home because of work and although Rose cries down the phone, she gets it. They have always had an understanding about money. She moves out of the halls and into the little bedsit at the end of her first year.

As the heat of late August descends on Brighton and the day-trippers crowd the narrow lanes, she receives a large brown envelope from Rose in the post. Inside is a birthday card; it smells faintly of alcohol. Wrapped in tissue paper, there is a pink love heart on a silver chain. The message in the card tells her that Rose misses her.

There is another envelope addressed to Bea. It's from a solicitor called Thomas Beresford with an address in the City. It contains the deeds to Falmouth Road. She takes a deep breath and fetches her pen to sign them.

Thirty-Three

Bea 1987

Bea cannot face Rose. She can't face Trevor and Rose together in the same space. She makes the same excuses and during the Christmas holidays lives in the bedsit. It's February when she discovers she's pregnant and with Trevor visiting less frequently, the bedsit has become a damp unloved space. She lives on soup and vegetables prepared on the two-ring stove. There's no fridge but it's cold enough for milk to stay fresh.

The job at the pub keeps her sane through the summer and the boss has moved her to the early shifts to make life easier. With this comes the end of her time at university. She is losing weight instead of gaining it and the skin on her face and inner thighs is covered with a pimply rash. The thought of going home to London becomes more and more attractive as autumn descends.

Trevor arrives one unseasonably cold night in September. A five-bar heater is on full blast and they sit on the bed under blankets. Before the pregnancy became obvious, he couldn't wait to get her clothes off. Now he can barely look at her. He stares listlessly into his bowl.

'What's the matter? Not hot enough? I've got some chilli powder. I think I'm getting a taste for it. Do you suppose it's a thing? Getting a liking for spicy food?'

'Stop gassing for a minute. Boss has let me go.' Trevor leans back on the headboard. He pulls on a sweater against the cold.

'So?'

'I won't be coming to Brighton. I won't have a job.'

'You could get a job down here. We could live here.'

'Yeah.' He falls silent.

She picks lentil skin from her teeth. 'You could sign on and there will be child allowance. There are ways to survive. You could get a council flat.'

'You need to go back to your mother's.'

'What? I can't face her like this.'

'She needs you, Bea.' He throws off the blanket and gets out of bed. 'And I'm going away.' The words hit her like he's thrown a punch. 'I've got an offer from a mate down in Dorset.'

'I could go with you. *We* could go with you, I mean.'

'I never wanted a bairn.' He hangs his head and she's grateful for his remorse. He is brooding and dark and Bea will miss his handsome face. People in the pub say they make a really fine-looking couple. 'I'm going. I'm letting you know before this gets any weirder.'

'Weird? There's nothing weird about wanting to hang out with the father of your baby. I love you.'

'You don't love me. It's an adventure. That's all.'

'Hardly Calcutta, is it?'

'There's the thing, Bea. You're so bloody clever.' He raises his voice and Bea flinches. 'I'm packing up at the market in a couple of weeks and I'm leaving.'

'I'm going to drop your baby.' She pulls her T-shirt up exposing the mottled white mound.

'I can't understand why you didn't get rid of it.' He stands and puts his hands on his hips. 'You're so smart.'

'I'm not smart.' The tears come and she lies down and covers her face with the blankets. The bedsprings shift as he lies alongside her.

'I'm sorry, pet. But you're right. Brighton Council will give you a nice flat and you can bring up the kid.'

'They won't. I've my own place.' Her voice is muffled by the blankets.

'Your Ma's. You should go home.'

'It's not Rose's house. It's my house.'

He was still. 'Rose never said.'

'She wouldn't, would she? She just acts as if she owns it, but my dad signed it over to me. It's mine.'

'It's a burden that house. Too big for you and Rose. Too many things that can go wrong.'

'What do you care? You won't be there.'

'I'll be with you for the birth and I'll pay for anything you need. I'll help out wi' it.'

The warmth from Trevor's body and sheer exhaustion makes her doze. She dreams of a tiny white baby, hair, eyes, limbs, as white as snow. She lifts it up, but it wriggles out of her hands like an eel. She tries again but the featureless thing keeps slipping. The dream alters, and she has dropped the baby from a great height. The muted dream-state shock makes her wake with a jolt. The first thing she notices is a length of cold where Trevor had been.

Trevor reappears at the hospital as he said he would. He tells her he's found farm work and lives in a caravan with some other blokes. He looks younger than she remembered, or was it that she felt older? The midwives like him. They smile a lot when he's around and they praise him saying he's doing a grand job. On the day she leaves hospital, one of them, Frances, takes a photograph and Trevor poses with the baby in his arms.

'You bitch!' Rose launches a plate at Bea's head. Thankfully the baby is sleeping in the lounge. Rose runs to where Bea is hiding behind the kitchen door and grabs her upper arms. She shakes her and lands a stinging slap across her cheek. 'I hate you. I hate you.'

'Stop, Rose. Please stop.' Post-pregnancy, Bea is weak. She allows her mother the outrage she is entitled to.

'You've ruined everything.' Rose sobs, collapsing on the kitchen floor. 'Trevor was a good man. You took him away from me.'

Bea takes it all. She takes the hours of howling insults thrown at her and dodges the plates that fly across the kitchen. She hides the baby in her room with plans to move them both up to the top floor.

Her mother drinks herself into oblivion every night and doesn't so much as look at the baby, doesn't touch it, tells Bea it makes her want to vomit. One morning Bea awakes to find Rose has ripped up every photo of Trevor.

There is only one left. Taken by Frances, the midwife, outside Brighton and Hove Hospital. She unpicks the lining of the old dressing table curtain and takes the precious photo from its envelope. Sewing it up, it's as if she has entombed the memory of Trevor forever. It is safe for when Bea will tell her daughter about him. Whenever that might be.

On the morning Rose receives her summons to court, Bea is forgiven. Bea says sorry. Rose says sorry. The baby cries and both women turn to attend her. Respectability, Rose says, is the deal. Rose will say the baby is hers.

'It'll be our secret. I can look after her. You can't be saddled with a baby at your age. You'll have to get a job.'

Rose's appointment to register the birth is booked and Rosemary Kathleen Fuller, according to the certificate, is registered as mother to Evie Frances Fuller. Father Unknown. Birth hospital – St Mary's, Paddington – all lies except for the date of birth.

It's amazing that no paperwork is required to register a birth. Just make an appointment and rock up. No one asks for evidence. A utility bill is required to ensure Rose lives where she says she does, but that's it. Nothing else. This baby could be anyone's. Bea could have found it on a street in Brighton.

Thirty-Four

Evie February 2020

Scarlet lies in a bouncy recliner. The silver birch sapling outside the window casts shadows on the living room wall. She watches the leaves as they flutter in the breeze. Evie sits and catches every turn of the head, every blink. She's fascinated by the way she moves her lips as if she's about to speak. What would she say? Evie is as besotted with her daughter as on the day she was born.

Scarlet. Evie's baby. Max's baby. Every day, Evie sees more of herself in her daughter: in the way she holds her head to one side when something takes her interest; the shape of her lips when she laughs or frowns and the expression on her face when she fights sleep.

When Evie left Falmouth Road on the day Bea told her she was her mother, it was as though her body had separated into tiny subdivisions of DNA. She went through the motions of driving home, concentrating fully on the road, all the while particles collided, distorted, shattered inside her. She felt them rearranging as if Bea had pulled the handle of a slot machine and sent the cherries spinning. Bea. It's hard to think of her without feeling pain even now they have gone over it. The magnitude of her lie, the way she betrayed her own alcohol-dependent mother and even more inexplicable, the subsequent collusion.

Scarlet's eyes are struggling to stay open, as if following leafy shadows is too much of an effort. Her little body flexes as a magpie takes up a frenetic cawing somewhere on the estate. Evie holds her head on one side and smiles at the baby who immediately responds in kind, lighting up the room.

Evie's memories of childhood: being held until she slept at night, being read to, Ma sneaking her sweets that meant Bea had to take her to the dentist for fillings, all have another meaning. Evie understands now that Ma was the indulgent grandmother, like Bea is to Scarlet.

The evening she learned that Bea was her mother and not her sister, she had fixed a supper as usual and laid Scarlet down for the night. When Max came home and asked after Bea, she had clung to him, soaking his shirt in tears. Max had gently pulled her away and sat her at the kitchen table and with Scarlet's snuffles audible through the baby monitor, she had told him everything.

'I have a whole drawer full of false documentation with the wrong information. My birth certificate is an outright lie, marriage certificate, a lie. I have photos of my christening with Ma holding me over the font. Not Bea. Not my *real* mother. My *real* mother is standing on the left.'

Max had squeezed her hand. 'It's odd. Feels like Bea is someone I don't know anymore.' He had fetched a bottle of wine and poured them both a glass. 'You should ring her when you're ready to talk. You'll need her birth certificate to change yours.'

'I don't want to talk to her ever again.'

'It will have to be you. Bea won't act first. And anyway, she's not well.'

Evie had rehearsed what she was going to say. She had attempted kindness and understanding but it wasn't genuine and she had no compulsion to be magnanimous. Instead, when she eventually got round to picking up the phone, she chose pragmatism. She wanted Bea's documents so that she could rectify her own.

Bea came over. She had placed a hand on the doorframe as if it were a prop to haul herself into the house. The lines around her eyes had deepened, she wore no powder, her skin was colourless and her hair thin. She had the demeanour of Ma on one of her bad days. Evie had stood in the narrow hallway and let Max take charge.

But watching Bea, listening to her gently cooing over Scarlet, a transformation took place. It was Evie in Bea's arms. The daughter looking up with searching, curious eyes was Evie. The mother looking down adoringly at the daughter was Bea. In that moment, Evie's sister became her mother. Scarlet's aunt became her grandmother. 'It's going to be okay, Bea,' she had whispered, but Bea was too engrossed with Scarlet to hear.

There are still wounds that need to heal. Bea's decision not to tell her the truth earlier stings and her betrayal of

Ma is still incomprehensible. It will take more time to process these transgressions.

The silver birch flutters, its shadows have sent Scarlet off to sleep. Evie has two deliveries. First, a bulky brown envelope containing her revised documents. Evie's birth and marriage certificates were incorrect so she had them put right. Life's labels amended, nothing to hide and all in accordance with the truth.

A moment later she receives a bouquet from Bea. It contains all their favourites: sunflowers, gerberas, lilies and more. It's been delivered from a supermarket. She's glad that Bea has dropped her snobbery about shop-bought flowers. They can be just as good as the florist and better than home-grown as they last longer. And look at how the seasons are irrelevant. Sunflowers in February?

She arranges them in a beautiful glass vase. It was a wedding present from Sarah, the only person she has confided in other than Max as yet. Scarlet will be christened soon and the photographs will show Bea in her rightful place alongside Judith as grandmother. Sarah will be Scarlet's godmother.

She has come to realise that Ma and Bea are both her heroes. Not suffragettes or resistance fighters. Everyday heroes overcoming whatever life threw in their path. The insecurity of grinding poverty, the spurious moral code they struggled to adhere to and the stigma of being unwed mothers was as present in the eighties as it had been two decades earlier. When she is old enough, Scarlet will learn about her grandmother and how happy Evie had been growing up in the big old house on Falmouth Road. She was loved by Ma and Bea just as deeply as Scarlet is loved. The old jealousy, that Bea was the favoured child has been completely dispelled.

She places the vase on the mantelpiece and rearranges the flowers to bring her favourite blooms to the front. The sunflowers seem to turn their heads towards the light. There is a memory associated with them that one day, all being as it should be, she will share with Scarlet.

Acknowledgements

With thanks first to Sally Keeble of Eleanor Press for encouraging me to take the leap and get *Shop-Bought Flowers* out there. Without your guidance this book may never have reached its audience. Thanks also to Jan Woolf for making the journey less stressful. Your networks are boundless. Your advice as sound as a trout in a stream. Thanks Beth Archer and your team at Troubador for your dedication and guidance throughout the process. Rebecca Baker, your attention to detail and your professionalism during the process of editing was awe-inspiring. I learned so much from you. Thanks to my great friend Dee for your inspiration and to Debbie for always being there. Thanks of course, to my big, extended family for sharing eye-witness accounts of North Kensington back in the sixties. Your memories helped me to paint a vivid picture of the area and its characters and I couldn't have achieved this alone. Thanks to Patsy and Pat for your help on all things Portobello and Kensington Markets and thanks to Paula for picking up the inaccuracies. Thanks to Jack, Matt and Chris for approving my silly ideas and putting up with me for all these years.

This book is printed on paper from sustainable sources managed under the Forest Stewardship Council (FSC) scheme.

It has been printed in the UK to reduce transportation miles and their impact upon the environment.

For every new title that Troubador publishes, we plant a tree to offset CO_2, partnering with the More Trees scheme.

For more about how Troubador offsets its environmental impact, see www.troubador.co.uk/sustainability-and-community